MADNESS

MADNESS

REBECCA GREY

To my son, Greyson. May you become all that you wish to be and not what the world tells you to be.

I love you.

Table of Contents

Table of Contents Continued

ONE

Dace

Flies swarmed over the trash that hadn't been taken out since only the gods knew when. Fluids of all different types dried in puddles and molding films on the long bar top. Drunken patrons didn't mind the less-than-sanitary conditions. Once I hadn't either, but something had changed. I couldn't view this bar as what it had once been for me; an escape.

Nothing here felt right, nothing helped to settle my thoughts that raged like a storm. Chatter rose and fell as conversations picked up and drifted away while the patrons flitted around the bar. Their dull roar was never enough to drown out my thoughts.

My eyes burned as sleep had eluded me last night. The lack of rest left its mark in the red rims and dark circles that surrounded my dull gaze. My head slipped from the fisted hand that had propped it up, nearly making my chin dip into some yellow liquid under my cup. Gods, I hoped it wasn't piss.

But everything had turned to piss in my life. I frowned as I lifted my head and looked around. This bar had been everything to me before. A small freedom from a reality I was convinced I didn't want. Now that it was gone and I could never return to my home, something in me felt broken.

Never again would my eyes trace the brush strokes of the paintings that lined our near-empty halls. Never again would I find myself tirelessly busy with tutors or trainers. My body wouldn't rest upon the finery of my bed or grace the expensive clothing stocked in my wardrobe. Nothing was mine anymore. My childhood memories were now just that, memories.

'Prince' wasn't a title I carried anymore, and without it I was an enigma. Dace. My name was simply Dace. It felt incomplete without the title.

Passing fae still stared at me, though none tried to greet me. It was a quiet, curious glance as they tried to see what I would become. My parents had been gracious enough to excuse prison time and instead sent me out to live on the streets, without help. Sometimes I had the thought that maybe the dungeons would have been best. At least there I was provided meals, unlike on the street where I didn't have a cent to my name and no one wanted to take in a 'traitor' as an apprentice.

MADNESS

All that remained of the refuge was smoke and ash. Footprints in the snow were overlapped and confusing to look at. I couldn't count the number of nymphs who had gotten away. The bodies remained though. I couldn't bring myself to count that number either. Guilt made my stomach turn painfully, like I had stabbed myself with a dagger and twisted.

I let my face fall against the counter, ignoring the pang of disgust at myself for letting my cheek touch the bar top. Nothing really mattered right now. Everything I was, everything I did, was a disappointment. At some point I would have to rally myself, move on from my self-pity. Right now didn't feel like the fitting time though.

Next to me two men sat themselves in the empty bar stools. The chairs squealed against the floor as they pulled them underneath themselves.

"Did you hear about the Heathern Court?" the shorter man said to his friend, who opted for another drink. He followed suit, dropping his own coin onto the counter. The waitress was fast to serve them, I noted. Regular customers, I thought, as I looked at them closer. Yes, I'd seen them before. Honestly, I think they may have been a few that lost to Shavarra's mad card skills.

The day had continued on without me, moving slower than I thought. Time did not move quickly when

3

all you did was stare at the back of a bar. The bartenders were not caring enough to make conversation with me when they knew I wasn't good for any money.

My eyebrows raised in interest as I listened intently. I wasn't in the know with my family anymore, mere gossip would be all that I had to hold on to. Ugh, I hated to resort to eavesdropping, but here we were.

"Oh, by the gods, yes," the friend mumbled.

"Ganglin was right, those nymphs are a threat to us." The short friend's voice was harsh, edged with concern and worry. My fists clenched in my lap at his belief.

"You don't really believe that, do you? I mean he had it coming anyhow. I'm just in awe of how quickly they took over his castle. Do you think our court will send help to aid him?"

I blinked. *Who did* what *now? Nymphs took over the Heathern Court castle? Where was Ganglin?*

"What did you just say?" I sat up, ripping my cheek off the counter with a disturbing peeling sound. Tentatively, I brushed my fingers over my reddened cheek.

"There, uh, was an attack on the Heathern Court. Nymphs currently hold the castle."

His words repeated in a chorus inside my head. They had done it. Someone had finally made a move and the nymphs were fighting back. My heart skipped and my pulse raced with the adrenaline of joy.

Slowly, my lips stretched into a large smile. The men before me exchanged a worried look. It suddenly didn't feel like the end anymore. I knew I looked insane, I just didn't care. I wasn't out of the game yet, I just had to get where I was truly meant to be, and it wasn't here.

"Holy fuck. Are you serious?" I gaped.

Together they nodded, concern evident in their furrowed brows. Their judgment of me no longer mattered. This homeless, hopeless, place I was finding myself no longer mattered.

"You look like you could use a drink," a feminine voice said over my shoulder.

The two men's eyes snagged on the woman, their eyes caught on her hourglass form, eating her up like she was dessert. Her face remained hidden in the shadow of her hood, her body curling into itself ever so slightly as she shied from their attention. Lifting my lip in a small snarl, I pulled their attention from her. They turned away with a roll of their eyes and continued their conversation more quietly. I twisted to meet her soft golden eyes, her short blonde bangs brushing against her eyelashes.

"I don't have money. I'm not here to purchase a tart," I mumbled waving her away. If she was a whore, she was a poor one at that. She should have picked her target better. Maybe she didn't realize I had been dethroned. Maybe she lived under a fucking rock.

"I'm not here to sell myself to you," she whispered, drawing nearer to me. "Shavarra sent me."

My breathing hitched. Shavarra, oh my gods.

"She's alive?" I coughed. "How many made it out? Where are they?" Questions rattled inside my brain. Who was this woman and why was she here for me?

"I'll explain it to you on the way." Her whisper was harsher this time. "Please, we must go."

The urgency in her words caught me off guard. A new nervousness rose inside me. I didn't know this girl, who was she to take me to anyone?

With a lifted eyebrow, I took her hand, letting her weave us through the crowd. The noise of the bar became muffled as the door swung shut behind us. Night had cloaked the streets in darkness. Fae firelight was glowing from a few hanging lamps to keep the drunks from hurting themselves on their travels home. I, unfortunately, was not drunk.

"Who are you?" I ripped the hood off her head.

The girl hissed, springing forward with a knife poised for my throat. She stopped just short of my Adam's apple, and my hand rose to grip hers. "I'm saving your life. There is a bounty on your head and some of us, me included, would like to see you on that throne again one day."

6

"Okay, first, calm down. Second, I'm sorry, but who would want me *dead*?" Well, a lot of people probably. I wasn't particularly a kind person. I may have done a few people dirty in my lifetime, too. Damn, I was a screw up.

"Not information I cared about." She lowered the knife, slipping it back into the sheath I hadn't seen, and pulled her hood back up. "Follow me."

"Well, now that I know my life is in danger, how do I know that you aren't going to try and kill me?"

"If I wanted to kill you, you'd be dead already." Her cloak flicked out behind her as she quickened her pace and surged forward into a dark alley.

"Good point," I mused under my breath, following her. My saddened state had left my instincts sluggish. Who I guessed to be a whore was actually an assassin.

She no longer looked the part of the tart now. Not with her overly-confident steps and the way that she seemed to blend in with the growing number of shadows that appeared as she led me quietly away from the bar.

We turned corner after corner heading out of the main village. Most people barely gave us a second glance. The rejected prince and the supposed whore he would spend his time with. It was an easily believed tale. She didn't technically *need* the shadows to hide.

7

"Just a little ways out," she assured me. Dirty blonde hair stopped in a blunt line at her chin, her lips a faded lavender pressed into a firm line as she pushed forward through the outskirts of town. Her words did little to appease me as the main path tapered to a small dirt trail. Homes passed sporadically, with spaces that grew farther and farther between.

A small, cozy looking home appeared in the distance. The porch was lit only by the smallest fae fire lamp. Winter vines had overgrown the siding, their blue buds sprouting every so often.

The assassin's eyes drifted from side to side, her hands brushing the fabric of her hood behind an ear as she listened. Her chin dipped in the smallest of nods before she led me forward up the old wooden steps that lead to the porch.

She knocked only once before the door cracked open. Lavender eyes peeked through the smallest crack. I could see the tangle of long blonde hair that fell over her chest. A strained breath escaped me. Gut wrenching tension released as the door swung open wide enough for us to enter.

"Shavarra," I whispered, ushering myself in and pulling her into my arms.

She wheezed, but wrapped her hands around me. "Gentle," she sighed. "I'm still on the mend." Her lips grew into a smile I could feel against my neck, her words damp across my skin.

I pulled away to examine her. A bandage wrapped around one shoulder, the wound still healing. My fingers brushed over it, and her expression tightened into a wince.

"I'm sorry," I said, my voice hoarse.

Her expression softened and she squeezed my hands. Shavarra was nothing if not forgiving. Her tongue slipped over her lower lip, moistening the dry skin. The intentness of her gaze drifted from me back to the woman who brought me in.

"I knew we would find you in a bar," she forced a chuckle.

"I, uh, didn't have anywhere else to go." Avoiding her sympathetic look, I let my eyes wander the small cottage for the first time.

The assassin stood with her arms crossed over her, her shoulder leaning against a bookcase that was filled to capacity with books. Literature with bindings ranging from two inches thick to thin slivers were stacked upright and on top of each other, shoved into whatever space was available.

Next to the bookshelf was a small fireplace, cold and dark. Dust from old ashes fanned out from the stones and onto the worn, wooden floorboards. The dirt neared two broken-down chairs and a couch that looked more like a deflated balloon.

Pictures were propped up of smiling faces I didn't recognize and one all-too-familiar face. This was, if I must guess, Shavarra's real home. And it was a far cry from the luxuries I had been living in.

"I heard they took your rights to the crown away," Shavarra nodded. "I'm sorry to hear that." Sometimes Shavarra liked to fill the silence that occasionally rose between us. I had never been a fan of small talk, specifically when it reminded me of what I lost.

"Yeah, well it happened and I can't do anything to change it, so..." I tried to shrug it off like it didn't matter, even though everything in me felt drained of what normally fueled me. *You're so stupid, Dace, it does matter.*

"There is some good news, though."

My gaze stopped the adventurous wanderings of the space around me and found its way back to my friend's face. Her mouth ticked up into a sideways grin.

"And what might that be?" I drawled.

"Resources tell me that there are a lot of people who are pissed that you lost your crown. Fae have been flocking to us from all over the court expressing their loyalty to *you*."

To me? People actually liked me? No, it wasn't me. It was my cause.

I laughed, running my fingers through my hair. "What resources may that be? Because so far, everyone has treated me like a disease they didn't want to catch."

Shavarra pointed at the assassin. "This is Jesseline. She represents a guild of assassins who represent a lot of really wealthy fae who want to back you."

Jesseline raised her eyebrows, but said nothing to confirm the statement. I blinked away my warring thoughts and looked between Shavarra and Jesseline.

"How many nymphs made it out?" I finally asked the question that had been eating away at me since the refuge was burned down.

"Only about a third of them." She nodded, turning toward closed doors that lead out of the living room. "Would you like to see them?"

"They're here?" the surprise in my voice was evident as Shavarra laughed.

"I didn't know where else to take them, so I brought them home. To my real home." Her cheeks flushed crimson and she wrung her hands in front of her. "I, uh, know it isn't much, but it's what I have and it's far enough out of town that it's easy enough to hide them."

This place really was a trash pit compared to the castle, or even the makeshift home of the refuge. No wonder she had practically lived at the refuge. But she was giving everything she had, and that's what mattered.

"Your home is lovely," I said, hoping I was convincing enough.

Her throat bobbed, her gaze trailing over me once more like she had to make sure I was still in one piece. Physically, I supposed I was. Though I knew I looked worse for wear. My brown pants were creased, dirt scuffed up the side of my calves. The white button up over it wasn't so white anymore. And I could still feel the stickiness of whatever was on that bar top on my cheek.

Mentally, I was fucked. But honestly, was that any different than normal? I thought not.

The door at the back of her room opened quietly as she twisted the knob. A small kitchen open to a dining room was filled with nymphs. They sat at the table chairs or propped up against the counters. A few were curled up on mats that cushioned them from the hard floor. They spoke quietly, their conversations quickly stopping at the sight of me.

If I had thought that I looked bad, these people were clearly in hell. Many of them were bruised, bandaged, or cradling makeshift splints. None of them looked as if they made it out without a scratch.

"Prince Dace," many of them murmured in greeting.

My heart leapt at the name. The title I had often rejected and now missed. Even without my title I was still the prince to some, and maybe one day even the king.

I turned toward Shavarra, "We need to get them to the Heathern Court."

Her eyes lit up and she turned toward the crowd, "You heard the man."

TWO

Ryker

Shouts rose from the crowd, angry and questioning. "What are we going to do about the fae?" "Why are there fae still living here?" "How do we get the rest of our people free?" "Where is Ganglin? We want his head!"

The purge of the Heathern Court castle hadn't been quick. Deep emotional wounds still festered, leaving the newly free nymphs confused and heated. They had a point though. All those questions were the same questions I had already asked myself.

As the fighting outside the castle had come to an end, they had seen me atop the steps. All of their gazes fixed on me, as if *I* knew what to do. Did they think I was Hattie? The one who had given them the medicine that helped to give their powers back? I was full of fury, untamed and hungry. So we did what I had always wanted. I led them to destroy this place that had destroyed us for so long.

14

Fists met windows, and glass fell like confetti. We ripped down every banner, every sign or image, that reminded us of the ruler who had just fled. Earthmakers, like me, sent shuddering earthquakes deep into the ground that brought down statues, and screamed at nature as vines grew from the ground and covered the walls and any available surface.

Their powers were awakening and messy, and it made it that much more satisfying when the castle looked like it had been abandoned for years. When the destruction finally stopped, some nymphs fled for the forest, while others stayed to fight.

Outraged questions pushed up at me as I stood on my tiptoes at the top of what used to be Ganglin's dais. Dirt and blood still streaked their faces, and mine. Their bodies pushed against each other as they surged forward with every new question.

"Everybody, please!" I waved my hands trying to calm them down.

Daethian stood on the bottom step, stretching out an arm to stop anyone who tried to get too close to me. His shirt was tattered and splattered in red. Dirt was smudged along his dark brown hairline and across his cheeks. His brown eyes glared down at the unruly crowd.

Behind me, I could hear Graceson using what was left of his strength to keep Randsin propped up.

Together they leaned against Ganglin's throne that was now covered in intricately weaved vines. A new throne for a new people.

In the raid of the castle, the prisoners had been released. One prisoner though, had not been nymph. Randsin was nearly killed. Had it not been for Daethian, who kept him safe, he would be in much worse condition than he was now. The long, protective clothing he normally wore no longer covered his chest and arms. Black, detailed images covered every inch of his skin, tattoos that still remained visible despite the blood that covered him. His breathing was shallow, but he was still alive. Ganglin had meant to kill him.

"Why are there still fae here?" People shouted in agreement as the question rose louder above the rest.

How was I supposed to explain that these were the good guys? That there were fae out there who wanted to help, who were not the enemy? I had known all too well those feelings of unease and distrust.

"There are fae who want to aid us. More than you would think, who want to right the wrong that was done to us." I clasped my hands in front of me, my body swaying with exhaustion.

"They aren't one of us," voices cried out, "They are lying!"

"Look, I can't calm your feelings of doubt toward the fae. Trust me, it takes time and action for them to show you that they mean what they say. But some of them are good," my voice broke, my eyes wide and red.

"We will do our best to make camp here. Make this our home as we decide the next step. We will not give up this territory to the fae." This sentence seemed to calm them. Their shouts lowered to mumbles and whispered questions.

"I'll continue to cook the meals," one nymph raised his hand.

"We can do patrols of the ground and bring any unwanted visitors into the dungeons," a group from the back agreed.

"Yes, this is good!" I clapped. "Feel free to claim a room and let's try to make life normal here. If there is a job you wish to do to keep this place running, please do. What you do will be your choice."

Daethian's head bobbed from where he stood. "Let's make this *our* home," his eyes bore into me as he spoke. I swallowed the feeling that left my throat dry.

"Please, take ease in knowing that we will get through this together," my voice was hoarse from all the yelling I'd done. "Because we are going to need each other."

The crowd nodded and began to disperse into smaller groups or leave the room altogether. Their attention no longer needed to be held. As soon as I knew eyes were no longer looking to me for answers, my knees buckled and I sat myself down on the dais. Daethian came to my side, grabbing my hand and supporting my back.

"You need to rest," he looked up at Graceson and Randsin. "We all do."

"Where is Hattie?" I whispered. My hands shook as I brought them up to cover my face in an attempt to hide the tears that gathered at my eyelids.

"I'm sure Hattie is fine. She is a big girl and she can take care of herself."

But could she? She had run after Ganglin, so wild and reckless. I was supposed to be the reckless one. Even after I had asked her to stay, she had still darted away. Worry sickened me, turning like food poisoning inside my stomach.

Daethian's hand drew long, soothing circles over my shoulder blades. He licked his lips, pausing, "Look we can't do anything more until you rest. Let's pick you out a room. One with a good view, you deserve it."

The skin on the back of my calf had knitted itself back together, but the wound was still incredibly pink and the muscle strained to keep from giving out at every movement. My neck stung every time I twisted my head. Burns that would likely scar.

"Here," he whispered, tucking his arm under my armpit and helping me to stand. "There are a few rooms back down this hall used for guests. Let's get you all laid down."

Graceson let out a long sigh as he lifted Randsin with a grunt. What was left of Graceson's wings was tucked close to his back, strips of the reptilian flesh moving with any small breeze. Sweat glistened against his forehead, but he didn't quit moving. He would have to soon though. There would be a point when he couldn't push through the pain any longer.

Daethian's trusted arms helped to guide me through what was left of the crowd. Fatigue made me lean into every inch of his warm body. His attention shifted between watching where we were going and glancing down to make sure I was okay. Muscles in his jaw chorded when he caught me flinch in pain.

"Daethian," my voice came out with hardly a sound, but he caught it and lifted his eyebrows in acknowledgment. "How are you here? You were supposed to be in the Acture Court."

He cleared his throat, pointing toward a door, "In here." The wood was smooth, detailed with intricate designs that had been burned into it by an artist who had taken their time on their work. The fanciest door I had ever been allowed to walk through.

It was clear as we entered that this room wasn't meant to house guests, but was made and designed to fit someone with particular interests, someone who lived here. Plush and perfectly white bedding was still pushed away and unmade. Nymphs hadn't gotten to making the bed back up before all hell had broken loose.

Sheer, blood-red curtains hung over the three large windows that ran nearly the entire length of the wall, only stopping where a wardrobe was still propped open. An array of clothing, of all shades and colors, poked out like the inhabitant had only just begun to peruse their options. Glitter and bits of sheer materials caught my attention. Gowns. This had been a woman's room. A mistress, perhaps? A lady of the court?

There were many women in Ganglin's court, but only one came to mind that had yet to be married. The seamstress. She had been sought out by so many people that Ganglin decided to scoop her up and keep her for himself, offering her an opportunity to stay here, should she fancy making his own personal attire. No matter how much the fae tried to not care about their appearance, they were still unmatched in their vain natures. The urge to own and wear one of the many gowns I had seen her in, or seen her create, was a nagging and impulsive thought that distracted me.

My teeth pressed together hard as I tried to breathe through the pain of my calf stretching with each step. Daethian sighed, giving me the gentlest of squeezes. He turned his head away to talk.

"There is a room across the hall that is in good condition," he called to Graceson.

"He is going to need to see a healer before long," Graceson shouted weakly in response.

"You're going to need to see a healer!" Daethian's shout was rough.

We all needed a healer. After the war that had raged on this land, not only had the building begun to crumple around us, but many of us were broken too. Had anyone stayed who had medical experience? I prayed to the Mother that they had.

Daethian set me on the edge of the bed, lowering himself to untie my boots. From this angle it was easy to see a bruise that ran down the length of his neck and under his shirt to his shoulder.

"Are you avoiding my question?" I tried again.

His easygoing smile disappeared as he looked back up at me. Both hands held on to my ankle. "Ryker Avery, where you go, I am bound to go, too. I'll chase you to the ends of the earth if I have to, to make you safe," he paused, his tongue racing over the fullness of his lower lip. "Windre received a tip that you had been attacked on the way home. I traveled with no rest to get here, only arriving as the fighting began."

"Weren't you supposed to be helping train? Wasn't Windre upset?" He had left it all to come find me in the pits of hell, even when there was a bigger picture to look at, even when I was barely somebody.

But hadn't I been willing to do that for him? Yes. I was willing to steal and hurt and try whatever I could to get sent to a place I thought would try to break me, just so he wouldn't have to bear it alone.

"I didn't give Windre the option." He glanced back down at my feet, slipping the boots off one by one.

Even though I felt too worn out to smile, my lips still turned up at his words, "I'm glad you came. This would have been a lot scarier without my best friend."

Daethian hummed, a poor cover-up for the disappointment in his face. "You're my best friend, too. Now," he grunted and stood, his frame tall and wide, filling the space between the bed canopy and me. "Rest."

With his tattered and dirty shirt, and the peek at his muscular stomach as his arms hung from the canopy posts, he looked so much less like a sidekick and so much more like a hero. My gaze traveled back up to his face. The seriousness of his reciprocal attention made my body go still.

One hand dropped from its hold, lowering slowly, as he traced the marks on my face. His thumb trailed down my neck, my skin burning with a blush, stopping just short of the tamer's claiming marks.

With time, those marks would fade, his scent along with them. He hadn't taken what would have made those two small imprints last my lifetime. Another reason to thank the Mother.

A cough broke the silence. Daethian's hand fell to his side as Graceson's pale face appeared in the doorway. "I hope I'm not interrupting you." His eyebrows still rose with mild curiosity despite the pain he was clearly in.

"No, no, you're fine," I shook my head, angling myself away from Dae and toward the door. My muscles screamed at the small movement of lifting my legs to the top of the bed.

"Don't move too quickly," Daethian reminded me, before his attention narrowed back to Graceson.

"Randsin is laid down in that room, but I think at this point it is in my best interest to return to the Acture Court and report to Windre. I need to seek medical help myself." He swayed in the doorframe, making my worry for him spike. "I'll return when I can, hopefully with help. It seems I'm not very welcome here anyway."

He was right. His presence was a sore spot for many of the nymphs here. It would take a bit more persuasion, and proof of their kindness, for fae to walk around these people without lingering glares and threats.

"Take what you need. And, please, be careful. Are you sure you can make it there in your condition?"

"I'm older than you think," Graceson winked. "I've fought through wars in worse condition than this." He turned to walk away, but paused and poked his head back into the room, "Oh, and I would maybe put someone with Randsin to keep an eye on him and make sure someone doesn't sneak in to kill him."

Randsin was high on many nymph's shit lists. As the head guard, there had been a lot of punishment that had to be dealt out by his hand. Not his own orders, but Ganglin's. Even though he had taken me to the Acture Court, I still had a thread of concern that his closeness with Ganglin made him a threat to us. A seed of distrust that was growing inside my head.

"I'll stay with him," Daethian managed, finally pulling himself away from my side.

Graceson gave him a small bow and disappeared from the room, leaving us alone once more. Daethian turned back to me, slipping his hands into his deep pockets.

"Well," he started.

"Well," I whispered in return.

"Rest and I'll see if I can find someone who can help us find a healer. You need to start healing." Anything else he had wanted to say stopped as he clamped his jaw firmly shut and closed the door quietly behind him.

I sagged against the bed, the fullness of the pillow cupping the sides of my face. Voices carried through the hall as nymphs made themselves busy. Either finding places to sleep, pillage, or work in the meantime.

My eyes closed, but my mind couldn't stop replaying everything that had happened over and over again. What was in that box that Ganglin needed so badly? Why did it seem so familiar? Like deja vu.

Whatever it was, Daethian was right. We needed to start healing. Because this was only the beginning.

THREE

Dace

Shavarra's modest home was our biggest blessing in disguise. Local traffic didn't travel as far as her front porch, which limited the number of wandering eyes. She had stocked the home well. Well enough to keep the number of people crammed into the small space sufficiently fed.

Old worn maps, which she said had belonged to her grandmother, were rolled and stored in cylinders along her bookshelf. They were dated at best, with the edges crinkled and the landmarks fading from the hand drawn images, but they told me everything I needed to know.

My city of Caratona was one of the largest settlements in the Twinity Court, not unusual given that this was where my royal family resided. However, people often commented on the fact that they were not central to the Twinity Court. Our castle was too near the border of the Acture Court, a foolish place to have our capital. But the location

26

had been picked many, many centuries ago by my ancestors who drew near their allies and placed distance between themselves and their enemies.

It was convenient now that we needed to travel with this large group that there would be less Twinity Court land that we would have to pass through. My finger drew a path over the crinkled map of an old, forgotten road that used to carry exports to the other courts before we created new, more direct routes. It would be an extra day of travel, but it was the safer option. As a group, we would travel along the Acture Court and Obtune Court border, within the Acture Court, until we made it to the Heathern Court.

The nymphs were bandaged as well as they could be, many already on the road to recovery, a few being transported on cots and carried by those who could.

Silently, I rolled the map back up, slipped it back into its canister, and deposited it into the side pocket of my backpack. The bag that I carried was stuffed to near eruption. Essentials only, clearly. But I had to carry for those who could not. A sense of regret echoed within me. My wasted opportunity as a prince. I could have stayed quiet. I could have upheld my responsibilities without bickering. Biding my time would have been good enough to get me to the crown, to get me in a position to actually help these people. The people that Ryker belonged to. She had been fighting for her freedom for so long in my dreams that her passion sometimes felt like mine. And I supposed that was okay.

Far to my left, Jesseline walked on the outskirts of the dirt road, her body relaxed as she kicked at the dirt with her boots. It was all for show. I could see the way her eyes drifted along the woods. On occasion her hand pulled her hood down as she listened intently to the woods that surrounded us on either side.

Another assassin had joined our ranks. A tall, muscular man, who surprised me with his nimbleness despite how broad he was. Jesseline called him Slyke. From the back, he helped carry a woman whose tendon had somehow been severed as she fled the refuge, her leg not able to support her. The woman seemed happy enough as she leaned against him and stared warmly up at his navy blue skin and metallic grey hair.

Slyke was the messenger, Jesseline had informed me. When he had appeared, materializing inside Shavarra's living room just before we left, I had nearly had a panic attack. Only royal blood carried that magical ability. Though it made sense, once explained, I was still in disbelief when they told me that all assassins distantly belonged to royal bloodlines. They were scouted and recruited because of this ability. My tutors clearly skipped that lesson in my history books.

So Jesseline could do it too, appear and disappear at her will. It's what made them good assassins. But their indirect bloodlines diluted the power enough that their ability to transport someone or something with them was limited to the weapons they packed.

I had just nodded. They didn't have to know that I had never been well practiced enough, or cared enough, to expand my powers to their full potential. I knew it was within me, but I wasn't strong enough. Yet.

To my right, Shavarra breathed heavily, supporting one end of a cot on her shoulders. Her cropped shirt lifted just enough to see a large blue bruise, that wasn't healing as fast at it should, over her ribs. All of her blonde strands were piled in a hastily made bun to keep the hair away from her face. Her attention was focused on the snow covered path. Perhaps planning her steps helped to distance her mind from the pain.

"Here," I stopped her. "Let me carry him for a little bit." The man on the cot was unconscious, so he clearly wouldn't mind.

"No, you already have enough to carry."

Shavarra was sometimes too strong for her own good. But mostly, too stubborn.

"You're injured," I flicked my finger at the hem of her shirt, meaning to point out the bruise. The material rose enough to reveal the indigo bra underneath. My lips lifted into a cheeky smile.

"I'm bruised," she panted. "*Not* injured."

"Oh come on, Princess, move over." I snuck a shoulder under the cot, bumping my hip against hers to move her out of the way. The weight of the cot combined with the weight of the backpack in a way that made my bones feel like they were moaning in protest. I wouldn't tell her that.

Her cheeks flushed and she moved, playfully swatting my arm. For a moment she walked in silence next to me, glancing from the ground to my face. In turn, I watched where I was stepping, then briefly made eye contact with her. She was amusing sometimes.

"What?" I finally laughed.

A shy smile warmed her still-blushing face, "You've never called me princess before."

I lifted my eyebrows. She wasn't wrong. For so many years I had been prince, and princess had been a title I was never willing to give to anyone. I had reserved it for Ryker, stuck so stubbornly in my head and my heart. But for once, princess wasn't a title I *had* to give out, it was just a word.

And I may have given it too freely. Shavarra's gaze held a want in it that I would never be able to give her. We both knew it.

My smile fell, "Shavarra, it's only a word."

Jesseline's intense stare narrowed on the two of us, our gazes making contact for the briefest second. Like she could feel exactly where the tension was coming from.

Shavarra laughed, "I know it's stupid of me, to think that you would ever share that title with me. But sometimes when you play like you do… it gives me hope."

Oh, I was a stupid, stupid man. I knew returning to her night after night would create an attachment. And it had. I had thought the attachment was only on my end. Though to be clear, it wasn't her love that I had been after all these years. If that made me a bad person, then so be it.

"Don't say that," I whined. "You know this thing between us is nothing. Casual."

"Casual in the way that you sleep in my bed more often than you don't?" she paused to chew on her lip. "And don't try to act like you are only there for the sex. How many nights have you slept next to me just to have a warm body at your back?"

She was right. I hated being alone. My dreams had ruined me so often that it hurt to feel the empty space in my large, cold bed. Shavarra willingly filled that hole for me.

"Okay, okay. So do you want to stop? Do you want me to leave you alone?" I tried to keep my voice low and soft to avoid gaining the attention of the nymphs that walked behind us. What was going on with her? Why bring it up now?

"No," she frowned.

"Then what is your problem?"

The instant I said it, I regretted it. Her face fell for a moment before she schooled her features into apathy.

"You asked, Dace. And maybe I shouldn't have said anything," Shavarra laughed coldly, falling behind me.

We both knew what the problem was, and it was my own fault that it was happening. Though, her hurt had been an unexpected dagger to my heart. Because even if I didn't love Shavarra, I cared about her.

She was like my sister. The sister that I fucked. Oh gods, that sounded disturbing. She was only supposed to be a fuck buddy, she wasn't supposed to be someone who became important to me.

Jesseline pulled herself forward from her position, casually walking over to me, then on by me. "Smooth," she whispered in passing. It was clear she was Shavarra's friend. Perhaps her real friend, since I seemed to only wreck her.

Half of me wanted to chase after her. My head turned side to side as I tried to find an able body to take the cot from me. It's weight pressed into my shoulders that were already sore from the straps of the backpack. But there wasn't anyone around who could take the turn.

The other half of me sighed in relief at the thought that I didn't have to confront that particular issue right now. And I had the excuse, no one could take this cot right now.

A few miles up the road we would run into an old trading post where there should be a well. When we rested, we could talk about this a little more. If she even wanted to talk to me.

I focused on the effort it took to carry all this weight on my back. Sometimes the physical equation to the mental struggle was a welcome distraction. We had already traveled relatively far, only stopping when we had to. Snow began to fade, melting away with the mild weather of the Acture Court. It's central location in Stylica gave it the more pleasurable weather, as it did the Obtune Court. The Twinity Court and the Heathern Court bore the brunt of the cold and the heat.

Tall trees cast their shadows over the dirt that we trod. Sunlight poked through the interwoven limbs and made up the contrast to the shadows in its own odd pattern. Mild chatter followed me. The urge to look over my shoulder for Shavarra rose up in my thoughts more often than I'd like to admit.

An unattractive amount of sweat built up over my brow the longer I carried the cot, the person at the rear getting switched out with someone I couldn't see. Before, with the title of prince, I didn't feel like I needed to worry about people finding me attractive. Beauty came with the title, it's what made them like me. But now... I fought with myself about whether or not I should wipe my forehead. If I was more attractive, then more people would like me. That was just math.

Just math of the upper class, I tried to remind myself. These people didn't care if you were attractive or not. So I let the sweat build, until it dripped annoyingly and I couldn't be bothered with the feeling any longer.

Miles passed like this. The rise and fall of conversations behind me, my mind starting imaginary conversations then stopping at the idiocy of it, and the ache in my back only growing stronger. The trading spot was getting closer, it had to be.

Jesseline materialized in front of me, her hand already pulling out a weapon. My feet came to a sudden stop, the cot smacking me on the back of the head as the person behind me took their next step.

"I suggest you put that cot down," she said, cocking her head to the side.

"And why is that?" I asked, already taking the opportunity to set it down. The nymph on the other end followed suit.

She opened her mouth to answer, but instead disappeared and reappeared five feet ahead as an arrow shot through the space she once was.

"We aren't alone any longer," she smiled, like the thrill of the fight was what she lived for. Then she vanished again.

This couldn't be happening. Not again.

Quickly, I twisted my body around, my gaze already looking for her icy blonde hair and persistent lavender eyes. Our eyes locked, the space between me and Shavarra an uncomfortably long distance, with more bodies between us than I could count.

Men's voices rose from the woods on either side of us. I reached for the knives on my belt. Metal, warm from being pressed against my body, met my fingers like an old, familiar lover.

A deafening boom sounded near the rear of our fleeing caravan. My heart stopped, fearing how close it was to Shavarra. Thick tree trunks shattered, shrapnel flying in all directions from the blast that shook our feet and sent nymphs hurling through the air. Even at my distance, I wasn't safe. The force of the explosion sent me flying backwards, my back hitting the ground and sliding through the dirt as the air was forced out of my lungs. The weapons in my hands scattered around me.

A ringing began in my ears, the muffled sound of nymphs crying out in surprise and pain all around me. Dust filled the air. My vision blurred, and I blinked to make sense of it all as I saw figures rush forward out of the forest. Blue and white uniforms with patches of thorn-covered snowflakes. Men from the Twinity Court army.

Soft, pliable dirt met my fingertips as I felt the ground for my knives. Anger flooded me as I found their beaten handles on the ground around me. I blinked, clearing my vision, and the body of a soldier hurtling down the hill neared our path. With one smooth motion, I sent a knife spinning through the air. It met his throat. His body toppled to the ground, the men behind him ran forward and jumped over him like they didn't know him.

Jesseline and Slyke appeared and disappeared with frantic swipes of their swords, just to keep the men on the ground from advancing on our already-broken group. Nymphs crawled from where the explosion had hit. But some of them had yet to make it off the ground. They drug themselves forward, leaving behind lines in the dirt of their mangled bodies.

Shavarra had to be one that was getting up, I assured myself as I stood with a new rage welling within me. There wasn't time for me to look for her, or to question her safety. I had to hope for the best and protect what was left of us.

I ran forward. Another arrow whizzed through the air. My head snapped in the direction it came from, the archer perched in the limbs of a tree. Magic welled within me, tingling over my skin. In the blink of an eye, the earth below me was gone and replaced with the bark of a tree.

"Hello there," I said to the archer, who jumped in surprise, nearly dropping his bow.

His hands reached to re-nock the arrow, as if that would help him, and I lunged forward. My shoulder collided with his chin as I wrapped my arms around him and we fell through the air together. At this height, the drop would kill him if he didn't have enough noble fae blood in him. At least, if he did, it would knock him out. Served him right.

"Sorry, but I can't stay longer, you'll have to take the rest of the trip by yourself," I growled as my power pulled me back to the trail.

I settled in a low crouch on the edge of the forest, catching his short-lived scream and the sound of his body crunching against the ground with a thud. Men still trickled over the hill, though not as many as I expected at the beginning of the fight. My parents had clearly underestimated us. Which was offensive, but whatever.

Pushing off the ground, I sprinted into the woods, flinging my knives into any uncovered piece of flesh available. Eye sockets usually worked the best when using plenty of force with my long tipped daggers, but getting them right in the jugular was also satisfying.

As their bodies dropped I darted past them, pulling my blades out as I went by. I didn't care if blood stained my belt line as I slipped them back into place.

Jesseline and Slyke still popped up, in and out of what was left of the men, but slowed as their numbers lessened. A few nymphs even gave it a go, slicing through soldiers with weapons they picked up off the ground. It didn't matter if you were trained if you were angry enough and had the gods on your side.

With the attempt on us coming to a quick end, I wove through nymphs to where I'd seen Shavarra last. I froze. Blonde hair spilled over the ground, blood trickling down her face, her body still. A nervous, stuttering breath filled my chest as I burst back into motion.

Dirt clouded around my feet as I ran the last few yards to her. Her chest rose with a shallow breath. The rustle of a soldier in the trees pulled my attention.

He locked eyes with me, his face freezing in fear as my unbridled anger ripped through me with a wild roar. The soldier turned to run away, scampering up the hill, though it was no use.

I appeared in front of him. My magic was tired from overuse. His eyes grew wider and his mouth fell open. He made a pitiful soldier if he was fleeing like this, or maybe he was smart to run from me. My arm shot out and grabbed him by the throat, lifting him up in the air as I listened to the gurgling sound he made as he fought me.

"Tell my mother I said 'hi'," I hissed before throwing him at my feet. "Now run faster, before I regret sparing your life."

The man gasped, his feet searching for purchase underneath him before he could even get air into his body. I didn't take any more time to see if he kept going or not as I dropped into the dirt before Shavarra once more.

Jesseline and Slyke seemed to be doing their final sweep of the forest, no more soldiers appearing. Nymphs around us were helping each other up and examining any new injuries. They were less frantic than the last time. Like they had come to expect that bad things were going to happen.

"Shavarra. Oh, Shavarra," I murmured, rolling her head to the side to examine her injuries. Her mouth opened, but no noise was emitted. Splinters from the fractured trees were embedded in her skin, none deep enough to do serious damage. No, the head injury was what had done it.

Carefully, I slipped my arms under her. The full weight of her body dropped into my arms. We had to get to the Heathern Court. We had to get to Ryker. And we had to get there *faster.*

FOUR

Milo

The white stone steps of the castle led down to the waiting buggy. A restless horse huffed and shimmied within its bindings, waiting for the order to carry us forward. It was a simple enough carriage, no flashy insignias or sparkling jewels embedded in the wood. Just an open cart, with enough space for two people to sit with the reins, or lay in the back with the packed food.

My throat bobbed as I swallowed. Princess Maggie lifted her shimmering auburn gown as she descended next to me. Her lips parted in an adventurous smile, her head constantly swiveling as she took everything in.

"Now Milo, I'm sending this scented parchment with you. Use it to correspond with me. Write me letters, I want to know everything that is happening. Every two days, I'll send my bird. You'll know him by his black feathers and the tie at his ankle." Without asking, the princess opened the bag

40

that hung over my hip and slipped the papers in. Her hand gave the bag a good pat after she closed it.

"Shouldn't I be sending that information to your father?" I hummed, trying to appear more bored than scared shitless.

"Oh, you will," she winked. "But he will send his bird every four days. So you'll need to write *a lot* of letters. Keep in mind, we're friends, and friends don't leave out the juicy details."

"I wouldn't dream of doing anything to the contrary." My feet met at the bottom of the stairs, my hand already clasping the side of the wagon. "Now, shouldn't we get this show on the road?"

"No need to rush. It's only a few days' travel. Just follow the sunrise and eventually you're bound to run into the Acture Court. Nevertheless… come, come."

The delicate flick of her wrist signaled the waiting guards, who prodded the unlucky nymph girl forward. Red's scowl had never appeared deeper, creating a sharp wrinkle between her eyebrows. Loud metal shackles rattled with every step she took down the stairs. Both her hands and ankles were bound. She didn't fight them, but she also didn't seem like she was coming willingly.

"I will miss your cooking, Red," Maggie pouted. "Well, have a nice trip." She pointed at a long slender finger at me, while I leaned impatiently by the wagon wondering how sincere her words were. "Don't forget. Every. Juicy. Detail."

"Yeah, yeah," I grunted, lifting Red into her seat at the front of the wagon. Her body slumped against me, legs and arms dangling as much as she could manage them with the bonds. She let all her dead weight fall into the lack of movement. If she had weighed any more it would have been an inconvenience, but even with her resistance she was still relatively light. "You're bound to make this rather difficult aren't you?" I hissed.

"Well, it would be very unlike me to make it easy," she sniffed, lifting her chin.

Despite Maggie's confidence that this would be a quick trip, I had the feeling it was going to drag on and on.

With a chuckle, I walked around the carriage and found my seat next to her. Leather reins warmed by the sun felt like silk in my hands as I scooped them up and looked at Red, before giving Princess Maggie a final wave, and gave them a yank. The wagon lurched forward. Our bodies rocked against the seats and we sat quietly until we put distance between us and Princess Maggie.

"You know, I've never seen you in bindings," I leaned over, letting my voice rasp softly into her ear. "Would it be ungentlemanly of me to say that I like it?"

Red stiffened. Her spine became impossibly straight as she tilted away from me with her dagger gaze.

"Oh, calm down," I smiled. "I'm taking those off as soon as we get out on the road."

"What makes you think that I won't run away?" Red huffed.

"What makes you think that I won't catch you?"

She sighed, reclining into her seat. It may be a very long ride indeed if she was bound and determined to hate me so. Not that I blamed her, she was a slave and I was the man charged with dragging her off to see how badly she could be tortured. Something inside me rallied with happiness at the thought. Not of it being Red. But at the idea that I may actually get to be a part of something I was good at, and something I actually enjoyed. I guessed that made me a sadist.

"So, since I'm being taken away to my death anyway, care to share your actual story?" Red had the audacity to look over at me with those half-hooded eyes, like this conversation was the only thing keeping her from dozing off with the sway of the wagon.

I glanced back toward the distant white castle walls, the gate on the perimeter passing and closing behind us. She did have a point. I didn't *really* think with how bad of shape she was already in that she could make it through whatever torture the Acture Court had in store for her. My head still got a little foggy when I thought about the idea that the king had spared my life and was instead going to use me as a mole in another court. It's like I was a spy, spying for the person I was spying on. A spy within a spy within a spy. Except for the fact that I wasn't, I reminded myself.

It would be nice to share something with someone while I was here, and there wasn't anyone else I could even talk to. My eyes roamed the passing city streets I had once strolled through looking for work. Only this time, I was wearing a simple guard uniform. Not too dressy for travel, but still presentable enough for when we arrived at the Acture Court. And of course, the material was suffocating. I slipped my finger into my collar, tugging it away from my neck.

"You wouldn't believe my story, even if I told you," I mused.

"Well, it isn't like I have anything else to amuse me on this long-ass ride to my death." She tilted her head up to the sky, letting the sun play over her features. For a second, the angular point of her nose, the paper thin line her lips were pressed in, and the narrowness of her far too small eyes actually looked... attractive. Like the sun was where she really thrived.

I squeezed my eyes shut, pressing them closed as tightly as I could, then opened them again. That had to be a trick of the light. That, or this clothing was actually causing me to be delirious. When I opened them again, Red cocked her head and stared back at me.

"Well, out with it."

"Why don't *you* tell me about what you were doing that night I caught you in the woods? Now that sounds like a story that needs to be told."

Red snorted, "Just so you can get those juicy details for Princess Maglehwhore, no thank you."

I didn't bother to hide the smile her word-play on the Princess Maggie's name gave me. Sometimes when Red wasn't trying to be, she was funny. Though I didn't think she ever meant what she said as a joke, it always tickled my dark humor bone.

"She won't entertain you, you know."

"Excuse me?" I glanced away from the road. A few other wagons in front of us moseyed about the street, unrushed in their morning errands. They called and waved on occasion to familiar faces and business owners. That sort of enthusiasm was just plain exhausting and I couldn't be bothered. When I gave Red my attention, my mouth sprung open, her words registering in my mind.

"If that's what you're looking for, I mean. A fantasy romp with the princess of the Obtune Court."

"And what makes you think I'm doing all this for a chance at the princess's virginity?"

Red snorted a second time, "She is no virgin."

45

"Doesn't matter. Answer the question."

Wind blew over us, carrying the scent of the freshly baked bread that sat in the bakery's window. One of the last stores on this heavily crowded merchant street. The breeze tossed Red's stick-straight black hair into her face, but she didn't bother to move it.

"Isn't that what most men who want to climb the ladder of success are trying to do?" her gaze remained forward, her knuckles taut as she folded her hands in her lap.

"That is not the wall that this particular ladder is leaning on."

Her dark eyebrow lifted in question. "Well that's good to know, because Princess Maggie prefers the company of women anyway."

She what, now? That can't be the truth. Not with the way she fawns over men. Had I actually seen her fawn over men though?

"I thought she was in love with what's his name… that Prince from over yonder." I pointed to my left, unsure of what direction that prince might live.

"By the mother," Red brought her shackled hands up cupping her cheeks and rolling her eyes as she stared straight ahead like she was talking herself out of screaming in frustration. Finally, she sighed and turned to face me. "You're so stupid. She doesn't *love* him. He is merely her means to ruling sooner. And if you are

46

going to pretend to be from around here you should probably learn the names of the noble fae. His name is Prince Dace, by the way. And he actually isn't the prince anymore, if the rumor mill is correct."

"Did he die?" I frowned. How could he just all of a sudden not be the prince anymore?

"No, his parents dethroned him." She shrugged her shoulders.

The busy streets faded away. Homes came and went in the following silence. Above our heads, the sun traveled across the sky, moving the shadows over Red's impossibly pointed bone structure with it. As the last of the houses blurred at the edge of my sight and the paved path to the Acture Court began, I slowed the wagon. Gently, I laid the reins over the wood panel in front of us. It was still an oddity to me that there was so much leather in this court when mine would kill for even a taste of that material.

"What are we doing?" Red sat up.

"I'm hungry, aren't you?"

I reached into the open dray behind us and lifted the lid of the wooden crate that carried our food. The very kitchen Red had worked in had packed this crate and something told me Red had been very loved in her position, not only by the king. A long sandwich was carefully wrapped in cloth. I undid the material and tore it in half, offering one portion to her. Metal clacked together roughly as she lifted her bound wrists with a frown.

"Oh, right." I shoved her half in my mouth, holding it together with my teeth, as I pulled the key from my pocket and undid her shackles.

Quietly, she rubbed her red wrists. Twisting in her seat, she turned to face me and shook her head. "I want the half that hasn't been in your dirty mouth."

With a roll of my eyes, I handed her what was supposed to be my half and tore my new half out of my mouth. The sandwich had a wonderfully seasoned spread on it. Thick cuts of meat, cheese, and a savory sauce that had soaked into the loaf.

"Shouldn't I be eating the soup?" she pointed sourly, while taking large bites of the sandwich.

My eyebrows furrowed as I thought. She was right, she probably should be. I just hadn't thought about it. The seat creaked underneath me as I stretched back and looked into the crate at the canisters of cabbage soup that waited.

"Oops," I said through my large bite.

The smallest tinge of a smile lifted the corners of her lips, but quickly disappeared as she continued to eat and turned to face forward again. She ate slowly. Her jaw worked unrushed, chewing every bite thoroughly. I had expected her to scarf it down. But instead she was trying to make it last as long as possible.

"Don't worry, there is more. Unless you want the cabbage soup."

"No, but I'll be happy enough if you undo my unwanted accessory." Red's attempt at a flirtatious smile looked much more painful than it should have been.

I huffed a laugh and leaned down. The metal key slipped right into the lock, the bindings on her feet opening to reveal the raw, red marks on her ankles.

"These must not be very comfortable," I mumbled, pulling the metal away and setting it in the wagon behind us.

"Neither is this," Red growled.

A jolt of pain bloomed at my nose and radiated up to the tears that formed in my eyes. Red's fist had met my face in an unexpected jab.

"Fuck," I snarled, grabbing my now-tender nose. My eyes had involuntarily clamped shut, and when I opened them all I saw was her thin frame frantically darting around the trees. "Are you kidding me?" I yelled. I prayed that the horse would stay put as I sprinted after her.

I didn't think Red was this stupid. She was clearly not going to be fast enough. It wasn't even a question of if or when I would catch her, but how on earth she really believed that there was a chance that I wouldn't. Even with that pathetic excuse of a blow. My arms wrapped around her waist as I snatched her up in my arms before she could make it any further. She exhaled loudly.

Keeping her tight against me, I slid my chest up her back until I was upright again. With one hand I grabbed her chin and forced her to look up at me. Then my heart stuttered. Red was grinning. Ear to ear, her lips parted in a brazen, unashamed, giddy smile.

"You had to expect me to at least try," she said.

I didn't know what I expected. Not that. Not her tiny, fragile little hand bopping me in the nose before she tried to outrun someone with five times her max speed on his worst day.

"Please, don't do that again," I breathed, lowering my head to rest my mouth against her ear. "I need to be more careful around you."

Like she was merely a small piece of luggage I needed to take with me, I lifted her, and carried her back to the wagon. As I passed the drivers seat, I snatched her bindings. She had brought this on herself. Without trying to be gentle, I set her down in the back.

"Welp, looks like you've won yourself some more time in these oh-so-glamorous shackles." I held them up, rattled them, and pretended to be a cheering crowd as I clamped the metal back on.

Red winced, and the smile she wore just moments before had completely vanished. "These things hurt, you know."

"I know," I whispered, but I couldn't hide my grin.

Red folded her arms over her chest, watching as I finished with her ankles. I pointed at her wrists. Her black strands bounced as she shook her head.

"I'm not doing this willingly, " she laughed haughtily.

"Oh, I don't need you to."

I tried to slip my hand between her arms and she pulled away. Every time I got near her she pulled away, until I had to climb into the back of the wagon and stand over her. The wood protested my weight with every step. I lowered my face to hers.

"Give me your arms," I said, before prying them away from her body and binding them in metal again.

"You seem to be enjoying this, Keeper."

"I would say that I wasn't, but since you think I'm a bad liar, I'll just admit that perhaps I am." Slipping my arms under her armpits, I pulled her upright, and led her out of the back of the cart and into her seat.

Making a show of it, I plucked the reins from where they rested, straightened my shirt, and sat down. "Shall we continue on then?"

Red sighed, but didn't bother to turn and give me her attention. If this was what every stop was going to be like, this might be the longest trip of my life. Without a thought, my hand rose and rubbed the tip of my sore nose.

FIVE

Dace

Blistering rays beat down on my skin. The excessive amount of sun that shone within the Heathern Court borders took perspiration to a new level. Sweat dripped off my chin, landing on Shavarra's top and darkening the material in that spot.

Shavarra hadn't woken up since we were ambushed in the Acture Court. I took relief in the fact that she was still breathing. Even if sometimes I would have to stop walking and press my ear against her chest to make sure. It was the subtlest movement of her breast bone and the faintest rhythm of her heart that pushed me forward at such a pace.

My feet ached. My whole body felt sore really, but I didn't give in to the pain or the exhaustion. I didn't let myself think about the blood that ran down my arms. Some of it was mine, I knew, but the majority was from small wounds that had already closed. Most of it was Shavarra's.

For her, I continued. Nymphs who had chosen to follow me, chosen to shape our future, or free a peaceful people, marched on behind me. Bodies were strung up in their arms like wilting plants. Though the crying had long since quieted from both the wounded and the grieving. Some carried the dead. Friends or family they couldn't leave behind. Once we reached our destination I would make sure we gave them all a proper burial.

I wished sometimes that my dreams would give me something useful. Would have shown me some sign of this attack during our travels. But no, somehow I still only saw *her*. Yet, I didn't resent her. My punishment for wishing away my crown was clear. It was loving someone so unattainable, for so long. It wasn't her fault that the gods had chosen to make me some sort of freak obsessed with a person who hardly knew me. Crown or not, here I was fighting. These people were no longer alone, and neither was I. It gave me pride, the same pride I suppose the other noble fae got from their courts, when this group looked at me the way they did. These people trusted me to show them the way. Trusted me to save them and their families.

Though, I had already failed. The grim cries of sorrow throughout the night were enough to tell me that.

But they still looked at me the same when the morning came, when we continued on as if the small attack couldn't hold us down.

I was thankful to the gods, to the nymph's Mother Nature, or whoever else was responsible for allowing us to make it here, mostly unscathed. The surprise attack had been scary and it left a few with additional injuries, but we had only lost a few nymphs. One had already been questionable and nearly paralyzed on his cot beforehand. I shrugged to myself. I tried to rationalize that his already declining health made him less of a valuable being. Technically, it did. *Shitty train of thought, Dace.*

We moved as quietly and unnoticed as we could as we skirted around the edges of small towns on the way to the Heathern Court capital, Meridat. It was clear as we traveled that the fighting within this court was not done. Some towns waged their own battle as their nymphs fought back. Even from our mostly-hidden path we could hear the clash of powers and raised voices. Some wanted to help, but I turned them down with a short shake of my head. We couldn't lose any more numbers. We just couldn't.

The fighting had faded, much of it so long ago that it was easier to pretend like I hadn't heard it at all. Still, the more I pretended, the worse the remorse got.

Now I could see the light at the end of the trail. Trees leaned away from our path, no longer keeping us in their cool shadows, and at the end was the long valley between us and what was now Ryker's castle. If I closed my eyes I could see it's sandstone walls atop the hill, and the absolutely absurd amount of steps it took to reach any entrance.

I leaned back, jostling Shavarra against me as I adjusted my grip. The stiffness in my back grew and throbbed, my backpack bouncing behind me. Just a few more steps and we would be at the valley.

"We are almost there," I grunted loudly to the parade of people behind me. A small wave of excitement pressed them forward. A few children in our company giggled and ran ahead of me. "No, please stay behind me," I shooed them. Better I be the first in the line of danger than them.

Slyke had taken his position at the back of the group once more, and Jesseline took her time walking up to my side. She pressed her fingers against Shavarra's neck, taking her pulse as she walked backwards, watching me.

"We'll make it in the nick of time. I think she'll be okay once she sees a healer," Jesseline nodded to herself. "I'm going to go ahead of the group, warn them of our arrival."

"I agree. Let them know we need medical attention."

The air around her blurred in a haze as she pulled her hood down from her face and completely disappeared. The last of the old trade route stopped. Blades of grass sprouted in the fading dirt and multiplied into the open valley that bloomed year-round with dots of purple and white wildflowers.

Every ounce of air within my lungs escaped me as we stepped into the clearing. Half of the valley had been turned into something like the training arena in the Acture Court. A little more pieced together, and a lot less polished than theirs, but I could see it nonetheless. Behind it, the soft tan walls of the castle were no longer visible behind layers and layers of green, leafy vines that had climbed and covered all of its surfaces.

Nymphs had paused whatever activities they had been attempting to complete as they saw us. My eyes scanned their faces looking for Jesseline. Looking for Ryker. Bodies moved in a swarm as we rushed forward, and the crowd of waiting nymphs parted.

Jesseline was next to Ryker, talking quickly and quietly. Ryker nodded, stopping to point at a nymph and call out an order.

I squeezed Shavarra tighter to my chest, "It's okay. We're here. We made it here. You're gonna be okay. You have to be okay."

Soft brown curls bounced behind Ryker in a taut ponytail that revealed her sun-kissed face. Light freckles dotted the bridge of her nose, her full lips pressed together in worry as we finally met in the middle.

"Please," I said hoarsely, as emotion swept over me, an unusual onslaught of happiness and fear. "I didn't know where else to take them that wouldn't give Windre away. Shavarra..." I took a deep breath to steady myself, "We were attacked on the way here. Shavarra hasn't woken up yet."

"It's going to be okay," Ryker whispered, pinning me with her citron green eyes. Gently, she brushed her hand over my fingertips, where they dug into Shavarra's leg. She pointed to the nymph who had appeared at her side.

The young man, with fish scales carved into his skin in a strip over one of his eyes, offered his arms. "I'll take her to the healer."

"Thank you, thank you," I murmured, passing her over. The sudden lightness of my arms left me swaying, feeling a bit unbalanced as I watched him carry her up the remainder of the hill and toward the vine-covered castle.

"How many do you have with you? How many more need medical attention?" Ryker tilted her head to look around me.

My brain felt frozen as I opened and closed my mouth a few times. How many had been at the refuge?

How many had died? How many did I find at Shavarra's home? How many? How many? How many of us were left?

"Dace!" Ryker grabbed both my hands and pressed them together between hers, bringing my attention back to her. I hadn't realized how badly they had been trembling until the shaking calmed under her touch.

"Your hair has grown again," I said roughly.

She breathed a laugh and shook her head. "Hair does that. It grows. Can you answer my questions?"

"No, yes," I pulled my hands away from her and scrubbed the sides of my face. It itched where the shadow of an unmanicured beard was growing in. "Um, maybe fifty total. The people on the stretchers are the most critical, but we have quite a few who could use a good look over. Some have dead they wish to bury"

"Okay. Follow me. Let's get everyone where they need to be."

She turned toward the castle, the end of her ponytail brushing between her shoulder blades. She looked different from the slave I saw in the Heathern Court, and still different from the version of her I saw in the Acture Court. She looked stronger. She looked like she was fulfilling her destiny.

She no longer wore the paper-thin servant uniform, and didn't wear the training outfit the Acture Court had offered either. A soft white, nearly sheer, button-up over a thick black bra, tucked into brown khaki shorts that had been rolled and cuffed mid-thigh. It looked like she had dug through my wardrobe and mended the clothing to fit her taste. Very fitting for someone who had taken over the castle and kept the grounds for her cause.

Nymphs turned to watch our party walk through them. Some jumped into the procession to help carry the injured and escort the few that limped. They smiled at each other excitedly. It was a feeling buzzing in the air, an electricity in the atmosphere that told us this was where we were supposed to be. This was their new home.

I winced with every step we took up to the waiting open doors. My body was screaming for the breaks that I didn't allow on the last leg of our trip. Even my lips were cracked and dry as I ran my tongue over them.

Inside the castle, the air cooled. Which served as a huge relief from the sun, one that we had all waited for. Vines covered most of the surfaces inside the building, too. Pictures and furniture were shattered or remade into something totally new. Bricks in the walls were clearly missing where the vines had dipped inside them. Honestly, I was surprised this castle was still standing after what they had done to the place.

Ryker paused at a junction in the hall, her voice carrying. "Those who need medical attention can travel down this hall to the infirmary. We will do what we can, with what we have, to help them. Anyone else who would like to find a bed to rest in can go that direction," she pointed down the opposing hall. "You'll find many unoccupied rooms that you may claim as your own. If you're hungry, you can continue straight to the dining hall and we can get you fixed up there as well."

Nymphs shuffled past us, deciding what they needed the most and followed the directions down the subsequent halls. Ryker watched them quietly as they moved forward, smiling at those who offered their thanks and ruffling the hair of a child that pressed against her in a quick run-by hug.

Once everyone had hobbled away, the two of us still remained in the hall. Ryker turned her pointed gaze to me, "You look like shit."

I brushed at the dirt on my shirt, "How sweet of you to notice." My fingers buzzed with the need to touch her again. I slipped them into my pockets to keep them from moving of their own accord.

"You can come with me," she finally amended, and turned to walk back the way we had come.

I followed her through the broken-down hallways, taking a few turns before she pushed open a door and walked into the room. Even dismantled, it was clear what the room had been used for, and what it was being used for now as well. Books that had at some point been pulled off the shelves, had their pages stuffed back in and were sloppily placed back where they belong against the wall. A large desk, propped up by more books to make up for a broken leg, was mended where it had been split down the middle, with a board and nails. All three chairs arranged before and behind it had been sliced open and sewn shut again. Ganglin's office.

Ryker had her own maps spread out over the available surface. Random weapons sat on the papers like very expensive paperweights. She pointed to one of the seats.

"Please, rest," she whispered, and reached for my bag. When she noticed my wandering eye she continued, "He is a terrible being, but surprisingly has good taste. I couldn't let all this stuff go totally to waste."

She had a point.

I groaned as I shrugged off the backpack, then hissed as the bag brushed my lower back. A long strip of skin felt excessively tight, like I might rip it open if I moved too quickly. A spot I hadn't noticed before.

"You're injured?" She let the bag drop to the floor with a thud. It toppled over, items rolling out beside us.

"No, I'm fine."

"No, you're not. Let me see." She pushed aside my hand where I gripped the bottom of my shirt and peeled the material off my skin.

I bit my lip to keep from growling at the pain, placed both hands against the desk, and leaned into it. The sweat that had cooled when we entered the castle was replaced by a new sheen and my head spun. I nearly jumped as one of her calloused fingers traced the healing wound.

The blood on my shirt hadn't been noticeable since I had changed into the oversized maroon shirt Shavarra had in her closet. I hadn't even realized I had the wound until long after the attack had taken place. How was I to know how I even received it?

It hurt like hell, but the thought of losing Shavarra had hurt worse. So I pushed through it. My noble fae blood had done enough to heal the majority of it.

"You should see the healer," she said again, her finger pressed against it.

I reached back and pulled her hand away. "I said I'm fine."

"Okay," Ryker deadpanned.

"I just need a shower and I'll be fixed up good enough. Maybe a meal and a nap wouldn't hurt."

"I agree." She sat against the desk and watched me fall into the seat in front of her. "What happened, Dace?"

I shuddered a breath. If I thought too hard the memories of everything came back in painful flashes. Fae guards rushing nymphs. Arrows flying. Fire burning their home to the ground. My mother and her booming voice. My father and his disappointment. The long dirt path that brought us here. The explosion that had left Shavarra limp in my arms.

"I lost everything," I whispered into my palm as I leaned into my hand. My gaze traveled to the debris-covered floorboards. "My ass-hat of a friend discovered the refuge. He ratted me out to my parents. They attacked the refuge. Burned it to the ground."

I looked up as Ryker sucked in a breath and continued, "They revoked my crown. Shavarra sent someone to find me and..." I trailed off, not wanting to admit the terrible state I had been in that bar. "We took everyone that made it out and brought them here. We lost a few in the ambush that happened in the Acture Court."

"Windre's men?" she asked, taken aback.

"No, no, these were definitely men from the Twinity Court."

"Wow, you must have really pissed your parents off for it to be that bad." She tried to keep her face neutral, I think she really did. But the hint of a smile still graced her lips. "Come, let me show you to your room, and bring you some food, and you can tell me on the way."

"Can't go against what has been foretold," I said as I leaned forward slowly, to avoid passing out in pain, and stood. I followed her, continuing when she gave me a questioning look, "They believe that what you see in your dreams is what is meant to be. That you should do everything in your power to make sure that dream comes to fruition as the gods have demanded."

"But you don't believe that?" Ryker stepped out into the hall, walking a different direction than the one she had pointed the survivors of the refuge in.

"No."

Ryker dipped her head in a small nod. She looked up at the ceiling in thought, as if the climbing green vines held the answer to her impending question. "Why is that?" she finally said, her eyes narrowed on me as if she was trying to figure me out.

At what point was it appropriate to tell a woman you've dreamed of her for nearly one hundred years?

I fisted my hands inside my pockets until my knuckles became white. Light shone through the cracks between the boards that covered the broken windows in the halls beside her. The light framed her face and gave her an angelic hue. But her expression was anything but angelic. It was determined and savage. Part of my chest became tight with overwhelming joy at how much the look reminded me of the girl I fell in love with every night. This was really her.

"Because I saw the Day of Ruin coming. Because I still saved as many nymphs as I could without being noticed, despite seeing every single one of them being taken into enslavement. And you know what?" I shrugged my shoulders and nudged her with my elbow as we came to a stop outside a door.

"What?" she whispered.

"Nothing bad came of it." I sighed, long and slow. "Until now."

Ryker chewed her lip, an absent motion that caught my eye. The white of her teeth dug into the pink flesh of her lip, raking over it slowly, until her plump lip was untouched once more. I tried to breathe through the desire to kiss her, choosing to slip my hands behind my back instead.

As my attention traveled back to her gaze, I found her staring at me, examining my face again. Damn, had I been caught?

She swallowed. Her hand caught on the doorknob and she opened the door with a forced smile. "I know this isn't the room you stayed in, someone already claimed it, but hopefully it will do."

I tossed a half hearted glance at the room. Medium sized bedroom, fluffy bedding, a bathroom, and a couple of broken windows. She could have shoved me into a broom closet and called it my bedroom and I would have happily cuddled with the hard end of the mop.

"It's perfect. One question though," I held up my pointer finger. "Where is your room? You know if I need to find you to… ask more questions... Or if I think of some other sort of important information?"

She hid a cough behind her fist as she cleared her throat and pointed with the other hand. I followed the imaginary line from her finger to the door she pointed at, just three doors down on the left.

"And Daethian is across the hall from me if you ever need him," she added.

Why would I need the boyfriend/not boyfriend? It was a battle not to roll my eyes. So instead, I took a step into my room.

"Lay down, someone will be back with food for you. Hopefully a healer as well, if she isn't too caught up with all the people already crammed in there. On second thought, I better go and check on her myself," she bowed slightly, reaching for the door handle.

"Ryker?" I asked, stopping her in the doorway.

"Yes?"

"I, uh, I tried to save you, too. On more than one occasion I wanted to come to the Heathern Court and bring you back to the refuge. But my dad always managed to stop me," I frowned, waiting to see what my confession might cause her to do.

My father had always dreamed about me. Every wrong was always reprimanded and corrected because of what he saw. And somehow he always saw himself stopping me from rescuing Ryker.

67

Part of me expected Ryker to be mad that I never saved her. She should be angry about every year she lived in this hell hole, being punished day after day for the smallest of offenses. But she chewed her lip, trying to disguise her growing delight.

"You've already saved me, Dace," she said quietly, flashing me the smallest of smiles before the door clicked shut behind her.

SIX

Ryker

The halls of the castle were busier than ever. Nymphs took full advantage of every resource that this location could offer and every activity they had long been deprived. And I mean *every* activity.

Good food was being eaten. Yes, lots of delicious food was being consumed at all hours, as the kitchen was rarely closed. Training was strengthening us, and we took turns pushing our powers to their limits in the long valley to the side of the main courtyard. And parties, lots of parties were being thrown. I had yet to attend, but I could still hear the music in passing, often catching glimpses of the small crowd of people that would gather in someone's bedroom as they danced in a small mob.

Then there was the sex. Loud moaning surprised you when you turned the corner and found two, or more, people intertwined.

Everything had been so strict for so long that it seemed no one felt the need to abide by almost any rule. Not that I had set any, but you would think common decency would. Ever since I was a child, my parents had taught me about the seriousness of choosing your mate. Every intimate action with someone would leave their scent on your skin in some way, shape, or form. Like the bite the tamer had left on my neck. But that was fading even now.

The scent of arousal and the heightened aura of consensual sex left the entire building reeking of sweat and orgies. These nymphs didn't care if they smelled like one, two, or three other lovers.

I saw the appeal, I really did. Sometimes I caught the perfume of lust that hung heavy like a morning fog in the air, or heard someone cry out in pleasure, and it struck me right in the gut. And by gut, I mean vagina. Mother, this place was quickly becoming some sort of brothel and I wanted to sell my virginity to the highest bidder.

But I wouldn't. These people kept looking to me for guidance. I couldn't be one to frolic around carelessly. My leadership was what was holding them steady. Freedom, with a dash of revenge.

Sometimes it was a welcome distraction. My mind still back-tracked over everything that had happened in such a short time. Hattie was still missing. Ganglin was still missing.

Squeezing my eyes closed, I walked by a room with the door cracked open, revealing two very eager bodies pressed together, on my way to my own private space. The shortsword that I fancied when training bounced against my skin with every step. My love for this weapon had grown on me, I clung to it even when I wasn't out on the field, just so I could be sure that no one else could claim it.

I hadn't a clue who it had belonged to, or if it was Ganglin himself who had owned it, but it was mine now. A large red jewel glittered on the bottom of the hilt, winking at me in the light. My hand often floated to my hip to rest against it, as I had seen Dace do on more than one occasion with his daggers.

My gaze traveled down to Dace's door. I hadn't seen him emerge from his room yet, though I was assured by the healer that he was doing well. At night I prayed that Mother Nature would bless Suzetta, our most gifted healer. She was a natural, even after all these years, and she had accepted the task of tending to all of the nymphs from the refuge with grace. I sighed, turning as I heard a door open and my name called behind me.

"Ryker?" Daethian smiled, slipping from his room and closing the distance between us.

71

I looked up at him, waiting expectantly. We hadn't seen a lot of each other in the past couple of days. Just the passing hello and goodbye. Though we always ended up sparring together if we found each other down in the valley.

"Want to grab something to eat? I could use a good conversation. Randsin has been like talking to a brick wall." He casually placed his hands on his lean hips, giving me his famous half smile and showing off the dimple in his cheek.

I hadn't caught Daethian's scent on any of the females here, and there weren't any lingering smells on him now. Part of me melted with relief. He stiffened when a particularly pleased moan carried down the hall.

My attention darted back to Dace's door. A split second thought to double-check that the sound hadn't been coming from his room either. Daethian followed my gaze.

"Uh, I don't know, Daethian," I hedged. I kind of just wanted to crash for the night. "How is Randsin doing? Healing nicely?"

He chuckled dryly, "He is okay, though he won't tell me what all his tattoos are from, or what they mean. Even stole one of my shirts to cover himself up so I couldn't look at them anymore."

I lifted my hand to scratch the back of my head, the gesture never fully making it. Daethian reached for my hand, interlacing his fingers with mine, and took one step down the hall.

"Ah, come on Ryker. It won't hurt to let loose for one night."

He tugged me another step forward. My feet dragged against the stone floor slowly. I tried to smile back, but my body still screamed with the need to be touched, and Daethian's hand held mine so tight that it scattered my thoughts. Something like that between me and him could ruin our relationship.

"No, no," I amended, trying to slip out of his grip.

He had turned away to face the direction he meant to take me down the hall. His body froze, his hold on me tightening so quickly that my hand screamed in pain, like he was about to crush it. Angrily, I ripped my hand away from him with a shout.

"Daethian, what the hell is wrong with you? That hurt!" I cradled my hand to my chest and flexed my fingers up and down to make sure they hadn't broken.

His boots squeaked against the stone as he swiveled to face me. Everything in his gaze was focused and tense. His normally caramel-brown eyes looked near black, as if someone had spilled ink inside his irises and left them cloudy and dark.

"Daethian?" I mumbled, stepping closer and touching his cheek with my palm. "Are you okay?"

He blinked, his eyes returning to their normal light-brown in the light again. It must have just been a figment of my imagination I tell myself, as Daethian laughs quietly and presses a kiss into my hand.

"Sorry, I guess I still don't know my own strength yet. Go ahead and enjoy a night to yourself. We can catch up tomorrow."

"That sounds lovely," I say slowly, not quite sure I believe him. Maybe I'll mention something to Suzetta.

Daethian's throat bobbed. He turned back the way he had wanted us to go, raising both hands to scrub at his face before they ran through his hair, leaving me to stand outside my room, confused. That had been an odd encounter. Maybe I needed more rest than I was letting myself have.

Stepping into my room, I pulled the door closed behind me and leaned against it. There were still a few hours of sunlight left, so it felt silly to go straight to bed. My gaze traveled over my room. I hadn't changed much since I had begun my stay here. Maybe I should make it my own? The room was a little too glitzy for my taste, a little too bold. It needed to be beautiful, but humble. This room was not humble at all.

I looked over the framed images of gowns that were in the planning stages, waiting to be made. Thick bolts of fabric were still stacked together by a desk that held pin cushions dotted with needles. Then my attention fell on the wardrobe. Fancy dresses ranging from floor-length to mid-thigh, voluminous to body-hugging, and overstated rhinestone-covered to understated satin. Maybe I should just try one on. It couldn't hurt to have just a little bit of fun. And I was in my room where no one could see me so...

Racing to the closet, I flung open the doors. Materials of all different colors burst out from their restraints like they had been stuffed in there for far too long. Emerald, mauve, lemon-yellow, jade, lavender, onyx, and indigo, so many colors to choose from, and the choice was all mine.

Gently, I lifted a hanger off the rod, pulling down a daring red dress. This dress was certainly not humble and it was something I would never set foot in public in. Light bounced off the crystal pendants that hung off of every inch of the material, they chimed together like the gentle sound of soft rainfall.

The sleeveless top covered only the smallest amount of skin before the neckline dipped so low it had to be near where one would imagine someone's belly button was. The back of the dress was simple enough with just a zipper to get in and out of the garment. There wasn't enough material for it to be one of those poofy, old-fashioned gowns, and the ruching at the sides gave me the impression that it clung relatively close to the body.

I pressed my lips together. My cheeks hurt from excessive smiling. With a small, giddy squeal I set the dress down and ripped off the plain clothes I had been wearing to train in, kicking them to the side. The zipper of the dress split open smoothly. Inside the gown, buttery fabric caressed my legs and I pulled it against me.

Sounding like a wind chime on a particularly gusty day, I shimmied over toward the long mirror that leaned against the wall. The gown was beautiful. But it would look better once I zipped it up. I grinned at myself in the mirror. Contorting my arms, I worked up a sweat pulling the fabric back together and twisting this way and that to work the zipper back.

I relaxed my shoulders with a steady exhale, finally in the dress. I turned, sending dots of light shining over the walls of my room. The dress was magic, utter magic. Somehow it had turned my lean, nearly-flat physique into the curves of a rich, well-fed woman. My hands slid from the small of my waist over the curve of my hips. My attention following the red gown to where it draped over my feet on the floor. This is what it must feel like to be beautiful.

Two rapid knocks at my door drew me from the fantasy I was building inside my head. Every bead clinked loudly as I twisted toward the noise, my face losing all color.

"Ryker?" Dace's voice called. "Are you in there?"

"Yeah... Yes," I stuttered, reaching behind me to find the zipper. The tips of my fingers swiped near the zipper but couldn't quite reach it. *I'd just zipped it moments before. Come on.*

"May I come in?" his beautiful, dulcet voice asked in a confident tone.

No. I wanted to shout as I arched and curved my back while my arms twisted in every odd angle I swore I had tried successfully before. Why couldn't I reach this damn zipper?

"Just a minute, I'm changing."

It was all I could manage, and it sounded more like a question than an answer to his. Dace was waiting outside my door for me, and every minute it took to try and pull this dress off me made the lingering silence between us feel more awkward. Even if I couldn't see him.

"Are you alright in there? Are you sure you don't need a hand?" he laughed, after a few more minutes passed.

I whined to myself, frowning at the heat in my cheeks as I tried and failed to snag the one thing that could get this gown off my body. "I'm fine! I'm fine," I tried again to sound more sure about my answer. But every single attempt was failing and I could live in this gown or make the prince *(oops, not prince)* wait outside my door forever.

Shit. I needed help.

I wondered what Dace thought of the noise the gown made as I kicked at the trailing fabric on my way toward him. Taking a deep breath, I opened the door and stuck just my head out. Dace tilted his head and gave me a questioning look, but I ignored him. The hall around him appeared empty, no wandering, gossipy nymphs to spread the word that I was about to snatch him into my room.

The silky, half-buttoned, mint-blue shirt on his chest bunched in my fist. Dace's mouth fell open as I yanked him into my room and slammed the door closed behind him.

"Woah," he laughed, holding his hands up. Then his jaw quickly clamped shut and his eyes grew wide. He cleared his throat taking in everything that was the, far too revealing, dress I wore. "I feel like I may be underdressed. What's the occasion?" he finally said.

This is so embarrassing, I cried internally. Suddenly, I was extremely aware of how much upper and side cleavage I had showing. Plus, now I was going to have to confess to being that stupid girl who wanted to wear stupid, fancy dresses when I was so clearly *not* that girl.

"I tried it because I thought it was pretty. And now I can't reach the zipper on my own. It's stuck," I whispered like someone was spying on us, as if me wearing this dress was something of significance.

"I'm sorry, what?"

"The dress is stuck. On me," I hissed again stepping closer to him.

He leaned down, his eyebrows scrunching together in confusion, "I don't understand."

"I tried the damn dress on because I wanted to feel pretty, and now I'm stuck in this damn thing," I shouted, my hands rushing to my cheeks to cover the way they burned crimson under his amused gaze.

He licked his lips, then smirked. "Are you asking me to undress you?"

"No," I paused. "No."

But wasn't I? This had been a foolish idea. I should have just greeted him and fed him some load of bullshit about me getting ready to wander off for some sort of royal meeting that there wasn't any possibility of. A ball. I should have told him we were throwing a ball. Damn, any lie would have been better than the truth.

"I just need help with the zipper," I finally frowned, dropping my hands and playing with the dripping crystals.

"All you had to do was ask."

He straightened the cuffs on his sleeves like this was an everyday thing. He probably had helped many girls out of their gowns over the years. The thought sent a sliver of want straight between my legs and a pang of unwanted jealousy clenched my heart. But I didn't want to be just one of those girls.

My tangled hair had fallen over my shoulders, covering the top of the dress. Quietly, I pulled the strands to the side and offered him my back. His breath hitched and I felt it drift over my skin. His fingers brushed just above the zipper before he tugged it down. With both arms, I clung to the top of the dress.

Dace cleared his throat and stepped away. "Would you like me to leave the room again?"

"Turning around will suffice." Holding the gown to my body did at least one thing, it hid how much my hands were actually trembling.

"Alright," he raised his eyebrows attempting to suppress his smile, not well I might add.

With his back turned to me, I waved an arm back and forth in the air, the other holding the gown as I shimmied. The dress made a little noise as I did my lunatic dance to ensure he wasn't looking. When he didn't laugh, I took a deep breath and dropped the dress.

My whole body stretched as I lunged for the clothes I'd kicked aside. Holding the material, I turned back to watch him as I slipped into the items. Better make sure he wasn't trying to sneak a peek. *What would you do if he did, Ryker?* The scandalous part of my brain, run strictly by hormones, performed a sexy dance that would seduce him. Though the more prominent part of my brain, the one riddled with the crippling fear of being overpowered, screamed in terror and clutched the clothing to my body like a child with a useless rag doll.

"So, uh, what are you stopping by for?" I asked, buttoning my shirt.

Dace tilted his head back and forth, keeping his back turned. "You mean other than to save you from the restraints of that dress?"

"Clearly."

"I just wanted to express my gratitude and maybe offer my assistance."

Fully dressed, I firmly placed my hands against my hips, already feeling less curvaceous outside of that fancy gown, and stared at his back. His shirt was thin enough, and damn near sheer enough, that I could make out the muscles in his shoulders. Dace sure liked to show off his muscular upper body. Not that I'm complaining. I shrugged to myself.

"Yes. Keep talking," I urged.

"You've really taken charge of this place. The nymphs here look up to you as a leader and you welcomed us, *me*, here without question. I'm sure I'm speaking for Shavarra as well when I tell you how much this means to everyone from the refuge." He turned his head to the side, his eyes scanning his periphery to get a glance at me.

"Hey! You're looking at me!" I pointed.

"You're dressed," his easy laughter filled the air, as he turned back to face me. "Were you just going to have me face away from you the entire time we had a conversation? Is my face not pretty enough for you?" His polished loafers took a step closer.

"The view from the back wasn't so bad." I blinked at the words that escaped my mouth faster than I could tame my tongue. My cheeks burned as another blush bloomed on my face. Why did that always happen to me when he was near? Curse that *not* prince for influencing me with his beauty.

Dace smiled, unfazed. He managed another step forward before my nervous habit of running away kicked in, and I scooped up the gown from the floor, moving to the wardrobe to hang it.

"Speaking of Shavarra, you seemed rather worried about her when you arrived. You must be pretty close. Tell me about her." I looked between the gown and the hanger. How did this hang so nicely before? It had no sleeves.

"I met her in a bar, during a game of cards. Don't ask her to play unless you want to lose. Speaking from experience, it doesn't go well. She was different from the other girls at the bar. She wasn't swooning on the arm of the man she thought would win, or drunkenly dancing to the band. She was there making money and she introduced me to a few of her friends. All traveling nymphs that had stopped in Caratona on their way through to visit. Her love for them was so deep, it didn't feel right not to tell her about my dreams of the Day of Ruin. She's the one who really hatched the plan for the refuge. I was just the means to do it."

I kept my back turned, fiddling with the dress and the hanger as a means for distraction. Dace did think rather highly of Shavarra. Even near death, as she had been when she arrived, she was stunningly beautiful. She had the curves that I envied so much.

Annoyed, I exhaled loudly and slung the dress sloppily on the hanger. I pushed at the other gowns, shoving them apart to make room for the messily hung dress I tried on. Dace's hand slipped against the dress on the other side, taking the hanger from my hand and slipping it back onto the rod.

Piercing blue eyes stared down at me, watching me expectantly. I should have said *thank you* but instead I blurted, "Are you lovers?"

SEVEN

Milo

Time does not fly when you are staring at a horse's ass.

My eyes had grown tired of squinting into the sun as it was beginning to set. Every hair in my nose had practically burned away with the rancid smell of the horse's shit as we traveled. What did they feed this thing before we left?

Red laid across the wooden boards behind me, still and quiet. She'd been laying that way for a while, so I assumed she was using her time more pleasantly than I was and was taking a little nap. Gods above I wished I could take a nap instead of steering this horse. But we were coming to a small town inside the Acture Court. Here I would take a much needed break from the travel.

Horse hooves and creaking wagon wheels, drew Red's attention. She sat up, watching as local traffic passed, uncaring of our presence. I glanced back at her. Sleep was still evident in her eyes as she squinted and looked around. It was hard not to wonder if she had risen to glare at her surroundings, assuming we had finally arrived at Windre's castle. Not quite yet, Red. Not quite yet.

Pulling on the reins, I slowed and steered our horse-drawn cart to the side of the road. A tall building with green shutters and a freshly painted sign that read 'Cassie's Tavern' waited. Hopefully with something good to drink and a warm meal. I didn't even want to look at the cabbage soup we had packed or eat one more cold sandwich. What I wanted was a steak. My stomach growled in agreement.

"Well sugar-puss, you want to hop out of that wagon or shall I fetch you myself?" I jumped to the ground, watching her with impatience while my foot tapped in the dirt.

"Where are we?" her scowl deepened, but she scooted herself to the edge of the cart and looked around.

"Some podunk stop on our way to Loutone. I fancy a warm meal. My treat." I lifted my eyebrows, but didn't give her any more time to question our stop as I grabbed the extra length of chain that connected her wrists to her ankles.

My eyes lingered on the raw, red skin under the cuffs. That was her fault. She could have had a mostly chain-free ride if she hadn't tried to act a fool. I guided her forward and through the carefully painted green door of the tavern.

The rich aroma of warm cooked meals greeted us pleasantly as we stepped in. The tables looked clean and full of enough patrons to tell me that this place had been worth the stop. Behind the bar, a short fae with shoulder-length red hair gave us a small wave. Her face was so youthful, I had to do a double take. Was this fae even old enough to be working behind a bar? She looked like she was only ten years old.

The chains rustled noisily between me and Red as I approached the bar. A few lingering eyes stopped to stare at my nymph. Red stared right back at them until they eventually looked away. She was a stubborn, headstrong girl.

"Excuse me, miss, can I speak to your mother?" I glanced back and forth behind the bar, waiting for someone who wasn't a child to serve me.

The red-haired child rolled her eyes, "This is my bar. How can I help you?"

"Cut the crap," I shot back with a look of disbelief.

"I'm nearing my eightieth birthday. My stilling happened when I was twelve. So you can either quit staring at me like I'm an attraction in a traveling circus and order, or you can turn around and quit wasting my time."

Red chuckled behind me. I gave her a hard yank, making her stumble, to shut her up.

"I need two orders of steak with whatever vegetables you have handy and, uh, what do you recommend to drink?"

The girl pointed down to the yellow ale most of the men were drinking at the bar, "I reckon our beer is good enough. Most popular drink on the menu."

My head felt dizzy and my stomach churned at the thought of another night drinking that terrible brew ever again. "No. No. I've found that I don't enjoy that. It's bitter," I scrunched up my nose.

"Hmmm," she nodded, thinking. "You know what, take a seat. I think I know what to get ya."

"Would you look at that?" I turned around, giving Red a big fake smile I knew wasn't reaching my eyes. "Lady can read minds. Why don't we go find a seat and see what she brings us?"

Red didn't respond. I didn't expect her to. But she did openly roll her eyes as she kicked her chains in front of her. There were plenty of seats to choose from between the already filled tables. Booths under large lamps that left little room for hiding. A thought that made me both thankful and nervous.

"Here," I pointed to the wooden seat.

The smell of the pine cleaner they used on the tables lingered on the wood. Every inch was sanded to smooth away splinters. A basket of warm bread already sat waiting on every table for the dinner rush. Carefully, I slipped into the seat across from her and let the long chain drape between us on the table.

"Do you wonder why you don't see any nymphs here?" Red pushed her chin forward to indicate the rest of the room.

"Because people don't normally take slaves out to dinner? Is this a joke?"

I flicked the thin layer of material that kept the flies from the food off the bread and plucked a roll from the basket. Warm, soft, and buttery, the bread made me excited for the rest of the meal. This was good.

"But don't they make them carry their shopping bags?"

I followed her gaze to a couple who chatted away while they picked at their meals, bags from their evening shopping sitting near their feet.

"Don't they make nymphs watch their horses or work in their kitchens, or hold their fucking umbrellas to shield their precious fucking faces from the sun?" she snarled quietly through clenched teeth, like I just wasn't getting something. "I didn't see any outside either. How am I the only one?"

She was right. There hadn't been any outside assisting their masters. From what I could see around the half swinging doors to the kitchen, it was all fae working back there too. But I didn't have time to question it further in private before the owner swept back through holding two pink drinks.

"One for each of you. Your food will be out in a minute. Why don't you give it a sip and tell me what you think? I can bring you something else if it doesn't please you. But I think it will."

I examined the short, fat cup with the long stem. Pink liquid with a dark to light gradient, and something floating in a layer along the top, with bubbles that didn't seem to pop. I sniffed it, pleasantly surprised by the fruity smell.

"What's in the layer at the top?" I asked. Intrigued, I swirled the liquid in the cup.

"Candy," she smiled, slipping her hands into the apron pockets.

Red's bored gaze traveled between me and the cup. She was probably hoping that the cup was poisoned so she wouldn't have to meet her fate with Windre.

Surprised at how good the sweet flavor sounded right now, I lifted my cup toward Red in salute and brought it to my lips. Creamy, carbonated liquid, flavored like a strawberry pie slipped past my lips and filled my mouth. I swished it around taking in the delicious flavor. This was beyond better than that nasty yellow ale the men seemed to enjoy. I swallowed gulp after gulp, until the cup was empty.

There hadn't even been time for sweat to form a ring on the table before I was setting it back down, completely empty. Honestly, I'd assume by the freshness of its taste that it lacked what caused that terrible feeling I had the next day.

"I'll take another." I glanced at Red, "Drink up."

The owner nodded with a polite bow, scooped my cup up, and gave Red a questioning look. It made me pause to think that maybe Red was right. Maybe there weren't any nymphs here.

"Excuse me, before you go, can you tell me why I don't see any nymphs around these parts?"

She stopped, holding my empty cup with both hands, and squinted, "You must be from another court. Heathern if I'd have to guess by your warm complexion. Windre does not allow common folk to keep nymphs. Only those in his court or someone with money rich enough to buy one from him."

"I'm not sure if that's a good or a bad thing," Red mumbled.

"Good for the nymphs, bad for me. I've got to pay the staff in my kitchen to work." She shrugged and headed back behind the bar.

Red watched the bubbles in her drink slowly rise to the top. She stared at it so hard I wondered if she had completely sunken into the deep recesses of her mind. Until she picked the cup up and took a tentative sip.

The owner dropped off another drink and disappeared without a word. I grinned, downing the glass as quickly as I had the first. Red merely continued taking sips here and there, her attention floating from face to face like she was waiting to find someone she recognized.

"Are you scared?" I finally asked. My body was feeling warm, it must have been the heat from the large light above.

"No," Red bit out, then took a large gulp from her drink. "I'm fucking petrified, and this is all because of you."

"Me?"

"Yes, you." She lowered her voice, "You just come waltzing into my court, my kitchen, acting like you are something you aren't, and when you get caught you can't just take your new assignment alone. No. You had to get me roped into it."

"Oh, trust me. I did not pick you. If I had a choice, I would have picked someone a little more docile, a little more sane."

"I don't believe you."

"Do you think I care if you believe me or not? You can turn up that crooked nose of yours all you want, but I had nothing to do with it. It just happens to be my luck that I got stuck with the one nymph with a fucking attitude problem."

Red shook her head in disbelief, anger quickly becoming amusement. "If you think I'm the only one that has an attitude problem, then you're wrong. I'm just the loudest. For now."

A full glass appeared on the table, replacing my empty cup. I gripped it and drank part of it down. The sweetness helped to cool the burning rage that Red liked to light within me. Thoughts bombarded my brain, and the filter I normally kept in place disappeared.

"You're fucking unmanageable and you'll get what you deserve when we get to the castle. So will any of your fucking little friends," I laughed, because it was all I felt like I was able to do.

The knobby bones in her shoulders lifted as she stiffened at my words. Her thin lips pressed together, nearly nonexistent, before she frowned deeply. Water brimmed in her eyes, but not a single tear fell. Red cared deeply for her friends, though she didn't have to say it for me to see it. I pushed the thought away. I didn't need to make her feel more relatable to me in any way. Red was likely going to die in the Acture Court. She wouldn't let them break her spirit.

Greedily, I drank the last of my cup. Just in time too, as someone emerged from the kitchen with our sizzling plates and another drink for both Red and I. I guessed she had finally finished her cup. She hadn't said if she liked it or not, but surely she had because it was empty and it wasn't like there was room in our argument to ask.

Steam rolled off the meat, still slightly pink as I cut it open. A healthy side of various vegetables filled the remainder of the plate. And there was my sweet, pink drink to top it all off like a liquid dessert. I took another sip before I cut into the meat.

Red waited till I dug into my plate then picked up her own fork and knife and started in on her own. Her shackles banged loudly against the table and plate, earning us a few unhappy glances.

"Here," I whispered before I dug the key out of my pocket and leaned forward to remove the cuffs.

"Wanna get my feet, too?"

I chuckled, lifting my cup back up to my lips, "Not a chance."

"Worth a try," Red muttered.

The remainder of our meal was mostly silent. Though my hands began feeling heavier and harder to manage. I blinked as liquid pooled on the table and ran off into my lap. My seventh pinkity drinkity. Eighth? How many have I had? What? Wait. Pinkity drinkity? Something was clearly wrong with me. My clumsy hands wrestled with a napkin, dabbing the liquid that continued to pour onto the cloth of my pant legs.

Red giggled. Then giggled again.

It was nothing I'd ever heard from her. For a moment it was sobering. I lifted my gaze up and stared. One slender hand was cupping her mouth as more laughter tumbled out, her eyes half-hooded as she pointed at me.

"You know those drinks have alcohol," she slurred. "And you drank a lot."

"How many have you drunk?" Mentally, I was adding up our bill. Thank the gods I had set aside some of that money Marcus had tried to steal.

"Two. I'm not drunk, you are," she hiccupped and both hands slapped over her mouth. "Shit, maybe I am drunk."

"Not a lot of meat on those bones to balance it out." I leaned into my seat, suddenly aware of how gravity was affecting me and how the room danced in circles.

With a wide, knowing smile, the owner took a deliberate step toward our table. "I own the hotel next door if you need a room for the night."

"No. No need." I pulled the bag of coins from my hip and dumped a heap on the table. That should be enough to cover our meal, plus a healthy tip for her quick service. Hurriedly, I pushed off the table and stood.

But standing wasn't happening very well. I exhaled, fanning the red bangs off her forehead as the fae gave me an 'I feel sorry for you' grimace. My chest was braced against her palms as she pushed me upright and I tilted back toward the bench. Smoothly, or as smooth as a drunk man with the top half as heavy as a cow could manage, I grabbed the back of the booth and leaned onto it.

"Totally fine," I laughed. "But maybe the nymph would like to stay the night. I'll do it for her. Draw out the suspense of our trip." I couldn't help the way I wiggled my fingers at her.

"I don't like you when you're drunk," Red pouted.

"I don't like you when you're not drunk." It was a pathetic rebuttal, a clumsy slur that tumbled off my tongue.

"Here," the owner plucked a few extra coins from my bag that I hadn't realized I had left out on the table, and handed me a large key. "Head next door and you can use this key for room twenty-five. Just make sure not to get too loud." She glanced from me to Red.

This would delay our trip. But since I wasn't able to stand upright without the world tipping me over, it was likely the better option to just make camp for the night in the hotel next door. It was okay. It was all going to be okay. I was already screwing up my assignment because of this stupid drink that tasted like fresh fruit. But maybe if I keep saying it... everything would turn out *fine*.

"Well let's go." I grabbed the bag of coins and attached it back to my waist, scanning the booth for anything else I may have misplaced. Red scooped up her wrist cuffs and scooted out of the booth. Together, we wobbled out the door and managed to make our way into the hotel.

"Room Twenty-Five," I said, holding up a key as we entered, to no one in particular.

A man dressed in a well-pressed suit looked up. His lips turned down in an unamused frown and he pointed to his left to a clearly marked hallway with doors with small painted numbers on them. Perfect.

"Onward," I coughed, placing my hand on Red's back and steering her toward our door. I could see the number twenty-five painted in green on the old weathered wood. Almost there.

Stumbling against the walls in between doors, I bounced back and forth like an eagerly thrown ball, until I stopped and shoved the key into our lock. It clicked and the door creaked open.

Inside, the lights were already on as if they had been expecting us. A single dresser, an understuffed chair, and a single bed. Quite frankly, it looked like the first dump I had stayed in when I entered this freaking realm.

"Great, another piddly slum like the last time." I grabbed Red's arm and pulled her along.

My foot caught against hers and we toppled forward, both trying to catch ourselves, only to collide again and bounce off each other onto the bed. We landed with quiet yelps as the mattress broke our fall and our shoulders brushed. Any words that we could have said didn't feel right anymore.

Every tense muscle in my back relaxed against the green comforter, and Red's head lolled to the side, a lingering smile still on her lips. Silence grew as we lay next to each other, breathing deeply.

"What's your favorite color?" Red asked in a whisper.

I squinted at the ceiling tiles like somehow that would help me sort through my muddled thoughts. "Red." I finally answered, knowing that was the answer that was required.

"Why red?"

"Red like blood. Red like lipstick. Red like the gowns my queen likes to wear."

"And do you fancy your queen?" she said even quieter.

"Hardly. But red is her favorite color, so it must be mine too."

"Is that how it works, then? You only are allowed to like what she likes?"

"I'm bound to her." I closed my eyes, shuffling through all the knowledge I had of what she liked and didn't like. Like files that were transferred from her brain to mine as soon as the binding was done.

"What color do you like?" she said again, turning to look at me. I could feel the heat of her gaze on my skin.

"I already answered this question. Red."

"No. Not what color you're supposed to say. Not what color does your queen favor. What color do *you* like?"

The answer had always been red. It had been red since the day I had been taken in to train in the castle. But I thought about it for a moment. Eydis often wore lavender. A particularly pretty shade of purple that I always thought complimented her fair skin. Then again, I only favored that color so much because it looked good on her.

"Brown," I finally said. Brown, it was a good sturdy color and most certainly underrated.

"Funny, you stuck me as a blue sort of guy. Like a deep, navy blue," her voice remained soft as she watched me. "That's the first I've heard from you that actually felt truthful."

"Shit." I sat up making the room spin in wild circles. Vomit rose, like flaming acid in my throat as I steadied myself and forced it back down.

"Don't worry. Who am I going to tell at this point that would believe me? You clearly are not from the

Twinity Court, so whatever region you hail from has certainly got to be far away."

A whole realm away to be exact. Yet, that didn't reassure me. Me and my big, fat, can't-keep-anything-quiet mouth. Whatever alcohol was in these drinks gave me a loose tongue.

"I'm never drinking again," I groaned, falling back against the pillows. My eyes drifted shut, lured by an overwhelming sense of fatigue.

"Yeah, until next time," Red giggled.

I think I love her laugh. The thought trailed through my mind. A drunken thought. Where her shoulder brushed mine was warm. It was a comforting thought, not being alone in this world, with someone who knew a little truth about me.

EIGHT

Red

I refused to let sleep pull me under like a capsizing boat, even if it could offer me vivid dreams of Milo drowning in pink, strawberry liquid. Instead, I relaxed and simply closed my eyes. As I felt his breath slow and his body slacken, I shifted on the bed. Slowly at first, just enough to make him think maybe I was rolling over to get comfortable. I waited there to see if he would wake. When he didn't, I reached with trembling fingers into his pocket. And it wasn't his family jewels I was after. My slender fingers curled around the key to my shackles. Milo still didn't move. Oh thank the mother. The key was long and slender and my release to freedom.

He was an idiot for thinking I wasn't going to take advantage of his drunkenness. Maybe he had thought I would take advantage of him another way, as I had noticed his nearly-hard cock pressed against his pants. Maybe in another world, where he wasn't him and I wasn't me. I hated myself for the way my gaze traveled up his muscular chest and traced the planes of his always-sad features.

No matter the smile he put on, no matter the anger that filled him, something about Milo was always just in *despair*. I tried not to wonder who had broken his heart to such a degree. His queen, perhaps?

Every move I made, I made sure it was deliberate. The lock on my ankle opened with a soft click, and I was careful to set the metal on the floor. My groan of pleasure as I rubbed my ankles was involuntary. Shifting my weight from side to side, I took a moment to shake out my legs. I felt like a different person when I wasn't dragging that anchor around.

I left the key to the chains on the floor and Milo as he was, practically snoring, on the bed. Freedom awaited. Without the chains, the only tell I had as a nymph was the tattoo under my hair, and my scent, should someone breathe in deep enough. Plus, I would need to steer clear of anyone who might recognize me as being with Milo. I thought I had the faces of the fae at the bar ingrained in my head well enough.

Our squeaky door whined on its hinges and I pulled it open wide enough to slip through and closed it behind me. My back pressed against the cold wood. I had made it this far, no need to let fear grip me now. Still, my heart thundered like a horse sprinting through the woods.

Pushing away from the door, I headed down the hallway that led to the entrance as quickly as I could without drawing attention to myself. Our horse and wagon were just outside. I hated to leave Milo high and dry, but *see you later, motherfucker!*

A door opened to my left and an arm reached out to stop me. "Excuse me, miss?" a man with short dark hair said. He smiled widely as he looked me over. "Do you work here, pretty thing?"

"No, I don't." I pulled my hand away, but he stepped in front of me. Fae were cruel and they treated women like playthings. I would not be his toy.

"Nevermind what I needed. I think I just found an answer to my question right here. Why don't you join me in my room and I can buy you a hot meal and a pretty dress, if you like?" He tugged at my stained, ill-fitting shirt. His lips smacked together waiting for my answer, though my repulsion had to be clear on my face.

"Do not touch me with your nasty hands," I scowled, pushing myself into his personal space. How would he like it if someone entered it unwelcomed?

At first his smile fell, but then it picked up again as he reached for my face and ran his fingers through my hair. I froze as the realization settled on his features.

"A nymph," he laughed. "Should have realized it by the ash markings on your chest. I just thought you may have needed a good shower."

The man lowered his mouth to my neck, speaking into the shallow dip between my tendon and my collarbone. Angrily, I tried to push him off, but he only came nearer, his eyes twinkling at the prospect of a fight. "Do you think your master would mind if I borrowed you for just a few minutes?"

His palm was clammy as he ran his hand up my arm. I narrowed my eyes, trying to put every ounce of my anger into the movement. I jerked my knee up to hit him, but he slid back, easily grabbing my lifted leg at the thigh, and slipping back into my personal space. His hips pressed against mine. A wave of nausea hit like a punch to the gut. He might do worse to me than Marcus ever did.

"Actually," a rough voice growled, "I do mind."

The greasy fae man attached to me stumbled back, getting a good look at Milo. I knew he had to be deciding if he was going to push the subject or not. But

Milo was nearly three times the size of him, and he looked just about livid enough to kill the man right now.

"Let's go back to our room now, Red. Can't stand the thought of someone using something that belongs to me without my permission." His attention remained trained on the other fae as he clamped his hand around my wrist and dragged me away.

I tripped over my feet as Milo practically threw me back into the room. The door slammed shut and he darted into the bathroom. Loud retches, and the sound of the contents of his stomach meeting the toilet with a sickening splat, filled the room.

"You're lucky," Milo emerged, wiping at his mouth, "I was awake and curious enough to see how far you were going to take it."

Damn it all to hell.

"You were fucking awake?" I dropped to the bed.

"I would never do to you what that man was going to do to you. You're an idiot for thinking you could get out of this town unnoticed. You're the only nymph for miles! Who was going to help you?" Milo planted his arms on either side of me, bending until his red face was level with mine.

"But you'll take me away to my death," I shouted back.

"You don't know that."

104

"Someone like me isn't going to survive Windre, Milo. I'm too stubborn, and he will kill me because of it."

"Because you won't break is exactly the reason why I believe you have the chance to make it out alive. You're an asset to King Ottack and not Windre's to kill," his chest rumbled with the growl. Milo pushed himself off the bed, pulling his hand through his long, dark hair. The brown of his eyes looked almost sunkissed as he stared at me. Maybe brown was a good color after all.

"Lay down and go to sleep," he pointed at the bed. Still fighting his drunkenness, he leaned against the wall, sliding down until he sat with his knees up in front of him.

"What will you do?" I asked.

"Make sure you don't escape again."

NINE

Ryker

The long stretch of silence should have said enough. Every passing second had me wondering if I had missed the signs. Were they something more than lovers? Had they had a rough fall out and my question hit an open wound?

Suddenly, I felt like a foolish girl. An idiot who believed in romance like my sister did. The thought of my sister made me squeeze my eyes shut. It helped to clear my mind of the fog that seemed to fill my head anytime Dace was near. It was that damn, sharp jawline of his, and those great forearms with intense veins. *Clear your head, Ryker.*

"No, uh, it's not like that," Dace finally said.

"But you have slept together?"

Why was I doing this to myself? I didn't really want to know. It was just so

106

clear that Dace cared strongly for her. I wish he would have just answered sooner and said something like, 'she's practically my sister'. Why couldn't she be like a sister?

Dace cocked his head, watching me with interest. "Why are you asking, Ryker?"

"I just assumed that maybe you were together." My hands met in a nervous twist. "I heard that she was awake and I didn't want her to get the wrong impression, should someone see you leaving my room. Which you should probably do."

"Don't worry about Shavarra. We are not together, not in that way. And," he held up a finger. "You never let me get point number two out as to why I came to your room." Unfazed by our awkward conversation, Dace pulled the chair away from the small desk and sat on it, balancing his elbows on his knees as he leaned forward. Everything in me yearned to sit near him, to listen to the velvet of his voice. The attraction between us was clear. But I couldn't afford to be a love-struck idiot.

I thought back to the night he took me out in the Acture Court. It hadn't been a date. Not a real one, not an official one. But it still felt like I was being courted. The same feeling of wishing we were not so different traveled through me now. I was nymph, only just now free of enslavement. He was a fae prince who had lost his crown.

Yet, I didn't want him to leave the room. Not yet. "Alright, give me your pitch." It took both hands to close the wardrobe, but I was able to finagle the fabric inside, enough to be able to lean against the doors and watch him.

"I can help you find ways to utilize your powers in combat," he shrugged. His scent was strong and I found myself taking a deep breath of the pine needle aroma.

"And..? What's the trade off?"

"And you'll help me keep it a secret that I'll be training too." One hand came up to rub the back of his neck. "I know I have the capability to transport items with me, people even. My power just hasn't been worked hard enough before."

"Why does it need to be a secret?"

Dace laughed and leaned back in the chair, hanging one arm across the back. He tilted his chin up. Ever the picture of confidence, even then, he spoke, "Because it's embarrassing, that's why. I'm a noble fae. Royal blood. I can barely manipulate my own travel, much less bring someone or something with me."

"It must be hard not being good at everything," I gave him a fake pout and ran my finger over the closet door. His teeth bit into his bottom lip, his eyes trailing my finger. Excitement made my heart beat harder, so I laughed to release the tension and gave him a playful smile. It was hard not to imagine that I was brushing my fingertip over his chiseled chest.

"Don't do that to me, Ryker," he hummed.

"Do what?" My arms folded over my chest as I watched him with raised brows.

"Tease me."

"Oh, learn how to take a joke. I'm only poking fun."

"I know." He stood, his loafers tapped against the floor, the only sound other than my trilling heartbeat. A wicked grin made the skin around his eyes crinkle. "I like it when you play with me. That's what makes it so dangerous."

I swallowed, trying to give life to my dry mouth and throat as I looked up at him. If he came any closer I could press myself against him, align our bodies in the way that my mind kept suggesting. We could brush our lips together in a moment of ecstasy that would, at some point, sizzle out. His teeth could scrape against the sensitive skin on my neck, douse the last of the scent from the tamer. Dace hadn't said anything about the lingering scent. But occasionally I would catch his eyes drifting to the exact spot.

"You can't sway me with your beauty," I lifted up on my toes to speak against his lips. *I could kiss him right now.* I could answer the lingering question of what his lips taste like.

He pulled away, just enough to be able to see the entirety of my face, "You've said that once before, yet somehow we always end up together." He leaned down, pressing a gentle kiss against my cheek.

Heat like I had never felt before burned up my cheekbones to the tip of my ears. Goosebumps rose over my arms. The air in my lungs was stolen by the smallest of movements.

"If you're ever in the mood to play, let me know. Or if you're done playing and you want to get a little more serious, I'll be around for that too." Ignoring the shiver he sent through me, Dace walked back to the desk chair and pushed it back into place. He paused at the door, looking at me with his blue sky gaze. "Meet me in the stables tomorrow night. We can start training."

***

Dace

I had said what I said and I hoped it wasn't too much too soon. Ryker couldn't tease me like she did. Not if she meant to keep me at a distance like she tried so hard to convince herself to do. It turned so sexy in an instant, and it damn near took everything in me not to act on the scent of lust in the air.

With the door shut behind me, I wiped my sweaty palms against my pant legs, my fingers roaming to touch the tips of the daggers on my belt to reassure myself that I was, somehow, still put together.

Hopefully she believed me when I said that Shavarra and I were not a thing. No matter how many feelings Shavarra may or may not have, Ryker was it for me. Ryker wasn't just my sun or my moon. She was my whole damn sky. She just might not be ready to know that yet.

It was a perplexing thing to be so near her, to know what we could be together, and not act like we were already there. I'd waited so many years, I could wait a little longer for her to figure it out on her own. But, damn, if I didn't want to fully kiss her just then.

Before I continued down the hall I adjusted the hem of my shirt, taking a moment to collect myself. It had been a shock to hear that Shavarra was awake. Why had no one told me? It almost made me ill to think that maybe no one had been there when she woke up. I should have been there.

The crumbling hallways were often filled when I walked them. Nymphs roamed as they had never been allowed to before. They made the most of it and I admired the joy that many of them carried once they got their freedom back. It made it feel like this war was worth fighting.

Rebecca Grey

It wouldn't happen overnight, and even this court still needed some mending. Occasionally, a nymph would walk by and still give me a dark glare or put space between themselves and I. Many of them still did not trust me. They only tolerated me because Ryker had let me in with open arms.

I came to the infirmary, one of the few rooms that hadn't been totally trashed. Beds had been lined up and filled with nymphs. Many slept or entertained themselves quietly, but I heard a bout of laughter as I entered and I recognized it in an instant. Shavarra had a blanket pulled up over her head and cocooned around her, her legs crossed under her, and her winning hand of cards sprawled out on the small table between her the bed next to her.

"Maybe next time, Rinny," she beamed.

"Can't let yourself get rusty, can you?" I whispered, wrapping my arms around her shoulders and pulling her up to me.

"I thought you forgot about me," she said squeezing my arm and leaning against me.

"No, though I'm mighty upset no one told me you were awake until now." I tugged the white blanket off her head, her blonde hair was pulled up messily. Through her pale strands I could see the long, dark-pink cut that was mending back together.

"You didn't wake up alone, did you?"

112

"No, there are like twenty of us in here." She gave me a sad smile.

"I'm so sorry, Shavarra," I said softly, brushing the frizzy strands of hair that had stood up when I pulled the blanket away, "For a lot of things. Listen," I glanced at the nymph across from her who took the hint and pulled away from their game of cards. "I don't want to lead you on. And if we need to be through, if you need me to stay away, I get it. Just know that I do care about you, Shavarra. You're more to me than just meaningless sex. You're my friend. You built the refuge with me."

"No, Dace. I'm sorry. You've been straightforward with me about everything from the get go. I knew there was never any room in your heart for me. It's my fault for letting myself catch feelings when I knew they could never be reciprocated." She grabbed my hand, pulling it away from her face and holding it between her palms. It calmed the chaos in my mind.

"So we can still be friends, right?"

"Always."

"Thank the gods," I breathed. "Scoot over then, let me get in here with you."

She laughed, making room for me on the bed, and lifted the sheet for me to shimmy under. Her bedding smelled like her, clean and sweet, like blooming lavender. Where she had sat was still warm.

"I think she finally hates me less." I leaned into the backboard of her bed.

"Well, tell me more," she answered, drifting back against my shoulder.

And so I did. Shavarra was my only real friend since Torrance had proven to be just as fake as everyone else in our court. Eager to use me for some sort of gain of his own. What did he get out of it though? Favor with my parents? My eyes traveled the expanse of the room, over the white bedding and quietly talking nymphs. Shelves along the walls housed oddly-shaped bottles with a rainbow of different color selections.

"Something about taking charge of this place... it chipped away at her anger. She's stronger now. Happier."

"Are you happier now?"

Me. It was always about me. Shavarra was always concerned about how I was doing and it was never about her.

"You know what," I patted her leg, "I'm happy right now. With you. Let's not talk about *her* right now, or me."

Shavarra's face flushed. "What do you want to talk about then?"

"You. You know what? Maybe you can tell me how exactly you got so good at playing cards." I smacked my lips, thinking. I didn't actually know that much about

Shavarra. Where was her family? What was her favorite meal? Or her favorite place to visit?

"Something's gotten into you, Dace," she laughed, pushing my hand off her leg.

"Call it a rude awakening."

"This may be good for you." She pointed a finger at me, the polish that had once coated them now chipping away.

"But we aren't talking about me, now are we?"

Her small, button nose crinkled with a smile. "Where do I even start?"

Crossing my legs at my ankles, I snuggled into her bed. I waited on her every word, determined that I would listen and learn for once. I would be better. Better to her, the friend who had done the most for me, even when I took her for granted.

"How about you start at the beginning?"

TEN

Ryker

Dace hadn't been seen out in the valley the entirety of the day. Rumor had it, he was in the infirmary with his friend, Shavarra. I still wasn't convinced that they were not an item, but Dace hadn't given me a reason not to trust him yet.

The sun was heading toward the horizon. Nymphs who had put in a hard day of work training and growing stronger out in the valley were turning back toward the castle. Men, who had organized themselves as our castle guard, switched positions and walked the perimeter.

Daethian unwrapped his hand, examining his knuckles. I leaned over the railing that had been made using the old frames of our tiny beds and glanced at his hands. As I expected, they were bright red and practically busted open. Daethian had pushed himself hard today when he sparred. A side of him I hadn't seen too much of. Almost like something else, something very angry and dark, had taken hold of him for a while.

"Maybe tomorrow you stick to just trying to manipulate your powers?" I pointed to his hand. "I think you should stay away from sparring, you nearly gave that one kid a concussion."

"Yeah." His eyebrows furrowed. "I didn't realize I had been going that aggressively."

A single strand of his dark brown hair fell forward into his face and he pushed it back into his sweat slicked hair. His shirt had long since been discarded on the side of the ring and his chest was still heaving with panting breaths. His tan had deepened, though a touch of sunburn had left his shoulders and cheeks flushed.

"Are you okay? You've seemed a little out of it lately. Just kinda out of touch with yourself."

"Believe me, I touch myself more often than a man should," he winked.

"Gross, Daethian," I laughed. "I'm being serious."

"I know, I know. It's just, I don't know what's wrong with me. I feel... off, but I can't quite figure out how or why. And I have these moments where time just escapes me. I'm doing things, but I'm not really present for them. Does that make sense?"

"Not at all," I shake my head. "Maybe you should have Suzetta take a look at you."

"Nah, I'm sure it will pass." Daethian gave me half a smile, leaning down to pick up his shirt and slip it back over his head. The material clung to his chest and his abdomen, darkening with sweat. "What do you say we go catch that meal together?"

"Actually, I already have plans."

He gave me a weary look, but we both started walking toward the castle. "Is it with who I think it is?"

"I don't know, who do you think it is?" I teased.

"Well it definitely isn't Randsin, because he hasn't left the motherdamned bedroom. But let me think... Does he look white as a fucking ghost? Is he overly cocky, despite the fact that he no longer has anything to offer?"

"Ouch. Man, you're really just trying to drive in the fact that you don't like him."

"Who said I didn't like him? What's not to like?" He shrugged his shoulders and bumped me with his hip. My steps staggered, but I swerved back on to my path.

"He saved me from Ganglin the night you were taken to the Acture Court. It could have been so much worse than some annoying fae chomping on my neck and taunting me. His scent will fade with time. Ganglin's, that would have stayed forever. And I don't think either one of us could have handled that."

"You're right. Okay, I get it. Generally, he is a decent fae. I'm just jealous because I wish you'd spend a little bit more time with *me.*" He batted his long lashes at me.

"Don't make me feel more guilty than I already do. I promise, tomorrow, we will have dinner together."

"It's a date!"

"It's not a date," I pointed out with a half-smile.

Daethian rolled his eyes. "Two people alone--"

"We won't be alone, a ton of other nymphs will be eating dinner at the same time."

"Alone. Enjoying a fine meal, with a couple of glasses of wine. Sounds like a date if I ever heard one."

"Daethian." I punched him in the arm softly.

"Fine, but if you change your mind, I promise I'll clean up really nice for you." He leaned down and pressed a small kiss against the side of my face, the hair of his beard scratching my cheek. But the kiss didn't do anything for me. Not like I thought it might. It felt practically platonic. "Hey," he straightened himself. "Have you heard anything about Ganglin? Or Hattie, for that matter?"

"No. It's been days since Graceson left, and he hasn't sent any messages. I'm hoping Windre's spies might have information for us. On either of their whereabouts." At night it was harder and harder not to think about the fact that Hattie hadn't returned. Sleep had been nearly impossible, and when I did sleep it was always a nightmare. "I really hope she's okay."

"I'm sure we will hear soon."

We stopped at the beginning of the mountain of steps that lead to the castle doors. Daethian turned, one foot resting on the first step, and looked at me. I couldn't help but stare back. We had come so far together. Starving slaves to practically running our own castle, and all because we never stopped believing in our right to freedom.

"This is where I leave you. I'm heading that way." I pointed toward the stables. "Why don't you go and talk to that girl. What's her name? Apaula. She watched you spar nearly half the day. Practically drooling."

"I don't know, I'm still pending a date with someone much prettier than her."

"There isn't a date, though," I laughed, walking backwards as he took his first step.

"For now, but things could change," Daethian yelled over the growing distance between us.

"Nothing is going to change."

"We'll see about that."

With a smile and a short laugh, Daethian turned and jogged up the stairs. I watched him for a minute, laughing to myself about how flirtatious, yet lighthearted, he was being. Careful not to trip on the dirt path, I headed for the stables. At this distance I could see the worn, sunbleached wood. The doors on either side were open, as they usually were, to allow some sort of a breeze in for the horses.

The valley had completely emptied now. Dew would soon form over the makeshift structures and targets we had created. Darkness covered them, but couldn't hide the way they made hope rise up within me.

Since returning to the Heathern Court, I had yet to come to the stables. Even the thought caused my chest to tighten and my stomach to knot. But tonight something else came with the idea of the stables. Excitement? Anticipation?

Rounding the corner, I could hear the horses braying and the flick of their tails as they brushed along the edge of their own personal prisons. There wasn't an intense odor, like I had expected, and the horses remained brushed and fed. Someone had been taking care of the stables. Guilt riddled me in an instant.

Most nymphs had taken back their regular jobs, something they were familiar with and could do well. Yet, I still had not done my part.

"Hello there, love," a voice called from the hayloft. Dace's feet hung over the edge as he swung them back and forth. He smiled down at me.

"Well, are we doing this or not?" I looked around wondering where exactly we were going to do this. When I looked back up, Dace was gone. "Dace?"

"Almost didn't think you were going to make it. Thought you might be getting caught up with that *not boyfriend* of yours."

I jumped as his voice came from over my shoulder. Whipping around, my hair smacked him under the chin as I faced him. "Yes, the same could be said of you with your *not girlfriend*. Didn't see you in the valley today."

"You see," he began, clearing his throat, "I'm trying this new thing out. I'm not particularly good at it. It's called 'being a good friend'."

"You're just now trying that out?"

"Yes, well, apparently it's a lot harder to have friends now that I'm not actually heir to a throne. And real friends are a lot more work."

"So that's what you were doing all day. Working."

"Exactly." He pulled his hand out of his pocket, holding an apple, and polished it against his sleeve. With one hand, he offered it to me.

Grateful, I took it with a nod. A snack was certainly needed before I tried to push myself any further today. Juice flooded my mouth as I took a small bite of the apple. The fruit had been cool despite the heat of the day. I wondered if it was Dace's doing. Through my full mouth, I asked, "Where would you like to begin?"

"Behind the barn perhaps. Keeps us out of view from the rest of the castle."

"Right," I say slowly, petting one of the horses' noses that poked out of their stall as I walked by, and pocketed the rest of my apple.

Dirt and hay crunched under Dace's feet as he followed me. He hummed an unfamiliar tune as he went, something surprisingly cheerful. Behind the barn, as he had pointed out, I wasn't able to see the castle anymore. Just the one side of the light colored barn wall and the expanse of manicured lawn on the other side. It was just the two of us. And that alone was a little bit scary.

Dace kept his distance, which did reassure me a bit, and stood against the wall watching me. The sun was nearly gone, just an orange blur above the distant forest. Stars were already appearing through the latticework of the clouds.

"What are you doing?" I asked, pacing slowly through the grass. Dew was already setting in as the wind blew in the evening chill.

"Looking at you," he bowed his chin, keeping his eyes trained on me with a coy smile.

I scoffed, turning away so he couldn't see the blush creeping up my neck. *This is about more than just a handsome boy, Ryker.* If I kept telling myself that, then maybe I could make it feel more real.

"Oh, so now I'm not allowed to look at you?"

"That's not what I said."

"True. You don't say anything. So I guess I'll take it as an invitation to keep on looking then."

Rolling my eyes and crossing my arms, I planted myself in one spot. "Let's get this going. I need to get some sort of sleep tonight. Would you like to start, or shall I?"

"Ladies first," Dace motioned for me to start. "What exactly are you working on now?"

"I--" I started.

"No, show me." He leaned forward with a stone-cold seriousness. A daring glare.

"Fine," I laughed, waving my palm in front of me.

Rock shifted under the earth, layers of soil, rock, and rooted plants peeled away. Under Dace's feet a hole appeared, dropping him out of sight with a quiet yelp.

He reappeared at my side, shaking his head, his arms crossed over his chest. "That was awfully cruel of you," he paused as I smiled, then continued with, "Nice move, must come mostly natural to you. But people like me don't fall for it. Or they have the opportunity to grab ahold of the edge, climb right out of your little hole."

"Not if I cover it up." Another wave of my hand and the rock and grass melded back together as it once was.

"In a real fight, you'll be too busy to close up every hole you open." Dace walked slowly, circling me like he was trying to examine me from all angles.

I put my hand out to stop him. "Not if I get really good at it."

"Oh, you'll get good at it. Just not quite yet." He grabbed my hand, lifting my arm over my head, then gave me a twirl like we were dancing again. He pulled me against his chest, my back against him and his mouth next to my ear. "You need to go for the kill." One finger trailed over my neck like a knife.

"Any suggestions?" I untangled myself from him with a sigh.

"Maybe instead of creating a hole, you create a mountain."

"That doesn't make sense." A strong wind blew across the lawn, ruffling the loose material of our shirts.

"Not like a big one. Think little. Think quick. Think sharp, like a spike." His fingers met at a small point in front of him as an example. The tiniest crinkle of his nose made me think that he was pulling this all right out of his ass. Maybe he was. Most likely, he was.

"Like this?" Inhaling, I imagined rock spiking up out of the ground. I fisted my hand. Cracking and crunching met my ears, and I opened my eyes to find a skinny slab of earth in the thinnest, sharpest, pyramid I'd seen.

It hit about Dace's height, and he looked at it, unimpressed.

"That took too long," he said mildly. "Faster. This time, keep your eyes open."

"Fine," I growled, annoyed by how blasé he was being. This was hard, and I had done it rather quickly for it being new. He was lucky I didn't knock him over with an accidental earthquake in my effort.

Keeping my eyes open, I shifted my gaze from him to the ground. I closed my fist and earth rose between us. Dace rushed forward, stomping it with his foot before it could build to anything more.

"Faster," he snapped.

I ground my teeth together and closed both hands. Sharp pillars began to rise on either side of him. His fist burst through one, his foot kicking through the other. Neither fast enough to beat his speed. But it wasn't just his speed I was trying to beat, I was trying to beat all of the fae just like him.

Heat flooded my body as my annoyance shifted to anger. So I tried again. This time with feeling. I closed one fist, a pillar rose and was shattered at the end of Dace's fist. Again. Closed a fist. Earth climbed over earth, sharp and angry, to the same end. Pebbles fell like a small hail storm.

My fist caught the air like I was snatching something up. Then I did it again with the other. Back and forth I went as Dace became a flurry of kicks and punches, slicing through everything I was creating.

Wind blew again, cooling the thin sheen of perspiration that was breaking out over my skin. But it couldn't calm my temper. Why was he being so hard on me? Wasn't this only lesson number one?

"Stop," I growled, yanking my fist through the air, "Doing." My fingers curled into my palm. "That."

"Why?" Dace taunted. "Does this upset you?" He spun around, kicking down the spike that I pulled up behind him.

"I said, STOP," I shouted, pulling both my fists to my sides. Spikes erupted like wildflowers around him, two touching his chest, and one pressed against his back.

His hands wrapped around the two stone pillars before him and he leaned into them. "That's it! Get mad, babe." Rock crumbled between his fists.

I sighed, wiping the back of my hand across my sweaty forehead, "I think that's enough."

"Why? You were just starting to get good," he laughed, slipping through the remains of the rock. "Although in a real life situation, you want to aim for the rock to impale them. But I do appreciate you not doing that to me."

"Aren't you supposed to be training, too? Your turn. Do a fancy little trick for me." I spun my finger in the air. *Show me what you got, Dace,* I challenged him back.

"I am not." he disappeared in one blink, reappearing next to me and sweeping his leg under me.

"A." My body toppled backwards through the air, my arms reaching for where he had been, but no longer was.

"Show pony!" He appeared where he had started and watched me land on my butt in the grass. He was mocking me, that asshole.

"Cool," I said. Pushing off the ground, I stood and dusted my legs off. "Now try that again with something in your hands." I tried to look bored, like Dace so often did, as I pulled the apple out of my pocket and tossed it to him.

"Well, if I put it in my pocket," he slipped it into his pants and disappeared. His voice erupted over my shoulder as he pulled the apple back out. "Not a single problem."

"But..." I said slowly.

"But, if I hold it in my hands." He gripped the apple and disappeared. Only the entire thing didn't disappear. A small sliver of the apple was shaved off and the majority of the apple fell and rolled in the lawn. Dace stood next to me. His shoulder rose and fell in a shrug as he held up the slice of apple and bit into it.

"I would hate to be that apple." We stared at the ground together for a moment. At some point he was going to have to carry something bigger than an apple. Bigger than the tiny slice he was chewing up right now.

Stepping through the slick dew, I bent down and picked up the apple remains. Red flew through the air and landed in Dace's quick hands. "Try again," I pointed at the apple. "But faster."

"My powers aren't fueled by my emotions, like yours," he laughed, gently tossing the apple back and forth between his hands. "Making me mad won't help me to improve."

"Then what helps motivate you?"

Dace licked his lips and tilted his head. He took a step toward me. The air next to him shimmered and he turned quickly. Jesseline appeared, hair mussed like she had been laying in bed, and her clothing sloppily thrown on.

"You have a visitor, Dace." Her hand rose to point toward the castle.

Her words took a moment to register. Our smiles slowly faded from our faces, replaced with concern and mild curiosity. Together we jogged around the barn. At the bottom of the long flight of stairs a dark figure waited, masked by the gloom of the sunless sky.

ELEVEN

Dace

Worry seeped through Ryker's features as she rounded the barn. The figure at the end of the path couldn't be made out at this distance in the night. The visitor was shadowed and a towering worry at the end of the path.

Jesseline walked between us, her voice low, "He is an assassin from our guild, but not one who works under the same people as us. I wouldn't trust him to get within arms distance of you."

The sounds of the night; hooting owls, croaking frogs, and chirping insects, felt muted now that my heartbeat filled my ears. I tried not to think too hard about how, from where we stood, the outline reminded me of an old ghost story my parents used to tell me about burgundy witches. It felt like they had brought them back from extinction to hunt me down now. As we neared, purple hair and deep, navy-blue eyes came into view. I couldn't remember a name, but his face was familiar, someone I'd seen in the castle many times before.

"He works for my parents," I groaned. "Do you know what he wants?"

"No, he said he would only speak with you." Jesseline pulled the hood of her dark cloak up over her head, and gave us a small nod before she disappeared. She wouldn't go far, not with this gentleman lingering around. Likely, she was finding herself the perfect spot to spy from.

The assassin took a step closer, but I held out a hand, projecting my voice just enough to sound assertive, "That's close enough. Why are you here?"

"Your parents are asking to have a word with you."

"Well, get on with it," I huffed, planting my hands firmly on my hips. I exchanged a look with Ryker, who waited patiently at my side. No doubt she was curious about what he had to say as well.

"They want you to come home to talk. They didn't tell me the message." His hands remained folded in front of him, a good sign that he wasn't waiting for his chance to slip something from his belt.

I laughed and then I laughed some more. "No, no, no. *They* disowned me, not the other way around. I won't be catering to their every whim. So you can just *poof* right on back and let them know."

The man fixed his gaze on me. Mother would not be happy with that news when he returned. "Wait here," he finally grumbled before his magic took him away.

Ryker turned to me, "What do you think they want?"

"The gods only know. As far as my mother goes, she's probably just reaching out to complain that I didn't finish something that she wanted done before she revoked my right to the crown."

As quietly as he had arrived before, the assassin appeared again, at the same distance he had kept before. His arrival came with the gust of the evening breeze. It spiked the anticipation that bubbled in my gut.

"Forgive me if I do not deliver this with the same *gusto* the queen would have. There have been riots and strikes throughout the Twinity Court since your crown was revoked. Your parents are asking that you return and calm them. Nip them in the bud, if you will."

"So we're asking favors now, are we?" I hummed, with genuine curiosity. Why would I help them? Why now? Were the people that supported me so influential that their fit-throwing concerned my mother that much? It was interesting food for thought.

Unless my father had seen something in a dream. Unless this was my opportunity to make a proposition. I looked at Ryker, then back at the man. If I could get my crown back, if I could be a prince again, I wouldn't need to train the world's smallest nymph army. I could provide an entire fae army. Holy shit. The revelation hit me like a bolt of lightning, the plan already forming in my head and tumbling from my lips before I could think it through.

"Those who did not support the decision to remove your crown are refusing to provide services or crops for those who did, including the castle," he continued quietly, his own plea for me to return. My mother would be too proud to divulge that information.

So they were going to starve the court out. Serves them right, those self-righteous assholes. With the crown, I could overturn the court, get rid of them all. Plus, there was still the matter of Torrance. May he rot in hell.

"Tell them that the only way I can calm them is by giving the people what they want so desperately. Give me my crown back."

I could feel Ryker shuffle next to me. The words repeated in my head as a coy grin spread over my cheeks.

The assassin pressed his lips in a thin line, preparing to leave and meet my mother's unyielding wrath. But I lifted a finger asking for a moment longer.

"And," I continued, "I want them to take my proposals seriously. I want our nymphs to be set free."

He sighed quietly, already preparing himself to deliver the news, and then he vanished. I stared at the spot where his feet had been, wondering how utterly, broiling mad my mother would be. If only I could see her face turn purple. It had to be truly out of hand if she was reaching out to me for help. It hadn't been that bad when we had left, and it had only been just over a week. I tried counting the days in my head. Was it? How long had we been here?

"Do you think she'll do that?" Ryker whispered. Her face was devoid of emotion and she had taken a step away from me at some point.

"Ryker, this is good." I closed the space between us, grabbing a hold of her arms. "I could gain back my power. I could *use* my power. Clearly, there are fae that want me there. They want it as it was before, they believe in your freedom."

"You have magic." She shrugged out of my touch. The shine in her eyes made me wonder if I was making the right choice. But of course I was.

"What about all those nymphs you brought here?"

"They'll stay, of course. This is where they belong." I stepped away, touching the hilts of my daggers in my belt.

"And Shavarra?"

I hadn't thought about Shavarra. She'd probably be ecstatic to hear the news. But what would she want to do? Would she want to return with me? She could be a new member in the court. She knew more about the general public than those stuffy old bastards anyway.

"Shavarra will have to make that choice on her own," I chewed my lip, thinking out loud. It was taking longer for the assassin to return. If he returned at all. Maybe my parents were laughing at me now and I had read this all wrong. "She could join me if she likes, but the nymphs from the refuge are like family to her."

A cough drew my attention. The assassin had returned and he didn't look like they had tried to take his head off. Not yet, anyway. His silence made me wonder how much of the conversation he had heard.

"The queen accepts your offer," he said slowly.

Internally, I cheered. Outwardly, I waited, because he wasn't done yet. "But…" I pushed.

His shiny white teeth glinted like sharpened knives in his mouth as he offered his own toothy smile. "But she has one condition."

I looked at him, waiting for him to continue. "For fuck's sake, what is with the dramatic pauses?"

"She wants you to take a bride. Once you are wed, your parents have agreed to step down from the throne, and you and your bride will become the king and queen of the Twinity Court. At that point, you can free the slaves."

Every ounce of air that had filled my lungs escaped me now. I wheezed like I'd been punched in the gut. Because, in a way, I had. My mother had always pushed for me to marry, and now this was her way of doing it. Her last hoorah before she couldn't force me into things anymore.

Plus, I never really wanted to be king. Not yet, anyway. I wanted my power as prince back. I wanted my parents to listen to me with the respect they showed everyone else. I wanted the nymphs to be free. I just didn't think it would happen so quickly.

My throat and mouth felt dry. Suddenly, the thought of doing anything but throwing up felt impossible. A warm body slipped near mine. Fingers intertwined with mine.

"It's okay, Dace," Ryker whispered. "Isn't this what you want?"

Had she seen the panic in me so easily? I blinked, trying to force away everything that terrified me about actually being the king. This was absolute madness, what they were proposing. Yet it had to be done. For the good of everyone involved.

My skin buzzed where Ryker's brushed mine. It felt wrong to agree to this with her here. It felt like I was turning away from everything that destiny had offered me. My mother wouldn't allow a nymph to be my bride.

"Tell my parents," I looked down and stared at Ryker's vibrant green eyes. "That I accept their offer. Give me time, two days at the most, to conclude my affairs here and I'll return."

"Thank you," he bowed, and vanished for the final time.

The reality of it was overwhelming. I was a prince again. Or would be soon enough. I was no longer going to be a nobody.

"I can't believe this is happening," I turned and shouted to the sky as Ryker slipped her hand out of mine. "This is insane!"

"It's a golden opportunity, really," she laughed quietly.

"Oh my gods." I ran in a circle at the bottom of the stairs, running up and grabbing her in a large hug. I pressed her slender frame to my body and spun around once. "We are going to win this fucking war!" Excitedly, I pressed my lips to her forehead in the briefest of kisses.

Ryker's cheeks were tinted crimson as I set her back down and she looked at her feet. With one finger, I lifted her chin so I could see the slight grin she wore. Moonlight filtered through the clouds, illuminating her face. I wanted to kiss her again. I wanted to kiss her directly on the lips.

"You're going to lead your people to freedom, Ryker. And I'm going to help," I whispered.

Jesseline appeared next to us, "Good news, I take it?"

"Great," I beamed. "Ryker, let me walk you back to your room."

Ryker hugged herself as another breeze lifted her ponytail. Ringlets had fallen down around her face as we had worked, and they framed her in the most beautiful way. Her eyes drooped, dark, telling circles had formed underneath them as she shifted her gaze back to me.

"That's a good idea after all this excitement." She waved to Jesseline, who disappeared with a smile. Her hand fell back to her side where her arms swung as she started up the steps. I wanted to take her hand in mine again. Press more kisses to her skin.

"So," she continued. "If you leave soon, when do you think we'll see you again? Or maybe Jesseline will go with you and her and Slyke can message back and forth."

If I leave, Ryker stays here. That didn't feel right. I didn't want to leave her again. Taking the steps two at a time, I caught up to her, trying to refrain from looking too deep in thought.

"Or I could come back and visit. We should still try to do what work we can on our powers." My unspoken *'and I want to see you again'* hung between us.

"Won't you be busy getting married?" She didn't look at me when she talked this time. Her attention remained focused on the last few steps before we reached the doors.

"I don't intend for that to be something that takes a lot of my time. Not if it isn't the right person." *Not if it isn't you.* I wanted to scream.

Inside, the hallways were mostly empty. Nymphs were either in the dining hall eating or having a party of their own in their rooms. Maybe some were sleeping, likely just a few. Ryker led the way back toward our rooms.

"Are you going to share the news tonight?" She slipped her hands into the pockets of her shorts as we approached her bedroom door.

I chuckled and turned toward my door. "No, I think that will have to wait until tomorrow morning at least. I need a moment to just soak it in." Carefully, I leaned forward, turning the knob of her door for her. "Here," I offered, "Holler if you need help with any more expensive gowns. I'm just down the hall."

"Not for much longer though," she pointed out, stepping into her room.

"Have Jesseline come get me, and I'll be here faster than you can say anyone else's name." I leaned into the door frame, but she pulled the door closed just a little bit more.

"I'll keep that in mind, Dace." The smallest hint of a smile graced her lips, but it didn't reach her eyes. "Goodnight."

"Goodnight," I sighed, as the door closed completely. What was I getting myself into?

TWELVE

Milo

No matter what I did, my eyes burned with the need for sleep. Red seemed well rested though, as she hummed a mournful tune with her lips turned down in a cranky frown. If I closed them even for one, slightly-longer-than-average blink, sleep threatened to take me under. But we were close enough now I could hear the calls of the capital that surrounded the castle.

The weather here was mild enough, similar to the Obtune Court. I was already beginning to think I'd never get out of these clothes and I'd die in a puddle of sweat. Leaves on the trees took on a different hue the closer we came to the capital. Green scalloped foliage faded into plum-y reds or sun-faded brown. Yet none of them littered the ground, like they would have in the shift of season back in Tierasia. It left me wondering if the city was spelled.

As homes and pedestrians came into view, I tested Red's cuffs on both her ankles and her wrists. She wouldn't be getting away this time. Sun glinted off the metal, making it even harder to keep my eyes open.

"Better make sure these are nice and tight," I murmured. This would be my first encounter with King Windre, the man who supposedly broke the nymphs of their rebellious spirit. We would have to see for ourselves what this king was all about. This was like a side mission to my main mission, not that I was complaining. The entire point of me working with King Ottack was to waste time and avoid the true reason for my visit to Stylica.

Finding the fae who took my queen's token had become more of a pressing need for her as she spiraled, feeling out of control. She lashed out against her own lands, just to appease the need to know what she could command. The way this had shaken her gave me hope that she could get rattled enough that we could knock her from her throne, as she had done many years ago to the king and queen who had ruled Tierasia in peace for their entire reign.

Whoever held the token, held the crown. Atarah wanted that token. She wanted the chance at more than just her own average gifts. But all that the king and queen had really had was half of the token. She would have to find the other half.

Queen Atarah hadn't wanted peace when she and her cult following ambushed the castle. The people didn't need peace, the people needed power, she had said. I'd heard this story time and time again. Atarah had only given herself power, not the people. In her attack on the castle, she had been successful in killing the king, queen, and their son. And, even though she fought hard to stop the rumors, sometimes people still whispered about the possibility that the prince had gotten away. His body was never found or publicly displayed as his parents had been. His father's corpse was found in the fury of the battle inside the castle, but his mother's, she had gotten farther. Her body had been carried back from the long expanse of forest behind the castle, along with the slew of men she had killed along the way. How far had the prince gotten? According to Atarah, not far at all. Perhaps the people were merely trying to hold on to the thread of hope that the rumor presented.

Along with her rule came a proclamation. The final words of a dying witch. Someone would come to Stylica, someone who wasn't meant to be there, and they would take what the queen treasured most. A.K.A. the token.

Then, Randsin had appeared, dazed and confused, in the middle of a gods-damned court nonetheless. And then he stole the love of my life. I didn't like Randsin, but I needed him alive. I needed the token to be protected or destroyed.

I sighed loudly. In my peripheral, buildings came and went, but I didn't give them enough attention to differentiate between home and storefront. Maybe it was for the best that I was here, away from Eydis, anyway.

"Why are you sighing?" Red pulled me away from my spiraling thoughts. "It's not like you're the one getting ready to be hurt."

"You could always just keep your mouth shut and comply with everything you're asked. That would probably help out your cause."

Red rolled her eyes, her body rocking with the sway of the wagon as we passed over uneven roads. Her attention kept drifting to the pointed towers of the grey castle; we kept getting glimpses through the tree line and busy, merchant-filled streets. She would try to distract herself by chewing at her nearly-nonexistent nails, or wearily watching people try to sell items to us as we continued by.

"Buy this beautiful hand-quilted blanket, sir," one offered, holding up a white cloth embroidered in gold swirls.

"Yes, Milo, why don't we stop for you to buy some souvenirs for this little trip. Maybe you can take one back to your queen." She turned to look at me. There was clearly not much hope that she could get out of this deal King Ottack had put her into now.

"Don't talk like that," I hissed through clenched teeth.

"I like it when your jaw cords like that." Red actually managed a small grin.

"You like to drive me bat-shit crazy, is what you like," I said as I fought to release the tension in my jaw.

Fae called to us and other passing pedestrians from their storefronts or wagon backs. Dark, blooming clouds overhead merged together to cover the sun. A few people, wise to the simple signs of an upcoming storm, plucked out umbrellas or scuttled back into their businesses. We did not have an umbrella.

Rain held off until we left the busy street and went through the small gathering of trees between the castle walls and the citizens of Caratona. Quiet grew where there was no longer the chant of sales to be made. Only the occasional caw of a bird as it took flight was left to listen to. In my humble opinion, that was a lot better than salesmen begging for my nearly-nonexistent dollar.

The emptiness between the rest of the world and the castle felt almost ominous in the shadows of the sagging trees. Through the last of the brush, the sound of water lapping against rock became apparent. Wood and plants met in a short bridge over the small, flowing river. The wagon jostled over the worn planks of the bridge.

And there it was. The outer wall that surrounded the castle was grey, tall, and spiked. Whether it was to keep people from coming in or from attempting to escape, would be determined. Two guards were posted at the gate. Their brown uniforms were trimmed in the same gold as the blanket the merchant had offered.

One man pulled himself away from the wall and stood directly in front of our cart, as I pulled the horse to a stop. "Name, and reason for visit?"

"Milo Piercing, I've traveled from the Obtune Court with a nymph King Ottack would like to place in King Windre's care." It made it sound like she was here for a vacation, and not the punishment she would undertake.

The guard grunted and motioned to his friend to open the gate, "Men will greet you at the door and bring you back to King Windre."

I mumbled a thanks, slapping the reins and urging the horse forward. Red had grown particularly quiet. I dared a glance at her. Her face was white, her arms folded over her chest, nails digging into her skin, and her legs were crossed. On top of that, her bottom leg began bouncing against the wagon floor. Red seemed to have lots of nervous ticks. She turned to me, not nearly as confident as she usually was.

The courtyard before the castle was filled with lots of miscellaneous devices, none of which looked like a lot of fun for the participant. Beams were nailed into the ground, ropes splattered with red lay between them. Even the grass near some of the other torture devices was stained with blood. It gave me an oddly familiar feeling of being home in my queen's own torture rooms. All different methods were available before we even made it into the castle. A few racks for stretching a victim's body, quite a few knee splitters, more than ten pillories to secure waiting victims, and even a tall, wooden box with its doors open and fitted with a number of spikes to penetrate the sufferer.

"There's still time to turn this cart around. You don't have to do this," her voice was hoarse and she spoke quickly. "Whatever it is that you want me to do, I'll do it. You want me to cry? I can fake a tear. You want me to beg? Hell, these knees have grown used to being pushed to the ground. We can turn around, right now."

"No, we can't." I turned forward, refusing to meet her red-rimmed stare. This wasn't like Red. Red didn't beg, she didn't bargain. She must be truly terrified.

"Fine," her pleas turned into a snarl. "Then what kind of price do you think King Windre would pay to hear that you're King Ottack's spy. Not only that, but you have an alliance with a far-away queen, and now you're here to sniff out his court. What would he pay for that information, Milo? What would he pay?"

And there she was with her quick and spiteful tongue. If sugar couldn't get her far, she knew that her menace could. But it wouldn't do the trick on me. My back practically cracked all the way up my spine with how fast I twisted, and my fingers dug into her cheeks as I pulled her to my face. Our wagon rolled to a stop in front of the waiting steps. A guard had already descended to meet us.

"You listen here, you'll shut your fucking mouth right now if you know what's good for you. Keep your tongue tamed and you won't make it worse than it already has to be." She didn't flinch as I spoke, but I could see the slightest tremble in her lip and water already building along her eyelids. But Red wouldn't cry. She would find a way to suck those tears right back up into her head and use the moisture to spit at us.

Pushing her away from me, I turned to the guard. "We are looking for King Windre, he should be expecting us."

"Right this way." The guard offered me his hand to help me out of the cart.

Already irritated, I waved him away and pulled Red forward. She stumbled out of her seat, the wagon tilting as all the weight shifted to my side. I didn't bother to be gentle with her now. The time for coddling her was over.

"Move it." I pulled the chain through my hands, stepping down and dragging her with me. To her credit, Red didn't say a word. I'd expected more of a fight, but maybe she was waiting a little longer for that. Only time would tell.

Her restraints rattled behind me as I led her through the tall black door and into the silence of the castle. I watched the guard's back as we trailed him, not bothering to make myself familiar with the castle just yet. He pushed through a final door, revealing the man I assumed to be king, reading while he ate some fruit, and a nymph sitting in the corner sobbing. I noted the way the nymph didn't have chains on his arms and legs, but rather around his scabbed neck.

"King Windre," I bowed low, dragging Red down with me.

The pages of his book slammed shut loudly, the nymph in the corner flinching. "You're late," he lifted his menacing stare to me.

I shifted under his scrutiny, "My apologies, someone tried to make a few escapes."

"No wonder King Ottack needs my help," King Windre spat. He stood, revealing a long braid down his back, and he shrugged into a long, auburn jacket. "You can't even keep one nymph tame enough to get here in time. King Ottack said in his letter that you should have arrived this morning. I don't like to be kept waiting," his voice dropped an octave, and that alone made me feel like my stomach was being filled with stones.

Expectantly, I pressed my lips together. King Windre was going to have to lead this show. I would take my own advice and keep my mouth shut.

"Let's get on with it," Windre sighed. "Step one, take responsibility for every time they step out of line. How many attempts did she make at escape?" His gaze traveled up and down Red's fragile body in disgust.

"Two," I said quietly. It was embarrassing, quite frankly. I should have been able to contain her. Somehow, in the kitchen, I had learned to let my guard down with her. I liked the way she entertained me with her quick wit, almost as much as I hated her unruliness.

"Twenty-five lashings then." He pointed at the guard still waiting at the door, "You may leave."

"Here? Aren't you worried you'll get blood on the carpet?" My boot kicked at the rug in the middle of the room. Shelves were filled all around us by various books, even those were in range to get some sort of splatter. And that looked like a very expensive carpet.

"Don't worry. She'll get it cleaned up after."

Windre pulled a whip off of his belt, looking at it a moment before he handed it to me. His whip felt different, but familiar, the handle surprisingly not as worn as I had expected. He must have seen it in the twitch of my brow.

"My whip is replaced monthly, if not quicker. I like a sturdy handle." Windre tilted his head, running his finger along his short beard. "Sit the nymph down."

I pulled at the chains, but Red didn't move. Her legs were stiff and her arms held close to her body like a statue. The only thing that moved was the rapid up and down of her chest as panic clearly raced through her mind.

It was better if she learned now. With more force, I wrenched her toward me. My hand met the back of her sweaty neck and I pushed her down to her knees.

"The shirt," Windre reminded sternly.

I took a breath. This was what I was good at. This is what needed to be done. So why did it feel so bad to do it? Maybe Red deserved it. But maybe, she really didn't. Either way, I needed to find a way to disconnect myself from the feeling.

The thin, flimsy material of her shirt tore easily as I ripped from the collar down and pushed the material aside. She was all bone. I had known that from the small glimpses I had when her clothing lifted, but looking at her back was almost scary. Every vertebrae, every single rib could be counted easily. It would take nothing to split her skin open right to her bone. Damn it.

Floorboards creaked as I took steps away from her, letting the whip fall loosely next to me. When someone screamed it was always my favorite part. A small thrill ran through me in anticipation that it would drown out the tiny taste of guilt that was souring my tongue.

Windre pushed his red jacket behind him, his hands on his hips as he circled Red like a hawk. A shiver ran down Red's spine as he lowered himself to her level and lifted her chin to him.

"Every time the whip hits you, you count. If you do not count, then our good friend Milo must start again, until he gets to fifty."

"I thought you said twenty-five?" I paused.

"Oh, it's twenty-five per escape attempt."

My fingers held the whip firmly, gripping it until I thought my hand might cramp. Windre stood and took a step back. His eyes flickered back up to me and he mouthed the word "go". I glanced behind me, the nymph in the corner had curled further into himself and his sobbing had quieted as he watched with wide eyes and gaping mouth.

Swiftly, I swung my arm above my head, getting momentum and warming up the muscles in my arm. The crack of the whip was felt with the entirety of my body as I pulled my arm back and carried the motion through with my torso. As if an extension of my body, Red lurched forward as the tip created a long red stripe down her back.

"Count," Windre said, kicking her leg.

"One," Red hissed, as I tugged the length of the whip back toward me.

Warmth traveled my body as I struck again. It had been too long since I had actually used a whip like this, and my whole physique, down to my legs, was waking up to the sensation of the movement again. Leather sliced through the air and slapped against Red's back as I struck again.

"Two," she whispered a moment after crying out.

"No, it wasn't loud enough," Windre said. "Start over."

So I started again. The whip cutting into her back over and over again. Her voice was a whimpering tremble I was certain would escape her, but it never did. Sometimes her screams made me smile. Sometimes the sound of her crying ruined it.

Rebecca Grey

THIRTEEN

Ryker

Waking up that morning was different. Something inside me had deflated. I tugged at the fluffy comforter on my bed, soaking in some morning laziness. Sunlight shone around my closed curtains, reminding me that I had responsibilities to attend to. I ignored the nagging feeling though and rolled over into my pillow.

My night clothes, a loose fitting shirt and cotton shorts, were bunched about as high as they could go from all my movement as I slept. But the sheets were warm enough it made up for the amount of bare skin showing. I spread my arms and legs out wide, reaching for the four corners of the bed, smiling to myself when I couldn't touch them. It was a huge upgrade from the tiny sliver of a bed they had forced us to sleep on before.

Two loud knocks on my door made me crack an eye, as if I could see through the door. I groaned and sat up. At this point I didn't care who was at the door, I wasn't getting out of bed.

"Come in," I yelled, pulling my hair up into a bun and securing it with a hairband I'd slept with on my wrist.

The door opened and Dace strolled in, his eyes wandering the room looking for me until they stopped, a little surprised, on the bed. He had obviously already been up and around this morning. Black leather pants, that screamed *I'm a prince again,* and another sheer shirt, this time gray. Today his hair wasn't as slicked back as it normally was, instead a few wavy strands twisted over his forehead. I hadn't realized he had any curl to his hair before, he must work rather hard to keep it slicked down. He took a few steps forward, stopping in the warmth of the sunlight that my curtains could not hide. Under the yellow rays his skin looked almost transparent, his veins bright icy-blue like his eyes.

"Good morning to you," Dace purred.

My traitorous body shivered at the words. Overly aware of my lack of underclothing, my thin shirt hardly hid the peak of my breasts, I folded my arms across my chest. "Nice to see you up and about." I crossed my legs in front of me.

"I actually came to see if we could do a little more of the training we didn't get to finish last night." He pulled yet another red apple from his pocket and held it in the light. "I could slice you off some pieces and we can call it breakfast."

"You want to do that right now?"

"Yeah, I'll just pop back and forth inside your room." He raised his eyebrows and whispered, "No one has to know."

"You think you can do any better than last night?" I challenged. "You never did get around to what motivates you. Since apparently, you are in better control of your emotions than I am." *I'm a wreck,* I thought to myself.

"Well, we can see how I do these first few times, and if I don't get any better, I'll let you in on a little secret."

"Okay then, get to slicing me up some apple." The apple in his hand did look rather nice and I remembered how juicy the last one he brought me was. Where was he getting these apples from? My mouth watered, my stomach rumbling in anticipation. "If you tried to bring me a cup of water, would it cut the cup long ways or up and down? I could really use a glass of water."

"Um, maybe let's not try that one just yet. I'm not trying to get glass shards on my clothes."

Images bombarded my thoughts. Glass shards on his clothes that he would then have to take off. Dace was far too handsome for my unchecked hormones. I smiled and placed my hands in my lap waiting.

"Okay, here it goes." He gave me a wink, vanishing. The apple hit the ground and rolled around where his feet had been. If he did this too many times my breakfast was going to get awfully bruised.

The air by my door shimmered for a moment and then he reappeared, already walking toward me with the slice. "Does it look any bigger?" he grimaced.

I took the chilled slice from his hand and looked it over. It was not any bigger. "Uh, maybe just a hair?"

"Are you just feeding me bullshit so I don't feel so bad that you made progress a lot quicker than me?" The tilt of his chin made the cut of his jaw extra sharp.

"Yeah, you really suck at this." I took a bite and smiled at the delicious flavor. Talking through the food in my mouth, I continued, "You sure you don't want to tell me how I could motivate you to do better? Honestly, I think pissing me off is what did it so well for me."

Though today I could tell my magic was tired. Sore, like a muscle, it ached at the thought of being used. But I would have to, I needed to make it stronger, build it up so I could be fast, smart, and deadly.

"Let me try again." He backed up from the bed, scooping the apple up again and vanishing without another word. The majority of the apple bounced off my floorboards. But he reappeared again by my bed holding out the same portion of apple as before.

My eyebrow ticked up as I took it out of his hand. "Not any better. Guess you'll have to fess up now." I leaned into my pillows, propping my head on my arm and popping the apple slice into my mouth. My fingers already felt sticky from the juices.

The mattress dipped as Dace sat on the edge of my bed. He pulled his legs up straight in front of him and leaned back on his arms, looking at the canopy above us. Small curls slid across his forehead as he tilted his head back and forth.

"Well, seeing as punishment has never worked on me, ask my mother, I can easily tell you that I work a lot better if I'm being praised and given rewards."

"Aren't you already praised and given enough as a prince?"

"I don't know what to say. I want it all," he cracked a sly smile.

"Okay, so you want treats and a pat on the head. Like a dog?" I snorted. Dace seemed less amused at my comment as he rolled his eyes and rolled onto his stomach.

"I think you should come with me, Ryker," he said seriously.

"Come with you where?" If he wanted to use me as the apple to transport, it was going to have to be a firm no. I wasn't getting my arm shaved off as an experiment of what he could or could not do.

158

"Come with me back to the Twinity Court. Come back for the formal they'll throw in order to give me my crown back."

"I can't just leave, Dace." I scrunched my nose, confused at the turn of the conversation.

"If I do better. If I can get a bigger slice, will you come? Call it my treat, *for being a good boy.*"

Laughter rattled my chest as I rested my body flat against the bed. I never knew what Dace was going to say and I never understood why he wanted to keep me around as much as he did. I was not nearly as beautiful as he was, even if all my training had helped to shape my body. It was weird to look at myself in the mirror now. Before the Day of Ruin, I was a child, a stick of a nymph. Now that I was healthy and thriving, the body of a woman looked back at me. It was startling.

"Do you really think that will help you get better?" I asked.

"I really, really do," he paused, then stood and retrieved the apple again. "Say you will."

"Dace, that's a lot you're asking of me."

"Oh, come on. Just say yes," he practically whined as he playfully stuck out his bottom lip. "Say it. Say yes."

"I'll say maybe. If you can get more of that apple to go with you, then I'll think about it."

"Damn, that's good enough for me." And he was gone. The still nearly-whole apple thudded to the ground. His boots hit the floor at the foot of my bed. He reached and handed me the slice, still the same size as before. He shook his head and darted back to the apple.

"I'm going again. I'm gonna do this. And you," he pointed at me, "Are coming to my party."

"We will see about that," I said to an empty room. He was moving quicker now. It felt more like a challenge, the atmosphere of it becoming more intense. This time the apple fell and a noticeable piece was gone. Holy shit, there was no way this was working.

The air next to me grew hazy and Dace smiled at me as he leaned against my pillow, with his head propped as I had been before. In his hand he held an actual thick slice, not just a tiny sliver.

"Mmm," he hummed. "Looks like you better pick out one of those gowns to take with you."

"Have you been able to do that this whole time and you're just trying to trick me into coming with you?"

The bed shook as he chuckled, "I wish, but no. I told you, I just needed a little motivation."

"I could use a little motivation to get out of bed today." I pulled the blanket up over my shoulder and peeked at Dace between the material that I gathered near my face.

"You know it's nearly afternoon," he drawled and ate the apple slice. *By the mother, I wanted that.*

"I know. I have to get up and get ready anyway. I told Daethian I would meet him for dinner tonight and if I back out of this again, he will probably kill me."

"You guys spent a lot of time together here, haven't you?" Dace looked at the back of his hand, curling his fingers into his palm and opening them back up again. It looked mildly threatening, especially when he looked at me from the side and flashed his teeth in a quick smile.

"Yes, he's my best friend," I admitted. Daethian had been the only thing that kept me going most days under Ganglin's rule. We were lucky to have each other. Without him, I would have lost my sanity or gotten myself killed, I was sure. "You should spend some time with him. You'd probably like him once you got to know each other. He is actually pretty goofy." I smiled, thinking about the abundance of jokes he's told me or played on me, or the way he made the keepers so pissed when he made a joke at their expense.

"Ah, I don't think that's such a good idea," Dace muttered. "Every time he looks at me, I swear he's thinking about murder."

"He's just nervous," I lied, as if I knew what was going on in Daethian's head. He had been rather odd lately, but there had also been so much change, so quickly. Some people just don't react well to change. Maybe Daethian was one of those people.

"Nervous? Ha. The only thing he is nervous about is that I'm gonna come in here and steal his girl."

I swatted his arm, "It's not like that." But wasn't it? Daethian wanted to have dinner with me, as a date. Daethian still gave me that look, the one he used to give me all the time when we were enslaved. It was a look that said he wanted to keep me all for himself. It had always scared me.

"Are you sure?" Dace hummed, placing both hands under his head.

"Are you trying to steal me? I thought this was an alliance thing." My lips felt dry as I ran my tongue over them. An annoying blush heated my cheeks. I was playing dumb, a game I often chose to play. Dace's obsession with the idea of making me fawn over him like every other girl did had always been clear. But to me, it had always just been that. Once he finally got me to fall, he would leave.

"I mean, I'm not trying *not to.*"

His smile became contagious. He rolled to his side and I followed suit. The softest hint of pink darkened his skin as we looked at each other. The air felt thick with lust. But it was likely just my own. I shouldn't have let him get this close to me.

"So," he sat up abruptly, "You better get packing for our trip. I wouldn't mind seeing you in that red number again." His boots thudded against the ground as he swung his legs off the bed. The noise was enough to clear my head a bit as I watched him head toward the door.

"I haven't agreed to go," I pointed out.

"Yet," he sang as he strolled out of my room.

And that was all it was. A moment of training. Some harmless flirting. And the sinking feeling that I would ask him to do it all over again if I could. This wasn't right, logically. *But it felt right.*

My hands scrubbed at my face trying to brush off my thoughts. The smell of him still lingered on my bedding. If I had to make a choice, whether to stay or to go, I would have to talk to Daethian about it at some point. Might as well get myself dressed and ready for dinner.

***

The world had continued on, as it always did, even though I hadn't left my room. It made me feel more humble about the way nymphs here were depending on me. Because in the end, they didn't need me. They just liked having me as the face for their cause.

Nymphs were coming in, laughing with each other, sweaty, and still red in the face from the overpowering sun. They still pushed themselves to do whatever they could to get faster and better with their magic, and with their physical capabilities, should Ganglin be able to take their magic away again. Daethian trailed behind a small group, his shirt slung over his shoulder, and a petite nymph girl talking quickly beside him. He laughed at her joke, his hand holding his flat stomach as he took a short breath in. It looked so natural. She batted her long eyelashes and smiled up at him. The girl was clearly smitten by him.

I pushed my hair behind me and fiddled with a few curls around my face as I watched him. See, he could get along with plenty of girls other than me. I wondered if he fancied this one at all. But he answered the question for me, when his gaze flicked up to me and he did a double take. Daethian left the girl, who was still talking, and jogged up to my side.

With wide eyes, I gave him an unforgiving glare and pointed at the girl who had stopped talking but left her mouth wide open. "Shouldn't you say goodbye to your friend?"

"Shouldn't I say hello to this one?" His strong arms wrapped around me and pulled me to his chest. The salty smell of sweat was overpowering as he gave me a tight hug.

"Damn, you need a shower."

"Oh, it's good for you. I didn't see you at all today, so I'm assuming you didn't get a workout in. Did you spend the day primping for our date?" He looked me up and down, hungrily.

I had spent a lot of time trying to find the perfect balance between looking like I do every day and looking like I wasn't trying too hard for my friend who I was *not* planning on dating. However, the part of the day where Dace laid in my bed and talked to me, I would maybe leave out.

"Not a date, remember?"

"Okay, whatever you say." The dark stubble on his chin had grown out a bit more. It was starting to look more like a real beard, making Daethian look even more like a man. How old was he anyway?

Together we began walking down the hall. I assumed Daethian would need to stop by his room and get clean. Maybe I could visit with Randsin while I waited for him to get ready.

"Daethian, how old are you?" I looked up at his tall frame.

He snorted, "You don't know how old I am?"

"Do you know how old I am?"

"You're twenty-five." He looked down at me with a frown. "I'm twenty-seven."

I wondered how old Dace was? Fae didn't age quite like a nymph. Another reason why we would never make a good pair. Fae aged until they hit their stilling and then they stopped. Depending on how much noble fae blood they had, they could stop aging young, or they could age well into their sixties if they didn't have much. So Dace may look barely twenty-five, but he was probably many years over that.

Nymphs, on the other hand, typically stopped aging at thirty. Though the wear and tear of enslavement had put many of us through the wringer and left us looking older than we should. But we didn't live for hundreds and hundreds of years. The lifespan of a nymph was, at best, one hundred and fifty. Dace acted like he wanted me, but he couldn't have me for his lifetime. It just didn't make sense. Another reason why he couldn't be serious.

"Why have I never known that?" My brow furrowed.

"That's a good question. You never really told me though. I just did a little bit of math." Our steps began to echo down the hall as nymphs dispersed around us and left us alone as we grew closer and closer to our rooms.

"You can do math?" I faked surprise.

"I can do a lot more than math." His carefree laughter carried down the hallway. He pulled his shirt off his shoulder and swiped it over his face and then his chest to soak up any remnants of his sweat. I tried not to watch, knowing it would only give him the wrong impression. But even though I didn't want Daethian like that, it was hard not to appreciate his body.

"I've just got to take a quick shower, then we will be off." He pushed open the door to reveal the mess of a room he was staying in. And I'm not quite sure that the mess wasn't his.

The bed was still unmade, blankets pushed aside and the sheets crumpled. Clothing scattered the floor that looked and smelled like they had seen better days. Dishes of meals that he had taken back to his room remained on the long dresser and the two small end tables. Sweat rings stained the wood under many of the dishes. Even the couch looked more like a heap of blankets than actual furniture.

A red chair was pulled up next to the only window. Randsin lounged in it, with a thick book propped open in his hand. He hardly glanced up as we walked in. His typical long uniform covered the majority of his skin, hiding the many tattoos Daethian had suggested he had under it.

"Make yourself at home." Daethian gestured to his ridiculous mess.

"It's a dump in here," I turned up my nose, unsure of exactly which corner the stink was coming from.

Randsin set down his book and looked up at me with a frown. One hand gripped the arm of the chair and his irises drained of color as his voice carried through the chair, then the floorboards, and up through my feet until it rang in my head.

"Try living with it," he rasped.

Daethian snorted and closed himself in the bathroom. Turning about, I looked for a spot to sit, but nearly everything was covered with something. Daethian sure was cute, but damn, he did not know how to pick up after himself.

"So how are you feeling?" I asked Randsin, whose irises remained drained as he anticipated our conversation. Last I had seen of him, he was being dragged away to this room, his head lolled to the side and his body unable to hold itself up. Blood had dripped from long, terrifying cuts over his torso and his face was beat up well enough that he was barely recognizable.

"I've always hated Ganglin for what he turned me into, almost as much as I loved him for acting like a father to me." His full lips turned down. "But I don't think a father would do what he did to me. Not that I have much of a reference."

One hand lifted and pulled at the collar of his shirt. Dark tattoos were broken by pink and white scars. The images that had been in his skin were not distinguishable through the long jagged cuts.

168

"No, you're right, fathers don't do that. Not if they love you. But I don't think Ganglin knows how to love." I thought back to my own father. It was like I had only had him for a second of my life. Twelve years with him hadn't been enough. But I knew my father had been good to me and Hattie. Many memories of him letting us braid his hair, or him dancing with us when mother had bid us good night came to mind. He had always fiercely protected us. Until him and mother got sick. They both passed away in the night, leaving me and Hattie to learn how to live in a world that didn't include them.

Resigning myself to gathering Daethian's laundry into a heap, I started picking up the clothes that littered the floor. "You should try and get out of this room and get some fresh air. This stink will poison you."

"These nymphs don't want to see me," his voice nearly quivered inside my head. "I'm a bad memory of the orders Ganglin had me carry out. I did everything he asked and it was never enough."

I glanced at the door where the water ran and Daethian cleaned himself, wondering if Randsin had shared any of this with him. Randsin looked more exhausted than sad, like all his years of effort had finally caught up to him. His normally perfect posture sagged against the chair.

Sometimes when I looked at him, all I saw was his whip. All I felt was the sting of the scars along my back.

In a way he was right, Randsin was an open wound to nearly everyone here. He may have saved my life from the gallows, he may have owed Windre a favor, but in the beginning he had been on the wrong side of this war. At least it looked like he regretted that decision now.

"At least," I lifted the heaping pile of laundry I'd gathered and dropped it into one pile near the door. "Let me clean this place up a little for you."

"Daethian will just ruin it tomorrow," he sighed. "Kid is a tornado of disaster, leaving a mess wherever he goes."

The bathroom door swung open, steam rolling out from the heat. Daethian leaned against the door frame in brown leather pants, a white button up, and a yellow embroidered brown jacket. His hair was still wet and dangled into his eyes, water dripping to his cheeks.

"How do I look?" He opened his hands and did a small spin.

I wanted to say he almost looked like Dace, if only he had a sheer shirt on to reveal his toned abs. Daethian, though, was a bit more modest than Dace. But I wouldn't dare say any of those thoughts that came to mind.

"Should I go change? You look absolutely dashing and suddenly what I'm wearing is not enough." I gave him my full attention, letting him bask in the way I

170

looked him up and down. Damn, it was hard to not appreciate what he was building here. But I only wanted to look and congratulate him on his hard work. I did not want to touch. That was the difference.

"You look perfect. Come on," he darted forward, grabbing my hand as he went. His steps stopped before the door as he pointed to the gathered laundry. "Did you pick up?"

"I couldn't look at this disaster any longer and just stand by and let it continue to be how it was." I gave Randsin a small smile as Daethian pulled open the door and led me out.

In the hall, I slipped my hand out of Daethian's and let my arms hang at my sides. Nervous butterflies tickled my stomach as I thought about how I was going to tell Daethian about Dace's proposition. He wasn't going to like the news. I could already picture his face dropping. The thought of making him feel that way really twisted my gut. But if I knew Daethian like I thought I did from our five years together, he would tell me that it was my choice how to live my life now that I was free. Just like the picture he used to always paint me in the stables about what our lives would be like after all this was done. Because we both knew one day it would be.

"Where are we going?" I glanced down the hall, pointing out that the dining hall was the opposite direction.

"It didn't sound like you wanted to eat with everyone last time we talked. So I thought maybe a little bit of alone time would do us some good. Just you, me, and some food that isn't cabbage fucking soup. *Almost* like old times."

But those old times were tainted with pain and misery. These would be new memories, happy memories.

"And where might we be eating then?"

"In here." He stopped and pushed open the door to yet another room wrecked by our rampage. It had been a bedroom, one it looked like someone was currently using. But all the furniture had been pushed aside so a spot was cleared for a small table and chairs. The curtains were open, with a view of the sun that was beginning to set in the clouds of pink and orange. Candles glowed from many surfaces, including one candle on the table that was already filled with steaming food.

"Daethian," I warned, "Why does this look like a date?"

"It's not, I just thought that maybe it would be more relaxing with the candles." He pulled me forward, even as part of me was screaming to run out of the room.

172

The legs of the chair he pulled out for me scraped noisily against the floor. His large hands gently pushed my shoulders down into the seat. I shot him a warning glare, but he only smiled in return.

"Don't look at me like that," I warned again. "I've told you we are just friends."

"And this is just a friendly dinner. Though," he picked up a wine bottle and poured some into the glass in front of me. "I've been thinking."

"It's never good when you do that."

Daethian chuckled, handing me my glass, and began filling his own. "Don't you think we work so well together?"

"As friends, yes." I took a sip of the sweet red wine.

"Everyone already sees us together and thinks we're an item. And damn, if we wouldn't make the cutest fucking babies."

I nearly spat my wine across the table. Babies? Who was thinking about babies at a time like this? I already had a hell of enough trouble dealing with being attracted to someone, let alone wanting to get myself impregnated! Damn.

"But friends don't have babies together," I muttered after I swallowed the mouthful of wine and wiped the bit that had dripped out of my mouth in shock with the back of my hand.

"I'm just saying, I think I could change your mind if you gave me a shot." He leaned back in his chair, holding his wine glass like this was a casual conversation everybody had. "I've loved you for five years and I want to show how much more I can love you than anybody else could."

"And if it didn't work? You don't think it would ruin our friendship? Things wouldn't just return to normal," I stuttered. My hands shook as I set down my glass and wiped my sweaty palms over my thighs.

"Who says it isn't going to work?" he laughed.

"Dace wants me to go to the Twinity Court with him," I blurted, my cheeks flaming red.

Daethian jutted his chin forward, his eyes narrowing. "What?"

"His parents are offering him his heir rights back if he soothes the riots in the Twinity court."

"Not to sound like I'm raining on your parade." He drug his hand over his face and looked down at the table for a minute before he brought his gaze back up, "But what does that have to do with you?"

And here was the part I was dreading. What was I supposed to say? 'I lost a bet.' 'I've been training with Dace and I'm trying to motivate him.' I couldn't tell Daethian how embarrassed Dace was about not being so great at travel manipulation. But not telling him also felt like a lie.

"It could be a great alliance to have another fae who backs our revolution," I stuttered.

"Yeah, I mean an alliance with someone of power would be good. So the fact that he has his crown back does work in our favor." His eyes squeezed shut. His eyebrows created deep wrinkles between them as they scrunched together. One hand rose and rubbed at his temple.

"It's good for us." I smiled gently. I knew this would upset him, but in the end he would be a good friend.

His eyes snapped back open, his pupils dark in the shadow of his downcast face. The hand that rubbed his temples slammed against the table, rattling the plates. "Who is us, Ryker?" he growled. "Because it sure as hell isn't you and me."

My smile fell as I leaned away from him. "It's good for nymphs. It's good for everyone fighting this revolution, Daethian. I don't understand why you're getting so upset."

"Upset?" he cackled, his lips spreading in a long, dark sneer. "I'm fucking outraged, Ryker. Are you blind?"

"I'm not blind."

"It would take nothing. *Nothing*. For Dace to slap some shackles on you and throw you into slavery again in his court. You can't leave this place. It's safe for you here, it isn't safe there."

"I get why you would be concerned for me, really. But I can take care of myself," I snapped, my hands gripped my wine glass as I took a long sip.

"You said that before. Remember? Then you and Graceson were taken hostage and you were nearly taken advantage of. You gave your word then that you could take care of yourself. How am I supposed to trust you now? I made a mistake when I told you to trust the fae, Ryker. This is different then you trying to give them a chance when we were in the Acture Court because they helped us get started. But now it's time for us to take control." His hands gripped the table, wood groaning at the pressure. "I told you to trust the fae. Not fuck them."

Anger flashed through me, but I didn't lash out. No, this was a much more dangerous rage. It calmed me. It stilled my entire body. I pushed myself out of my chair, knocking it to the floor behind me.

"That's not true, and you know it. Don't you dare speak to me like I'm some common tart. Why are you being so cruel?" I hissed.

His head bobbed in a funny small smile for a moment. Then his eyes pressed shut once more, and he brought both hands up to hold his head. A growl passed over his lips. I was sure he would stand up and scream back. I'd never seen him this mad before.

He let go of his head and let out a long breath. "I, uh," the red glow of anger in his face faded. He stood up out of his chair. "I have to go. I can't. I'm sorry, Ryker. I'm sorry," he muttered under his breath as he dashed out the door, slamming it shut behind him.

By the Mother. That didn't go well. I inhaled long and slow, setting the chair back as it was. Slowly, I walked around the room blowing out the candles. Maybe me and Daethian's friendship wasn't meant to work outside of enslavement. Maybe we couldn't exist as friends in a world such as this. Maybe we just needed a break from each other, and if I went with Dace it would make him realize that it was better to be friends than nothing at all.

FOURTEEN

Dace

My excitement to share my news with Shavarra had me practically skipping down the ruined hallways. It was a shame that a castle such as this one had to be destroyed. But I understood why it had to happen. Sometimes you had to take something that had caused you so much distress and make it into something of your very own. That's what I intended to do with the power I would have back in the Twinity Court. This time I would do it right.

I skittered into the infirmary, rushing right in the door and to Shavarra's bed. A curtain had been pulled around the bed, but I flung it open. A fluffed pillow and neatly tucked sheet met my elation, my mouth already opening to share the news. No Shavarra.

Twisting, my leather pants creaked. As I slowed myself to actually take in my surroundings, I realized many of the nymphs that had been here had been released. Suzetta, the

178

healer, poked her head out from the bunk at the back of the room where she helped a patient. "You just missed her. I released her maybe five minutes ago. Healthy as a horse. Kinda. Don't let her start messing around in those training rings they have out there just yet."

"Yes, ma'am," I said as I started out the door. Taking a few steps back into the doorway, I leaned back and tried, "Would you happen to know where she might have run off to?"

"She said something about being curious how the kitchen was being operated at this time. She wanted to thank the chefs for the meals they brought in for her and the others."

Classic Shavarra. Always going out of her way to make others feel appreciated. I didn't deserve her as a friend. I couldn't hide my smile as I weaved through the halls. It clearly startled a few nymphs from the refuge who had known me for a while, as their conversations fell quiet as I passed with a wave.

The doors to the kitchen were propped open. I noticed the windows were opened as well, letting in a nice morning breeze. Knives sliced through vegetables and bounced off the cutting board in the hands of the skilled nymphs who had been forced to do it for far too long. It seemed now that they had some control; it was something they didn't entirely loathe.

I spotted Shavarra with her back to me, talking enthusiastically to a few nymphs while they worked whisks through whatever it was they were baking today. As quietly as I could manage, with my heart trying to rattle right out of my rib cage, I snaked between a large table and snuck behind her, wrapping my arms over her shoulders. Pulling her into me, I swayed back and forth as she gasped.

"Trying to sneak away without letting me know they finally set you free?" I whispered in her ear.

Her shoulders shook with a laugh as she untangled herself from my hug. "I was getting around to that. I didn't think you'd be looking for me so early in the morning."

"But you see, I have news." I perched my hands on her shoulders and steered her away from her conversation.

"Uh," she waved quickly as the nymphs giggled. Knowingly, her feet carried her out of the kitchen and into the hall where she turned to look at me. "What's the news?"

I could hardly stand to keep it in much longer. I felt like somebody again. Both of my hands gripped the sides of her face as I lowered myself to her height. Oh, I could just kiss her right now. But.. I wouldn't. Because that's leading her on and we aren't doing that anymore, I reminded myself.

"I'm getting my crown back."

"I'm sorry, what?" She pulled my hands off her ears. "I'm certain I heard that wrong."

"If you heard that I'm going to be prince of the Twinity Court once more, then you heard me right." I pointed at her.

Shavarra gave me a nervous smile. "This feels like a trick. How? Like, how can you even get that back?"

"The people love me!" I spun around with my arms held out. "I don't fucking know how, because I'm a total dick, and I've only been nice to like three fae and one hundred nymphs in my entire lifetime, but here we are." I placed a pretend crown on my head. "The people's king."

"Don't your parents hate you? Don't you hate your parents?"

"Details. I negotiated. I return, thus settling the riots within our court, and I get my heir rights back, with a little more say in the running of our kingdom. Now, for the good or bad news first?" My arm fell over her shoulders as I steered her down the hallway.

"Oh gods, the bad news."

"Okay, bad news is that I agreed to take a bride."

"Who?" Shavarra said in surprise.

I rubbed the back of my neck, suddenly feeling like maybe I had jumped into this a little fast. "I don't actually know, yet. I'm assuming I'll have a say in it."

"You're assuming? Gods above, what's the good news?"

"I want to put you in my court, as a spokesperson for the people." The sounds of the kitchen finally faded completely away, leaving us in Shavarra's stunned silence.

"Dace, I-" she shook her head, "I don't have any money. I'm literally the most common commoner you'll find. There is absolutely nothing special about me that would make sense for me to be in your court."

I grabbed both her hands and made her stop and look me in the eye, "Everything about you is special, Shavarra. You deserve to be in the court more than half of the people who are currently in those positions. I don't care how common you think you are. Your voice, your opinions need to be heard. You can keep me on the straight and narrow better than almost anyone else."

Shavarra brought her hand up to her mouth and began chewing on her nails. "I don't know Dace," she mumbled.

"I'm the prince," I tutted. "Doesn't that mean you have to do as I say?"

She dropped her hand and gave me a pointed look. "When are you leaving?"

"Soonish. I asked for enough time to finish up my affairs here. Will you come with me then? I've asked Ryker to come along, too."

A couple of nymphs wandered down the hall, heading toward the kitchen. Our conversation paused as they passed, looking at us with cheeky smiles. When we lost sight of them, Shavarra began again.

"Dace, I think this is my place. Not to say that one day that won't change, but right now I can't leave. Not yet."

I blinked, sure that she was playing a joke. Shavarra had always been there for me, and to think that I would leave her behind in a day... No, I didn't like that.

"Are you sure?" I tried again, this time my throat felt dry.

"I'm sure. Plus, having me and Ryker together, that sounds like it could be awkward for you."

I knew that one day I'd have to explain it all and lay everything out on the table for the both of them. But I didn't think that would be any time soon, even if they both came with. Ryker flirted, she let me flirt back. It would take time before we were really an item. Though I wished it was sooner.

"Whenever you're ready, Shavarra, there will always be a seat at my table for you," I nodded, more to reassure myself than anything.

"I appreciate that," she smiled, but tried to distance herself from me. "You better get some rest before you have to put all that work in to make mommy and daddy happy. I've got to hunt a room down. I'll likely be staying in one of the keeper's quarters at this rate."

She was right, I needed to prep myself for everything that was going to hit the fan as soon as I made it home.

This was feeling more and more like I had made the wrong choice. It's good for the war efforts, I reminded myself. It's who you really are. Damn, if this didn't feel like some sort of identity crisis.

"Fine, yes, you're right. As usual," I hummed, shrugging my shoulders and backing away from her. "The keeper's rooms are down that way and to the right," I sang, pointing down the hall.

She made a vulgar gesture and turned the way I suggested, leaving me alone. These were confusing times, but I had the feeling that everything was still going to work out in the end. Cleary, we weren't there yet, and I hadn't a clue how they were going to work out, but like everything else I do, winging it typically worked.

I followed the hallways filled with nymphs drifting about their business until I found my way back to my room. Pushing open the door, I turned abruptly to the figure perched on my bed. Ryker had her legs crossed under her, one of the books I had been reading on and off in my free time propped in one hand, and what looked like a muffin in the other.

With a mouth full of food she looked up, "It took you so long that I ate the muffin I brought you."

Instantly, I wanted to run my fingers through the curls she had left loose down her back. My tongue ran over my front teeth as I suppressed the urge to laugh. "What are you doing in my humble abode?"

Quietly, I thanked the gods that I had done some version of picking up after myself. I'd even taken the time to somewhat make the bed, though I'll admit it didn't look as good as when the servants back home did it.

"I've come to tell you that I'm coming with you."

Stay calm, Dace. Fucking keep it cool. My hands rubbed together in front of me as I walked over to the small couch I often read at and leaned against the back so I could face her.

"I thought you might." I ran my hand over the end table. A small envelope waited there with my name elegantly written across the front. My family's seal closed the back of it, and I looked up at Ryker, confused. "What's this?"

She closed the book, keeping her finger in the pages to hold her spot. "Haven't a clue, it was there when I got here."

Though I knew it was likely delivered by an assassin or the messenger who had visited, I still walked quietly to the window and tested the lock.

"Is it bad?" she asked.

Since when is anything that concerned my parents good? Apart from getting my entire fortune and reign back, of course. I turned the letter over and over in my hands, wondering if I should read it now.

"Do you want me to leave?" Ryker started to stand, still holding the novel.

"No, no," I waved. "Please, stay." My fingers still trembled from the excitement of her agreement to come to the Twinity Court. It felt like all those visions would finally start to come true. Cracking the wax, I pulled the envelope open as I sat on the edge of the bed.

Dace,

Because you are my son, I hope that this letter finds you well enough. I'm reaching out to advise you that your promise to me must be kept, and that I expect your end of the bargain to be upheld immediately. Wear your best suit, and arrive no later than seven for your reinstatement and bridal proposition. Don't disappoint me again.

Love, your still reigning queen,
Mother

Though she didn't have to specify, it didn't surprise me that she had felt the need to remind me of her title. She had lorded her power over me since the day I was born. I swear as an infant she was singing me songs about how she brought me into this world and, should I be anything less than she expected, she was going to take me out. Is that not what typical mothers do? No? Just my psychotic one. And yet, she was somehow fit to wear the crown.

Dread built in my stomach, like the bubbling of a meal that was about to set my asshole on fire. I'd successfully avoided a bridal proposition since I was eighteen. Always a pressing matter, but never one that was urgent enough to evoke real action, other than snide comments from my mother. Now the day was approaching, tomorrow in fact, that I would be presented with options that I was expected to choose from.

Mother was tricky like that. The image of Ryker appeared on the inside of my eyelids, a memory of a vision of what was to come. An oxymoron, if I ever heard one.

"What does it say?" She tried not to lean too close, to look over my shoulder, but she couldn't hide the spark of curiosity in her eyes. I hadn't noticed how close she had grown as I focused on the letter.

"It says that I'll have to make arrangements for your travel. Hope you don't mind if I talk to daddy dearest so you can try some travel manipulation yourself. Oh, and you'll need to pack one of those dresses you have hiding in your room." I smiled back, as her cheeks bloomed red. I hoped she'd never quit getting flushed like that around me, I loved it so much and currently, it was just so easy to get her to do. "I have a feeling there may be one in there, a lovely blush color, made of silk, that would just look absolutely stunning."

"When should I be ready?" she said, quietly.

"Tomorrow morning, I expect that you'll receive the full princess treatment once you arrive as my guest, and you'll need time for all the pampering they'll do to you. Hopefully you'll enjoy it, and not hate me for all they'll put you through."

Her laugh echoed my own. "I better go back to my room, then." She jumped from the bed and sprinted to the door. Before she disappeared she grimaced and added, "One more thing, maybe do try and steer clear of Daethian, he didn't exactly take the news well."

"I mean, I would say 'I told you so', but it seems you've already gotten that point." I set the letter down on the bed and took in her sun-kissed face.

"Just avoid him. Okay?" Her fingers drummed against the door frame.

"Got it."

I didn't come all the way to the Heathern Court to spend time with Daethian anyway. Avoiding him will be the easiest task I'd ever been assigned. Though, I'd do almost anything Ryker asked, to be quite honest. She wanted someone to dance around like a monkey to entertain the nymphs? Damn, call me her baboon. I was smitten.

FIFTEEN

Milo

Blood ran down her back where her skin had split open. A zigzag pattern of welts and cuts weaved over the top of old scars. Scarlet had long since seeped into the carpet and soaked into the thin cloth of her pants and torn shirt.

Sweat drenched my top as I panted and curled the whip up in my hand. Windre hardly even watched. Instead, he disappeared behind me and picked up the book he had been reading. It made sense if this was an everyday occurrence and he was bored with it.

"Fifty," Red sobbed, falling forward and curling into a ball with a pain-filled moan.

Windre's book clapped shut. The chains of the prisoner, because that was a better word for him than servant, in the corner chimed as Windre pulled the boy up to stand. "Show the girl where we keep the cleaning supplies. She can clean up her mess."

I doubted any cleaning concoction he has could help pull the color of her blood from his ancient looking rug. But who knew? Maybe he had a cleanser with a little bit of witch magic in it. Something like that had to be at play here. Witch magic. How else were they able to suppress the nymph's powers like they are?

"You know," I leaned against one of the bookshelves, rubbing my shoulder with the opposite arm. "I was wondering about the Day of Ruin. I never understood how it *really* happened."

"How what happened?" Windre arched a brow, his mouth pulled in a deep frown.

"How exactly were we able to nullify their powers?"

Red and the other nymph limped together out the door, but I could feel her attention snag at my words. They didn't know either. I mean, I guess, they couldn't know or they would have somehow reversed the effects.

Windre laughed heartily. "That, I'm afraid, is above your paygrade. What are you, even? A simple mutt? A keeper?"

I watched as the pair left the room, blood trailing behind Red. How she was even standing at all was a credit to her mental strength. This visit was going to be twenty times harder for her because she was so strong willed.

"Keeper," I muttered. "Well if you won't answer me that, can you at least give me a little insight as to how you'll break her of her strong will?"

"Simple," he finally smiled, a long, face-splitting grin, revealing an entire mouthful of teeth. "Make her life so miserable and lonely here that the thought of serving as a maid or a stable hand, or whatever the fuck her job was, sound like a damn vacation. She won't step out of line again when I'm done with her."

"And what if she's stubborn?"

"Oh, even the stubborn break at some point," he whispered.

Both nymphs finally entered the room, the boy from the corner carried nearly everything as he dragged Red in behind him. Her face was tear streaked and swollen. Her eyes never reached mine.

I didn't like it. I didn't like the way she ignored me instead of taunting me with her mean and clever tongue. And I didn't like the fact that *I didn't like that* more than anything else.

She's just a nymph. She's just a pawn in someone else's game. Red is nobody and nothing to you. If I could, I would have slapped myself right then to knock the thoughts right of my dumb, thick skull. But even whipping her hadn't brought me the same sort of joy I thought it might.

"We can leave this mess to those two and my keepers can watch over them if you would like to return to your room and clean up. We will be having dinner soon."

"And what of her once the mess is clean? Where will she go? Sorry for the questions, but her misery is partially in my charge as well, and I'd hate to disappoint King Ottack." I watched Red as every movement she made caused her face to scrunch up. Then my gaze flipped back toward King Windre, who looked annoyed that I even bothered to ask.

"She'll go down to the dungeons, of course."

"I'm sure I can expect to see where she is being kept."

"Certainly," Windre purred, pulling himself away from the wall and walking out the door. In the hallway he snapped his fingers, beckoning one of the fae guards forward, a slender man with large, black reptilian wings. He looked fae, he smelled like fae. I didn't want to gawk at the rarity of it, but I hadn't seen a fae with wings in my entire lifetime.

"Jerydin, can you please show our guest to his room?" Windre glared down the tip of his long nose as he passed me off to the fae guard.

The man, Jerydin, nodded. It wasn't until I looked at him, and not just his wings, that I noticed how large his eyes actually were. It was almost unsettling. Maybe it was a trait that came with the wings. Something to counteract the attraction the wings created.

Jerydin didn't speak, but walked quickly. I averted my gaze to the floor, the walls, or the ceiling to keep him from feeling the heat of my attention on his spectacular wings. Damn, I wish I could fly. The more I focused on the ground, the more I noticed the red splatters that dotted the floors here or there. So much for making them clean up after themselves, someone had sprayed all sorts of fluid through these halls.

I'd seen many things in my time working under Queen Atarah, but it didn't give me the same feeling that I had while I was here. While I still loathed being bound to her, I had found joy in my work. There was something in the air here, something that felt like a lie. Something Windre said, or maybe it was this Jerydin character that was giving me a reaction. My gut, that wasn't often mistaken, knew something here was fake. I just needed to figure out what. I'm sure the news would please King Ottack, or even better, Princess Maggie.

The fae stopped outside a door without a word. I stopped walking to look at him, then at the doorway. "Oh, is this supposed to be me?"

He nodded.

"Thank you." I brushed past him and into the room. If I had thought that my arrangements as a guard were nice, then this was absolutely fucking spectacular. This room was fit for a king. Wait.. was I in the wrong room? I turned, but the door had been shut behind me. Guess it's mine.

A huge four-post bed with sinful red sheets sat as the centerpiece. Large orange and brown sitting pillows were scattered around the floor. Even the lighting was dim, making it look this room would be great for an orgy. I mean, pillows everywhere.

I squeezed my eyes shut and shook my head. What the hell was I thinking? A good place for an orgy? What had gotten into me? It had been years since I had a good orgy, but I hardly thought this was the place or time for it.

A double door sat propped open to the right of the bed, leading off into the bathroom. I hummed, trying to pull my head out of the gutter. I didn't know it was possible for a bedroom to turn someone on, but here the fuck I was, getting a hard on from this set up.

Walking into the bathroom, I expected something like the showers or large tubs that I'd seen already in this realm. This bathroom was different. It wasn't a tub, it was a whole freaking swimming pool. Steam rolled off the clear water. With a chuckle, I pulled my shirt off over my head and shimmied out of my pants.

The boner I'd gotten was not easing, if anything, this ridiculous bathroom was going to make it worse. I mean, I am alone. Breathing a sigh of contentment at finally being without the restrictive clothing, I tiptoed into the pool. The water lapped against my dirty skin. I hadn't been very fit to be in the presence of a king upon my arrival.

I reclined against the steps, my sinner hand drifting to my cock. My gaze shifted from side to side, nervous, for whatever reason, that I was not alone. My eyelashes fluttered against my cheeks as I began stroking from base to tip. Images already littered my thoughts. A memory of what it felt like to rock my hips into a woman's wet sex. I groaned as mild pleasure built. The speed of my hand quickened.

Oh, I missed the warmth of a woman, but for now this would have to do. The friction of my hand was uncomfortable, so I cracked an eye and reached for a jar of soap that sat near the edge. It poured out readily into my hand and created an easy foam to rub against my cock. I let out a trembling breath and cozied back into my lounging position.

Picture after picture came to mind. Memories of the orgy the room so easily reminded me of. And other images, too. The swish of black hair, a snarl that somehow still hinted at humor. An uninvited kiss that felt too good to be true.

Pleasure overtook me in wave after wave as my hand pumped up and down, my hips moving of their own accord with the motion. Cum poured out of me, thick and creamy across my fingertips and dripping over my lower stomach. At the peak of the orgasm was the memory of Red's body pressed against mine in her first escape attempt. Her sly, knowing smile as I gripped her to me and threatened her.

I coughed, looking down at myself. Something was wrong with me. Maybe I just needed something to take off the edge. I'm sure Windre's court had prostitutes or something of that nature. That's all I needed. Some good cunt and I'd be well on my way to sanity again.

A few towels lay folded, waiting to dry me. One would have to be good enough to be my cum rag. Oh, the joy the nymphs would have when they cleaned my room later. Though I tried not to think too hard on that, praying it wouldn't be Red who found the soon-to-be crunchy towel. Of all things, that might be the first here to actually embarrass me. I'm sure she would have something to say about it. She always had something to say.

Tossing the towel toward the corner of the room, I dunked my head under the surface and began scrubbing my body. If only baths could scrub away all of our sins. What a shame my soul had to reside in this meaty, lustful, shell of a man.

Once I was satisfied that the dirt and grime I had accumulated since leaving the Obtune Court was thoroughly washed away, I climbed from the pool. Water dripped off of me, creating a small puddle at my feet as I ran a towel over my skin. The material soaked up most of the moisture, leaving me only mildly damp as I drifted from the bathroom. The bag that I had brought had been carried in from our wagon at some point. It rested near the bed. Another uniform waited for me inside. Quietly, my mind drifted over all the dirty thoughts that still tormented my mind while I dressed. I gave the room one last look, sighing, knowing that there would not be any orgies in this room while I stayed here.

Trying to divert my mind to the idea of dinner with King Windre, I opened the door. In the hallway, I turned to find Jerydin waiting for me. Had I known the man was going to stand outside my door until I was ready for dinner, maybe I wouldn't have taken the time to jiggle the jewelry, if you get my drift.

"Oh," I stopped awkwardly, wondering how good his hearing was. "Are you here to show me my way to dinner?"

Jerydin raised his eyebrows and turned on the tips of his toes, walking off down the hallway. I watched his scaled wings sway behind him for a moment before jogging after him.

"Are you just a guard then? A man like you, with wings like that, should have surely found himself in a better position than that," I called after him, trying to keep pace and stay at his side. It would keep me from staring at his legendary wings anyway.

"I am more than a guard, but less than a king, if that tells you anything," Jerydin said roughly. "Though if my dear, but annoying, best friend ever returns, you'll find I'm not the only one in this court with wings to be ogled."

How utterly unlikely. Maybe by the time this so-called friend returned, I would be done staring at Jerydin's wings and would be less likely to appear like a buffoon around him.

"I'm not meaning to make you feel watched," I grumbled the half-hearted apology.

Jerydin paused and looked at me with his huge saucer eyes. "Watch away. Sometimes I find that watching people reveals more about them than what they actually say." His words were a quiet warning before he blinked and continued to lead me into a dining room.

Food was already heaped on platters and scattered over the table Windre sat at the head of. His sharp teeth dug into a leg of whatever animal had been cooked. He still smiled through the mouthful he chewed and pointed at the high-backed dining chair near him. His hand glistened under the fae firelight chandeliers, multiple rings adorning nearly every finger.

Jerydin walked to the other end of the table, pulled out a seat for himself, and sat down in it. His eyes remained trained on me as I approached the seat the king had offered. I hadn't been able to see when I walked in, but as I neared the table's edge I caught a glimpse of Red. Bound in chains, and gagged to hold back her fiery tongue, she sat in the corner. Her shirt hung off her from where I had torn it. The peaks of her breasts were clear where her shirt had fallen down. Both shoulders were slouched, but she leaned away from the wall to keep her bare, still-bleeding back from touching.

Just looking at her like that felt wrong. I turned my eyes away from the image, my cheeks warming. Instead, I focused on pulling out the chair and examining the food options. What was the protocol for eating with a king? In Tierasia we didn't eat with Queen Atarah, not unless she meant to use your body later in the night. And even then, you really only ate sweet dessert and fruit. I'm assuming Windre didn't want to use my body as his late-night sweet treat after dinner.

"Go ahead and eat your fill. You must be hungry from your travels." Windre took another bite of meat.

Happily, I lifted my plate and began scooping and setting things onto it, until the porcelain was no longer visible underneath. The smell drifted to my nose, creating a flash flood of saliva inside my mouth. If I was starving, Red must be too. I picked up my fork and began shoveling food. If there was meant to be a conversation between me and Windre, I didn't know what I was supposed to say.

I looked up and caught Red's unforgiving glare. I pointed at her with my fork, a roasted vegetable hanging off the end. "What will she eat?"

Windre glanced behind him like he forgot she was even there, "Oh, she won't."

"Nothing?" I laughed.

"No, I don't feed them till they are on the brink of starvation. Helps to bend their wills and keep them weak. We have to do a total mental reshaping, and that's hard to do if it takes time to break their will power."

He didn't know how stubborn Red was. She was likely to refuse her meal when it finally came, and die out of spite. But the question was more for Red than it was for me. Gave her the chance to hear what was being done with her to prepare for it as best she could.

"Sounds like a fun game," I mumbled through my full mouth. For the remainder of the meal, I wondered what else would be done with her. What sort of conditions was I going to have to endure? That thought felt selfish, too. Red would have it far worse than me.

But that felt like my own punishment. Something in my gut had been twisted. And it didn't seem like it was a good thing.

SIXTEEN

Ryker

There was a flash of hurried movement through the halls. Nymphs scurried after friends, whispering quietly behind their hands. I hadn't reached my room yet to pack for my small adventure. What would I bring? None of anything I owned really belonged to me. It felt more like I was borrowing them.

One of the males, who had volunteered to walk the grounds, acting as a guard, sprinted around the corner and stopped at my side. I paused wondering if what I always feared would happen was happening. Every day there was a small spark of fear that Ganglin would return to take back his home.

"What's happening?" I grabbed his arm and gave him my full attention.

"Graceson is back," he panted. "We've been looking all over for you. He is waiting in your office."

203

"Say no more." Everyone around me became a blur as I raced toward my office. The door was closed, but I quickly leapt inside and slammed it shut behind me.

Graceson's green eyes flashed as he looked up from under his loose red hair. One hand pushed the hair from his face and he gave me a small tick of a smile. "You're looking rather well, Ryker. Glad to see it." He set down the paperweight he had been rolling over in his hands against the desk.

As he stood, I couldn't help but notice his wings. Healed. Scarred and more terrifying looking than ever, but they looked like they were in working condition, which was all I really wanted. He had been tormented because they had thought him to be something to me. Something more than a friend.

"Your wings... they look..." I stuttered.

"Ah, yes. The healer in the Acture Court is very gifted, and she did me up rather nicely. Even gave me a thorough body massage. Happy ending and all. So I mean, I can't complain," he laughed with a smug shrug.

I shook my head. Typical Graceson, which told me that he was probably doing even better than I had expected. Again, good news. But surely there was more he had to say than that.

"I've come with information I thought you might enjoy." He strolled around the desk, his fingers trailing along its trim.

Ah, there it is. Tell me, Graceson. Let's hear it from your terribly tempting playboy lips. I bounced on my toes, unable to keep my anxiety and excitement tamed.

"Tell me, then."

"I don't know." He jutted his chin out and sat on the front end of the desk. "I'd rather hear about your time here. Rumors travel pretty far, you know."

I thrust an arm out, pulling a brick from the wall with such force that the book on the shelf in front of it flung forward and smacked against his arm. "Tell me now."

"Ooph. Fine, you don't have to play like that." He frowned and dusted his sleeve. "Hattie is alive and well."

I let loose the breath that had caught in my chest and refused to be let go. I wanted to melt into a puddle of joy. Thank the Mother, Hattie was all right. And now I could quit using resources to scan the Heathern Court for her.

"I'm assuming that means she is in the Acture Court then."

"She is. With Windre, of course. She trailed Ganglin once he left, trying to get this, um, *box*. Followed him all the way to the border of the Obtune Court before she abandoned her self-made mission and returned home."

"That's great news. So now we know where Hattie is and we know where Ganglin is. Did she say if she knew what was in the box?"

"No, she didn't. And I think it's safe to assume that Ganglin is rallying his dear friend Ottack, which is why he has moved his army from the Acture Court border to the Heathern Court."

That wasn't good. That was actually really terrible. We weren't ready to fight an entire fae army. We didn't have the numbers, and many nymphs were still trying to fine-tune their magical abilities.

"I thought you said you were bringing me good news," I said plainly, trying to mask my nervousness. Did this change anything about me leaving tomorrow?

"No, I said I brought you information. No where did I say it was good."

"You said I'd enjoy it."

"Well you enjoyed some of it? Right?" His eyebrows shot up.

"Just the part about my sister," I sighed and finally moved away from the door. Crumpling into the torn up chair in front of the desk, I looked up at Graceson. "You wanna tell me what the rumor is that you heard?"

"I heard that Dace is here. I heard that he is a prince again. And I heard that you're planning on leaving the Heathern Court to follow him." He said it plainly, not a stitch of emotion attached. Just fact.

"How did y--" I sat up, blinking.

"I have my sources."

My mind tried to connect the dots of how the word had gotten out so quickly. If Graceson had this information, who else did too? Did that make someone within these walls a lying rat? I didn't want to think about making consequences to actions like that. I was not Ganglin. And technically, I wasn't an authority at all.

"But," he held up a finger. "I support this decision."

"You do?" I said slowly, waiting for the trap it felt like he was putting into place to clamp shut around me.

"Of course I do. An actual alliance between the nymphs and the Twinity Court could hold some real power. Windre is just biding his time at this point. If you can talk them into something real, something tangible, then Windre doesn't have to hide anymore. That makes two courts openly backing you. Not just one in secret."

"You still think I should leave even though Ottack is directing his troops in our direction?"

"Absolutely. And the faster you leave, the faster you return." His wings flared, knocking a folded map off the desk that he snatched from the air before it could hit the floor.

It was nice to get his opinion, and I must be doing something right if someone like him, who has been in his position for as long as he had, agreed with me. My fingers picked at the arm of the chair, pulling at a loose thread. "You don't think it's a trap, do you?"

"A trap in the Twinity Court?"

"Yeah," I said under my breath. Daethian's suggestion that they could just as easily take me in as their slave was still a prevalent thought inside my head.

"If it is, I'd say Prince Dace has nothing to do with it. I mean, I don't want to necessarily encourage what's going on between you two, but I'll be damned if he doesn't look at you like he has been enchanted." He fiddled with the map. "But if you say you're not interested in him and you get cold at night, I happen to know a perfectly good warm body that's pretty good for snuggling." He gestured toward his body. "And other things."

I laughed, enjoying the bit of sarcasm in his voice. "I'll keep that in mind. But I don't think Dace is actually serious about anything with me. I'm just his entertainment for now. One day, when he gets bored of me, he'll find someone else. Best not to get my feelings too involved, right?" For a split second I had the thought that maybe this would have been a good conversation to have with Daethian, but then again, Daethian wouldn't want to hear it right now.

"Why do you think that?"

"Because it doesn't make sense for a nymph and a fae to be together," I laughed to brush off the awkward tension that started to settle on my shoulders and looked away from Graceson. "And he is a Prince. I'm a no one. His mom has set his bridal proposition, anyway.

He'll have to choose someone then. And as I currently believe that I am not an option on said list, I'll maybe stay a little bit guarded."

"Hmm," Graceson nodded. "It didn't make much sense for Windre's parents to get together. But you can't help who you fall in love with. But remember, if you get cold, you know who to call." He sucked on his teeth and walked around me to the door. "I think I'll go have myself a little look around and maybe visit our dear friend, Randsin."

I waved at him, but didn't turn to watch him go. As much as part of my mind said 'don't go', there was a bigger piece that held on to an immense amount of excitement, I was almost hopeful even. Hopeful for an official alliance, of course. No other reason, I thought again as I chewed my lip and tried not to picture Dace dancing with potential brides.

The Heathern Court had quickly changed from being my first nightmare to suddenly feeling like I had a hand in building what it was now. It had gone on without me, nymphs easily filling the roles that I played from day to day, but it still felt like there was a chance it would crumble without me. Maybe I was thinking too highly of myself.

Even though I knew I should pack a little something and catch some sleep before we left tomorrow, I still pushed off my chair and headed outside. I practiced the move Dace had shown me. I pushed my magic to build faster, smoother, deadlier, points until my head spun and my body felt drained. It could be done and it would be. And I wasn't about to head into unknown territory until I had mastered something.

***

Somewhere past the daze of sleep that kept my body immobile, I could hear someone knocking, and my name being called a few times. It felt distant, like a dream that I had no control over.

"Ryker, are you in there?" the voice called.

I wanted to say "yes", or more likely "go away, I'm still sleeping". But my lips couldn't move. My body still felt drained from all the effort of my work yesterday. That, and I had stayed up far later than I should have, only giving myself the opportunity for a few hours of sleep.

They tested the door handle. I could hear it jiggle, knowing somewhere inside my head that I had locked it. The rattling stopped.

"Ryker? Are you okay?" My boot shook. No, not just my boot, my entire leg.

Consciousness began to return to me slowly. My eyes were unable to open until I felt the soft brush of fingers against my cheek, pushing the loose strands away from my face. I cracked an eye first and smiled at the blonde-haired prince who leaned casually against my mattress.

"Good morning, princess," he whispered.

I groaned and rolled to my back, becoming overly aware of the fact that I was still in yesterday's clothing, shoes included. "Damn, I pushed myself a little too hard last night, I guessed. What time is it?"

"Well, it's about ten minutes away from time to jet on over to the Twinity Court."

"No," I whined and tossed him a pouty look.

"No?" He cleared his throat and sat up to give me his full attention. "What do you mean no? Do you not want to come any longer?" His voice was tainted with disappointment.

"It's not that," I laughed, finding my hand traveling to his and touching his knuckles lightly. "I haven't packed."

"Oh," he breathed. "That isn't an issue."

Dace slipped off the bed, the daggers on his belt tapping against the brown leather of his pants, his white button shirt snug against his lean torso. He had traded his boots for a dressier loafer, which made his steps quiet. With both hands he dramatically opened the wardrobe and gave me a quick wink before making a show of stepping into the chaos that exploded from it.

His fingers skimmed over material, pulling out soft pink hues until he finally clicked his tongue and pulled a hanger out. "Ah, here we are. This is all you really need. I can have new clothing sent up to your room. My parents will want you to dress formally for most occasions anyway. Hope you like dresses."

"I don't really."

"Shame. Because I know just how beautiful you look in one." He shrugged his shoulders and held the dress at his side. His chin ticked up and he turned to face the bedroom door. A knock sounded from the door. "Hope you're ready because Daddy dearest is here to give you your free ride."

My heartbeat sped up and my gaze traveled to the door. Dace twisted the lock and pulled the door toward him. His father, King Henrick, stepped into my room.

"It's time to go, love," Dace whispered, and disappeared with a flash.

SEVENTEEN

Milo

Sleep had eluded me most of the night. I thought that after traveling so much, and missing so many hours of rest the night before, that I would hit the bed hard, and only wake once my bodily needs couldn't be ignored any longer. But instead, my mind kept telling me how wrong I was to be here.

This was a side quest to my main quest, and it included hurting someone that... I didn't really want to hurt. When had that changed? The idea had come and gone in a fleeting thought that haunted me the rest of the night. Some sort of deranged nightmare I had found myself in and I couldn't escape my consciousness.

I washed in a hot bath, hoping to soothe myself into catching a moment of sleep, but instead found my hand reaching for the bottle of soap that lathered up my raging stiffy. Something was clearly wrong with me.

My rough hands smoothed down the fine materials of my uniform. I watched myself in the long mirror,

213

waiting to see it shine red at the call of my queen. Expelling the breath I couldn't hold any longer, I walked away in relief that she hadn't called. But she would soon. The long span of time between her calls left me wondering what was happening at home. Be it good or bad.

The door to my room remained unlocked, as I wasn't a prisoner here. But guards had been posted outside my door. I could hear them shifting their weight and chatting throughout the night as they stood post. They would be my guides in this foreign castle, and that I was thankful for.

As I opened the door, the men froze like they had been caught in the act of doing something unforgivable. But they both remained on either side of the door, facing forward, utterly harmless. I stepped out. They watched me with blank, well-trained faces.

"Can you take me to the girl I brought?"

They exchanged a small look, but peeled themselves away from the door frame. One walked in front of me, assumingly leading the way, the other trailing behind us. Was this the way I was to be watched or was this a gift of protection? I thought I could handle whatever was thrown my way.

I followed him down a dark stairwell, watching the back of his maroon helmet, the long red feather drifting in the momentum of the wind the guard created. The dungeons, I expected. My presumption was correct as the sounds of hissing and moaning met my ears.

An angry scream rang out in the darkness, the glow of torches lit with fae firelight waited at the end of the hall. We turned the corner and entered their radiance. The light revealed large, barred cells surrounding an open space in the middle. Cells circled what I assumed was the main torture arena. An easy way to terrify those who waited. Let it build up the suspense as they watched others flinch in pain. It was smart, really.

A weeping groan hit my senses like a galloping horse crashing to a stop. Leaning away from the table, Red's face was twisted in pain. Though I imagine it hurt to press her back against the chair as she tried to pull herself free.

"I wouldn't do that if I were you. You'll sit with this for one minute," the fae said. He twisted the knob of an instrument that held Red's finger, lowering a corkscrew until it pierced her flesh clean through. She yelped, her face drained of all color.

It was a tactic I had used before, though I often liked using a hammer, and I didn't go clear through their fingers like he had. It made it more of a game when it was a race to see if I could crush their bones before they pulled away. This didn't look nearly as fun. Specifically, because my hands itched to undo Red's bindings.

"How's it going?" I tried to sound uninterested.

"Ah, come to check on your nymph. Well, she's doing great," he laughed. "Got a good tongue lashing from her this morning as I pulled her out of her cell. Girl has spunk. I'll give her that. But she'll break before long. She's scared. I can smell it."

"I'm actually," he pulled the corkscrew from her finger and ripped her hand from the device, talking over her scream. "All done with her, now. I'm getting ready to toss her back into her pit."

"Well in that case, just leave her there. Thought I may be able to get a few hours of my own fun in."

"A man after my own heart. You like torture?" he cooed, throwing his tool back on its mount on the wall, still bloody.

"Oh, I love it. My favorite pastime, actually." I smiled, an actual smile, because I knew how true it was.

"Good," he hummed. "Materials are behind you on that wall. Do whatever you wish, just keep her alive, even if she's on the brink of death's door at the end. Windre will be glad to hear how involved you're getting."

"I'm sure he will."

Simple enough. But as the men filed out of the room and I turned toward Red, who sagged in her seat, I couldn't bring myself to pick up any tool from the wall. I took small steps, watching her watch me, until I sat at the table with her, and her gaze shifted away.

"Your mind is telling you to say whatever you need to, to get out of these chains, isn't it?" I leaned forward, looking at the blood that was drying in small patches on the table. "But there is another part of you that just can't give up your control yet."

Red swallowed. The stench of her fear was definitely apparent the closer I came. "A war is brewing in your mind. Do you feel crazy yet?" I tried again.

"Why are you talking to me, Milo?" she whispered, "Just do what you're going to do and get it over with, okay?"

Taking my own sweet time, I licked my lips and examined the dirt that clung to dried tears in black streaks down her cheeks. Her grey eyes flicked up to me, then away.

"Do you want me to tell you that I was a part of a rebellion? Is that what you want to hear? That the very night you found me out of bed, what I really was doing was forming a plan to escape?" Her lips trembled as she spoke.

It had always been clear to me that she was up to something. For some reason though, it never occurred to me that she was going to run away.

"I'm not strong, Milo," she panted, finally meeting my stare. Her fingers cupped over the metal cuffs that kept her hands on the table. "I'm too scared to fight back. But I'm willing to do what I have to do to survive. If I knew any more, I'd tell you, if it would get me out of this mother-forsaken place. But all I have is my will to get through another day, and a couple of names."

"I'm not going to do anything," I finally said, pushing the tools still on the table off to the floor. I reached into my pocket and pulled out a folded cloth and dipped it into the bucket of water next to my seat. I'm sure it was meant to be there for some sort of dunking, but it worked for my purposes too.

Carefully, I took her hand and began wiping the blood from her fingers, applying pressure when the blood didn't stop. Her lips pressed into an almost nonexistent line.

"Do you have feelings, Milo? Are you regretting bringing me here?" she growled under her breath.

"And if I said I did, would that change anything?"

"No." Her chin jutted forward.

"You remind me of me. You are bound into slavery like I am bound to my queen. Except that to save you, all that needs to be done is someone to stand up and fight for your freedom."

"More than one someone has to stand up. But one person is a start." Hope flashed in her eyes.

"I hope one day I'll be able to visit this realm again. And maybe one day you'll be free." I pulled the cloth from one hand and began dabbing at the other. "Or maybe we will meet in another world, in another lifetime and things will be different."

"There is no other world for me. When we die our bodies are given to the Mother. Our flesh melts into the dust that keeps this cruel world alive," Red sighed. "Maybe one day you could be free, too." Her face twisted as she flinched, the rag snagging on a still-fresh wound.

"There is only one way out of the bond, and I'll never do it. That's how I know I'm stuck." It was my turn to sigh as I leaned back into the chair that had never lost its warmth from the fae who was last sitting here. Fire-like pain singed at the back of my throat. Even saying the words of how to break the bond was painful. Few men had actually done it.

"How do you do it?" I barely caught her words as I undid the shackles holding her before me. The large, heavy, metal clamp around her neck was still on, rubbing her throat raw.

"You have to give Queen Atarah the person you love the most," I spat the words out quickly, clenching my jaw tight trying to work through the pain of saying the words out loud.

"But what does she do with them? Keep them as pets?"

"If only it was that easy," I laughed dryly. "She slits open their throats, collects their blood in a bowl, and then you must bathe in it."

"That's terrible," she agreed.

"That's why many sworn to her don't do it. That's why many of us don't even get close enough to love people. Or people stay guarded and don't let us love them. One or the other."

"Who do you love most?"

Patting my pocket, I remembered what I had stolen from dinner for her. I pulled out a roll and placed it in her hand. She cupped it, careful not to touch it with the tips of her broken fingers. My mind drifted to Eydis as Red ate. Who did I love the most? For a while it had been the woman I had been engaged to. I had built her up to be this perfect, angelic being in my mind, and she didn't even love me in return.

"I don't love anyone enough to break the bond," I finally admitted, pulling out a small canister of water and setting it on the table between us. Listening intently, I could hear the guards breathing at the top of the stairs, no one near enough to see what I had done.

"So you're the type to keep your distance," she mumbled through a full mouth. "I figured you were the type people stayed away from because you're annoying as fuck."

"Excuse me?" I coughed. "Would someone that annoying be kind enough to bring you something to eat in the midst of your planned starvation?"

"Well, clearly, because you did." She pushed the last of the bread into her mouth, one hand already reaching for the canister. Pain laced her features as she tried to extend her hand.

With a shake of my head, I picked the water up. I pushed off the table and walked over to her side. "I'd hate to be annoying, but let me help you with that."

Red rolled her eyes. With one finger, I tipped her chin up and she propped her mouth open. Careful not to drown her, I slowly tipped until water drizzled out. When I stopped, she nearly moaned. A noise that sent a spike of interest straight to my groin. Twisting the lid closed, I tucked the bottle back into my pocket. I had to force myself to take a step back.

"Thank you." Red nodded.

"I thought you would deserve whatever it was you had coming," I started. "But being here, it doesn't feel right."

"You're right. Something is wrong. Not just with how they treat me, but look around, Milo." She tossed a glance to her right and left. "Look at all these cells. Shouldn't a king so famous for breaking nymphs have a dungeon full of crying nymphs? Where is everybody? Why am I all alone?"

I followed her gaze. My trained eyes passed over cell after cell, all completely empty. She was right. Where were the nymphs?

At the top of the stairs the guards shuffled. It made me wonder how much of our conversation they were listening to. Was I incriminating myself just by being down here?

"Windre said part of the process was to make you lonely. I'm sure they are hiding somewhere." I stalled, still glancing around. Only to mumble, "Hate to do it, Red, but that's my cue to leave."

She felt like a feather as I pulled her chair away from the table and pointed her toward her cell. To avoid catching any more unwanted attention, I mouthed, "I'll bring more food." As she stepped forward, I closed the door loudly, sealing her back into her prison.

A small mound of hay waited as the only comfort in the all-stone keep. I tried not to imagine being magic-less, wounded, and stuffed into a hole like that. My hand brushed the bars in an awkward goodbye. Red was already curling into herself and ignoring me as I left.

The musty smell of the hallway greeted my sensitive nose, while I took the stairs two at a time. Both guards turned to watch me from the small platform at the top. Their faces remained blank. Whether or not that was a good sign was beyond me.

"Think I'm going to head back to my room. Maybe get a little bit of light reading done," I chuckled, smacking my hand off one of the guard's chests lightly. His face remained blank. "I can show myself back."

Their heavy boots followed me down the hall as I turned the direction we had come from. "Or not," I said to no one in particular, as they trailed too closely behind me. The moment I reached my room, I stepped inside and closed the door, leaning against it for a moment to hear them shuffle back into their original spots. It seemed Windre wanted to keep a close eye on me. But it didn't feel like *I* was the one trying to fool the other.

A soft caw came from outside the ledge of my window. Light tapping followed the noise as the bird outside pecked at the glass. I blinked with each hit of the thin panel that separated us. Was I confused, or was Princess Maggie's bird a day early? I thought for a moment, frowning as I remembered that our arrival here had been delayed. So I guess that meant that the bird was right on time.

Crossing the clean, colorfully decorated space, I reached the window. It creaked as I opened it, the hinges were not often used or managed, I supposed. "Come on in, I guess. You'll have to wait for me to write the damn letter."

Another soft caw and the bird dipped it's head as if it could actually understand what I was saying. It's wire-

223

looking feet tapped against the stone before it flew to the small desk and cawed again. Its eyes were pure black and reflected my emotionless face more clearly the closer I came. Feathers ruffled as it made itself at home and tilted its head. Those bottomless eyes watched me.

"Okay, then." I stretched out my arms and cuffed my sleeves. My fingers brushed over the knobs of the drawers as I pulled them out. Many were empty, but eventually I found stationary and a pen to use.

"See?" I held the paper up for the bird to see. If birds could scowl, then this one totally was. Clearing my throat, like I was about to begin a speech, I set the pen to the paper and began.

Dearest Princess,

My arrival at the Acture Court was not met with much welcome. The king and his court give the appearance of business, though I find this land to be not as I thought it would. It may be perfectly normal, or it may be as off, as I perceive it to be. Only the excessively rich keep nymphs as servants. Shouldn't there be more than enough to go around, as there is in your court? As King Windre is the self-proclaimed breaker of nymphs, I've found his dungeons to be rather empty, with the exception of the servant I brought along. I have yet to explore the castle further, maybe I'll find more nymphs hiding elsewhere. In two days I will write to your father. I'll share the news of my arrival and the King's appearance of business. But perhaps I'll keep my speculations to myself until I have physical proof to provide.

Truly,
Milo

"Are you happy now?" I sighed. I waved the letter in the air, letting the ink dry before I rolled the crinkled parchment up and secured it to the marker on the bird's foot.

He gave one last caw before he scuttled off my desk, claws tapping loudly, and took flight out the window. I watched as he blended in with a small flock of birds that flew away at his startling outcry.

Pulling the window shut, I stared at the back of my closed door. Maybe I should be more direct. This uneasy feeling in my gut had to be telling me something. There was a dirty lie in this court. I just had to sniff it out.

EIGHTEEN

Ryker

King Henrick's touch had been light as a feather. His power was so strong that he needed only the barest contact to pull me, and my belongings, into the snap of travel manipulation. It had felt like getting whiplash, my neck aching like I'd been thrown forward through space. I guessed that I had. My stomach rolled from the momentum. Vomit burned like acid at the bottom of my throat, begging to be spewed out the moment I blinked into what I assumed was the Twinity Court castle.

He had left without a word. An entire band of servants rushed in soon after and began picking and pruning every inch of my body. They had provided me everything, as Dace had suggested. But the feeling of not being deserving still nagged at me.

They ran brushes through my hair. They scraped the dirt out from under my

226

fingertips. Shining pink paint was applied to my nails, and with a hot iron, they replaced my natural curls with larger, more elegant ones. The washing, the primping, the stuffing into the gown, and smoothing the sharp edges of my typically too-casual look took the entire day. I'd watched the sun fall toward the horizon through the large windows of my room.

The servants, nymphs like me, gossiped in a familiar way. They didn't appear as underfed as I had been under Ganglin's rule. They even smiled as they made me beautiful. Windre was right, they treated their nymphs with more respect than the other courts.

"You're going to look so beautiful," they whispered to me.

"We've heard about you, Ryker Avery," another one said, wide eyed. "I can't believe everything you've done. Maybe after tonight you'll make us more free than we've ever been." The girl had nodded encouragingly.

When someone else said it it felt less real. I hadn't done much, not more than being angry and loud. But she was mostly referring to making an alliance, I assumed. That was the entire reason I had come. Dace was in alliance with me, with the nymphs, so as his crown was placed upon his head, the bonds that will lead us to victory would be strengthened.

"What," I stuttered. "What should I expect tonight?"

"Oh, don't worry, Miss Avery. You are going to do wonders. I heard the queen already had a dream about it. She's very confident in what will happen tonight," one had responded while applying the subtlest pink color to my naturally very pale lips.

"You'll wait to be announced with the other guests. There are women here from all over the Twinity Court who wish to take Prince Dace's hand in marriage. As they say your name you'll walk--"

"With straight posture and your head held high," the third girl interrupted, pulling my shoulders back.

"Yes," the other continued with an annoyed glance at her friend. "You'll walk down the flight of stairs. Prince Dace will be waiting. He will give you a nod in acknowledgment and you'll be pretty much dismissed to go and enjoy the party."

"That's only if he is still waiting at the stairs though. He could be off dancing with a guest that arrived before you, if he favors her."

"If he favors her?" I gulped. Just thinking about the beautiful fae women that I was supposed to walk proudly behind made my palms sweaty.

"Whomever Dace favors at the beginning of the night to be his bride, when they reach the bottom of the steps, he will offer his hand. If she agrees and takes his hand, he will escort her to the dance floor and the party will officially begin."

"And if she doesn't accept his hand?" I asked, almost hopefully. Under the heat of their attention, I pointed my gaze bashfully to the floor. What was I even asking? He would offer his hand to a gorgeous fae and then he would dance the night away. And that was just how it was meant to be.

"No one would deny the prince's hand and the chance to be queen," the third nymph had laughed.

Her laugh still echoed in my thoughts now. My hands were just as sweaty as they had been all morning. Beaded, beautiful gowns filled my vision, before and behind me. Fae women mostly, a few accompanied by fathers or brothers, waited in a long line to be introduced to the royal family.

Many of the women sent me unwelcoming glares as they twisted in curiosity, wondering why a nymph was even standing in line with them. It didn't feel very much like I was a wanted guest.

The call of an attendant, the one who had organized the line we stood in now, rang out from the platform before the marble staircase. Every name that was called was accompanied by a murmur. The noise of their gossip growing with each woman. I wondered if Dace was still standing there.

I tried not to let my eyes wander. I tried not to appreciate the beauty of all the women in line with me. My hands clenched into fists to keep them from visibly shaking as I waited. My ankles felt weak with anxiety, making me a tad wobbly in the sparkly silver heels they had shoved my feet into. It made me appreciate the nymph tradition of attending a party barefoot.

The line before me grew shorter. I twirled a curl with my fingers as I watched. Voices behind me grew loud and excited.

"LaBelle, oh don't you look gorgeous!"

It was the name that made me twist in my gown to find the source. *LaBelle.* That was who was rumored, as the nymphs who readied me had said, was favored to be queen. It was simply the most obvious match for Dace, everyone thought. Who was this girl? I had to know. Was she beautiful? Was she kind? Would she agree with the alliance with the nymphs?

Her skin glimmered a deadly blue, like she had been drowned at some point in her life, and sea-green hair was piled on top of her head. Her dress was a lavish white gown. She was ready to walk down these stairs as a bride.

I glanced down at my blush silk dress the prince had picked out for me. It was so much more plain than LaBelle's. And she was otherworldly beautiful. I could already imagine her and Dace's babies toddling around with their perfect skin, perfect hair, and incredibly expensive wardrobe.

Forcing myself to keep the worry from my face, I plastered on a pathetic smile. It was the only smile I could manage. The attendant's voice grew louder. Every step I took maximized my nerves, until it felt like any strong wind could blow my trembling body away.

Until there was no one left in line in front of me.

"Miss Ryker Avery, Leader of the Nymphs and guest from the Heathern Court."

The rumble of voices that gossiped as each name was called spiked to an overwhelming commotion before it completely died. I stepped forward onto the platform.

Large white columns held up the artwork that was considered the ceiling. Paintings of cherubs and gods alike, dancing amongst the moon and the stars. Glowing silver chandeliers with sparkling fae firelight twinkled and cast their light down on the marble floor.

Fae were gathered in a half circle to watch as guests arrived. At the opposite end from the staircase were three thrones, two occupied by the king and queen, whose faces had fallen to flat indifference. Between us, the dance floor remained empty.

My heart stuttered, not once, twice, or even three times, but enough that it felt like it might finally stop beating and kill me now, in front of this disapproving crowd. What a way to go. Not my way.

It must be LaBelle then. I prayed she would make a good wife for Dace, and a worthy alliance to my cause. Tossing my hair over my shoulder, I caught a glance of her. Her eyes were narrowed and her mouth puckered. It was wrong of me, but I gave her my best 'eat shit' grin and began my descent.

Dace, dressed in a blue suit, embroidered with white flowers, with a pressed white button up, waited. A sly smile rounded the apples of his cheeks. He lifted his chin, beckoning for me to continue down the stairs.

Yes, that's what I was supposed to be doing. I needed to walk down the stairs, and for the love of the Mother, I needed to not fall while doing so. With one hand, I reached for the railing, the stone chilled, as if I was the only one who had bothered to use it. Maybe it was bad etiquette. Maybe it would keep me from bouncing my face off the steps on accident.

Swallowing my nerves, I took a long, deep breath, and stepped down the stairs. Such a silence had fallen on the room that the only noise was the chords of the string quartet that played in a corner, the click of my heels, and the ferocious beating of my heart.

Part of me wished LaBelle had been before me. That I wouldn't have to watch him pick her out of the line up and take her to the floor. It would be easier if he wasn't waiting for me now. If I didn't have to look him in the eyes as I walked right past him, and pretend to smile as he offered LaBelle his hand after me.

At the last step, I smoothed my silk dress over my thighs and turned to look at Dace, awaiting his direction. But it felt like more than just looking at him. I was really seeing him. His white eyelashes danced like crystals of ice as they brushed his sharp cheekbones. They framed the intensity of his lingering gaze. The line of his jaw tightened and chorded, his lips pressing together before they opened in a wild, healthy, grin. He looked the part of the prince. And I wanted him to be *my* prince. My heart ached with a wish that I finally fully admitted to myself.

The point of his chin lifted. The nod that I had so much wished for and dreaded all at the same time. I lifted my foot to drop the final step and meld in with the crowd.

Dace's hand appeared in front of me. I couldn't hear the sharp breath that was stolen from my lungs over the exclamation of the crowd. Their constant need for validation of every thought and outrage rising once more.

I glanced up at the king and queen who hadn't moved, hadn't altered their uncaring expressions, and looked down at his waiting hand. It didn't feel real. This was all some sort of messed up dream. Surely, I was about to wake up and be totally deflated.

I could turn him down, I thought. The girl's voice still rang in my head, *'No one would deny the prince's hand and the chance to be queen.'* No one, not even me. Not when it was all I secretly wished for just a moment before anyway. If this *was* a dream it wouldn't hurt to say yes.

Yet, Dace's hand, as I hesitantly took it, was firm and inviting. Completely, and utterly real.

Confident, as he always was, he led me to the empty dance floor and pulled me up to his chest. The smile on his face never faltered, his attention never drifting from me to the crowd. Because Dace never needed validation in what he was doing, he just did it. Behind us, the attendant called the name of the next girl, who would be upset to find that the nymph was somehow favored.

"What are you doing?" I whispered, letting him lead me in a simple step around the floor. All around us, fae watched with displeasure. Though I caught one knowing smile. Jesseline held a bubbling glass up in salute as we made eye contact, her hair slicked back behind sparkling diamond earrings. She looked like a different person in the green, skin-tight gown.

Dace leaned closer, his soft lips brushing against my ear, "I'm choosing my bride."

"You still have time to change your mind," I breathed. "I've only been favored."

Dace straightened himself and watched me with furrowed brows. He licked his lips, looking around me for a moment before he said, "I've already made my choice."

"You can't marry a nymph."

I wanted to laugh, I practically did as I spoke. This was a moment of insanity, that's what this was. I was probably crazy too, for thinking this could really be an option.

"If I can't marry you, then I won't marry at all. And if my mother cannot accept that then she'll have to find another way to keep the people on the streets from throwing her ass off the throne."

His eyes fixed on his mother behind me as he spoke. The seriousness in his voice curled through me. The sound of his rich voice at my ears sent heat down to my sex.

"Did you not notice the way I've flirted with you? Is my game so far off that you never saw my attraction to you?"

"I, uh, I just thought that you were making a game of it. That you couldn't be serious. You just wanted me to fawn over you, like every other girl."

LaBelle had made her way down the stairs. I could feel her eyes zeroed in on my back, burning against my skin. The dress Dace had picked revealed my back completely, a self conscious worry. Scars marred my skin. Divots of skin were missing and uneven from my beatings over the last five years.

Dace ran his hand over the planes of my back, pulling me closer to him until there was hardly any space between us at all. "I've wanted you for all my life, Ryker."

Fear zapped through me, making me rigid. It was everything I'd just admitted that I wanted, and it was terrifying. Under the scrutiny of an entire court of people who didn't want me here, it was overwhelming. I wanted to hide, I wanted to run to Daethian or Hattie and tell them everything just so they could tell me it's okay. That if this is what I wanted, then we would find a way to work it out. But my best friend and my sister were not here right now.

"What do we do next?" I said as the song came to a close.

"You'll come stand by me, while I sign a public decree accepting my rights to the crown back. Unfortunately, after that I will have to take dances with all the other *options,*" he said the word with a hint of disgust. "But it doesn't change anything." He squeezed my hand, walking us up to his parents.

His father's hand had lifted to rub at the shadow of a beard that was growing along his jaw as he watched us approach together. Queen Couley's back was straight as a board, her hands resting against the arms of the throne. Her features were frozen, her skin an even porcelain. A beautiful statue.

"This is who you present to us as your favored bride?" she finally said slowly, enunciating every single word.

"It would seem that way, wouldn't it, mother?" His smile grew cocky as he lifted my hand in offering.

Standing from her seat, the queen's navy-blue gown danced with gems that tinkled against the ground like tiny bells. She flicked her wrist and a few nymphs carried out a table and a chair. A scroll, pen, warmed wax, and a crown rested on the wood. The nymphs looked up at me with genuine smiles as they set it down before us and scuttled back to wherever they had come from.

The crown was clear crystal, almost like it was carved out of ice. It didn't melt against the table, which put my theory to rest. Dace let go of my hand and sat down at the table.

"It's really been such a pleasure doing business with you. I'm so lucky to have parents just as *loving* as you." Every word was a pointed dagger aimed for his mother. The tension between them felt like a thick fog in the air.

No matter how much I wanted to believe that he meant it, I couldn't help but believe that he'd change his mind. There was the rest of the evening for him to talk with other girls, for him to talk with LaBelle.

Here my mind became a terrible rebel to the way I tried to smother my hope. I watched Dace as he smiled, leaning over the documents. He brushed the hair away from his forehead with those long fingers. It made me wonder what it would be like if he touched me like that. A reckless, mindless caress. It wasn't a fun game my thoughts made me play. He was a prince, the people's king. I was merely the face of rebellion. A nymph who has bewitched her way into winning a prize so much bigger than her.

NINETEEN

Dace

I know it was right of me to entertain these other women, just enough to make my mother feel content. But it was much harder to keep my gaze from drifting her direction. Everything about her was as my vision deemed it, down to her hesitance in taking my hand. She looked more than the part of a dream come true, she looked like a fucking angel.

"In my spare time, I like to sew, or occasionally tend to the gardens with my nymphs. Father says I have the greenest thumbs," the drone of LaBelle's voice went in one ear and out the other. I nodded along, though.

"What do you do in your free time?" she continued.

Ryker stood on the edge of the crowd, a sparkling brew made here in the Twinity Court in her hand. She smiled and laughed with Jesseline, who still managed to look like a killer. On occasion she looked up to watch me. Something was distant in her gaze. Was she enjoying her time here? I hoped to the gods that she was.

"Dace?" LaBelle said with a little bit more force, drawing me back into the conversation I was supposed to be having.

"I," I cleared my throat, thinking. "I like to drink. I enjoy training with my daggers." The feeling of their weight at my hip was sorely missed as I changed into my formal wear. But for comfort, one was tucked into my sock.

"Those sound like a dangerous combination," she giggled, trailing her finger over my shoulder.

"Yes, but that is why I refrain from doing them together."

With the exception of that one time. But I don't really talk about that. The point was, don't drink and play with knives. My arms felt tired from constantly keeping one hovering over her waist without actually touching her. I knew my parents wanted me to like LaBelle, but she was incredibly boring. Not to mention, overly perfumed.

I missed Ryker's scent. Even from this distance, if I took a deep enough breath, I was able to catch the smallest hint. It was probably just clinging to my clothing.

As we spun with the music, the other couples finally out on the dance floor, I caught a glimpse of long blue hair and silver eyes. My attention snapped to my friend-turned-enemy. I pulled away from LaBelle with the smallest of bows, keeping Torrance in my eyesight.

Torrance was the reason I had lost my crown to begin with. He was the person who led my parents to the refuge. The bastard had some serious explaining to do. That, or I could rip his head off his shoulders here and now, that seemed fair enough to me.

"Please, excuse me," I mumbled, turning on my heels before the song was even over. LaBelle was already flabbergasted behind me before the words had completely left my mouth.

Torrance's eyes lit up as he saw me approaching. He plucked a second drink off the tray of a server walking by and extended it toward me. "Dace, I'm so glad to see--"

His words were cut off as my fist traveled through the air and struck his face. Blue hair and the slur of the words he meant to say were tossed over his shoulder as his head snapped to the side. Liquid from the drinks sloshed from their cups and covered his suede shoes. Fae around us gasped, some even took a step back.

"You fucker," I hissed. "Do you know how many nymphs you killed?"

Torrance rotated his jaw and handed both drinks to the nearest fae. "Okay, I may have deserved that."

Rebecca Grey

"You deserve to meet the same fate as those whose bodies couldn't even be laid to rest." Anger boiled inside of me, my hand reaching for the knives that were not on my waist. It would be fitting for Torrance to have a slow, painful death. That idea was the only thing that kept me from using my bare hands to rip his head from his spine.

"Well, would you let me explain," he said with a smirk.

"You can explain from your grave if you don't knock that nasty little smile off your face."

The smile faltered, but he didn't lose it. "I was only following my commands. It was seen that I was supposed to lead them to you. I'm not about to test my fate with the gods. A simple misunderstanding, you see."

"What I see is a man whose nut sack is about to be up his damn throat in about five seconds if he doesn't get the fuck out of here. I don't care about the visions from the gods."

"Dace, you know I'm not one to miss out on these free drinks," he laughed easily.

"Dace," Jesseline coughed at my side.

"What?" I snapped.

The crowd around us watched with wide eyes. My father stood from his throne to watch our interaction. If Jesseline wasn't about to stop it, he sure would,

242

especially if it meant keeping my mother from getting embarrassed by my rash behavior. I pointed at Torrance.

"It would serve you well to disappear from my sight." I closed my jacket where it had come unbuttoned and forced myself to walk away. My fingers itched to wrap around his throat or to string him up by his toes. Torrance deserved to pay in some way for his actions, and I didn't care if it was god-ordained or not.

My attention trailed the mass of partygoers. I observed the fae who drank and danced and cheered. Some remained reserved, I noted that it was mainly members of my parent's court, the ones who strongly supported my absence. But it wasn't them I was looking for.

"Ryker stepped out for a minute," Jesseline said, her eyes never stopping her swift surveillance.

"Stepped out, where?"

She shouldn't have left. I should have made it more clear that with her being my favored proposition, she was a target to those who wanted that position. I cursed under my breath and jogged up the stairs and out of the ballroom. On the platform, I could hear the keys of a piano randomly being plucked at in no particular rhythm. I followed the sound to one of the small rooms that was also often used for parties, smaller gatherings of course.

Ryker was perched on the edge of the piano bench, her fingers pushing at the keys. The servants had ironed out her curls and they hung loosely over her shoulder. I stepped into the large, empty room and just took a breath of her intoxicating scent.

Her eyes jumped from the piano to me, her body jerking upright in surprise. "Oh, you scared me," she laughed, tilting her chin down. The curtain of her hair covered her bashful blush.

"Why did you leave the party?" My hands found a home in the pockets of my pants as I moseyed my way to her. I looked at her, then the piano, and quietly sat beside her.

"You and Jesseline are about the only ones who want to see me there. Just needed a break from all the judgmental stares, I guess."

"Ah, yes. My parents' court is famous for that. I'll tell you a not-so-secret secret." I looked around the room, then whispered, "They look at me like that, too."

Ryker's laugh was effortless, a small chuckle she swatted away, her hand coming to rest on my arm. Her smile melted as she noticed what she had done so easily without thought.

Despite the way she drew her hand back, I pulled up my sleeves and reached for the piano keys. The instrument was like second nature to me. Growing up, my parents had said I was to practice at an instrument of my choosing, and since Torrance and every other boy who came along to my classes wanted to pluck at the strings of a guitar or ukulele, I knew I had to be different. So I was rebellious and picked the piano. Though I could easily pick up a ukulele if I wanted. Practice had been nearly every morning for an hour or two, for almost fifty years. My favorite maid helped to teach me when I wished to sneak away from my other lessons.

Without a thought, I played a simple melody I'd learned so many years ago. Music filled the room. Awe sparkled in Ryker's large eyes as she watched my hands move. The melody was cheerful, but led into a long bridge that suddenly made the song feel more mournful. It was one of my favorite songs.

"You never told me you could play piano. But I guess I shouldn't be surprised," she mumbled, her body leaning closer to mine.

"I can do many things that I've never told you." I winked and ended the song in a simple chord. My hands slipped from the keys and I folded them in my lap. "I know that it sounds insane, but I meant what I said before we came here."

Ryker studied my face. An eyebrow lifting ever so slightly as she thought. I scooped her hands into mine, my thumb stroking along the back of her hand. In my dreams this was easier, but now my chest felt tight, my mouth drier by the second.

"You could stay here," I continued. "You don't need to go back to the Heathern Court. I could take care of all of that for you and maybe *we* could be together."

There I had said it. The silence that followed made every moment that much more intense. Ryker gave me a light smile.

"Dace, it isn't that simple."

"But it is! *Ryker*, please just listen to me, if you could only give this a chance. You can live your life however you please now. You can decide to live it with me. The Twinity Court could be your home."

Her curls bounced as she shook her head, one hand rose to touch my cheek. I leaned into her palm and let her pull away to trace my jaw and then my lips.

"Will it always feel this way?" I squeezed my eyes shut.

"What way?"

"Like every time I'm near you, I'm totally consumed by you. Like every moment I touch you," I opened my eyes and leaned forward, pulling her face to mine, "I become a drunkard without sense."

"Aren't you a drunkard without sense already?" she teased, her lips brushing mine.

Fire from her touch burned across my skin. The space between us, as little as it was, felt like miles. It was a distance I needed to close. My soul felt raw and vulnerable and Ryker could destroy me in an instant if she chose to. But I couldn't think about that. All that filled me was the urgency to kiss her.

With a short inhale, I pressed my lips to hers. Her mouth parted in soft surrender. It was everything I'd ever wanted and ever asked for, and it was finally happening in real time. My heart might very well explode from my chest, a feeling she was surely aware of, as I was of her racing pulse. She leaned into me, parting my lips further with the sweep of her tongue. The taste of her was as exhilarating as I thought it would be. I could savor her kisses all day.

Ryker pulled away, resting her forehead against mine. "As much as I would like all of that to be possible, I'm not free yet. Nymphs are not free, and I can't just run off and play princess and assume that everything is going to work out."

The sting of her words made my eyes flutter shut to try and hold back the overwhelming sense of disappointment. I loved Ryker, but she didn't love me back. Not yet.

"I was sericus too, when I said I was picking you to be my bride. One day you could be more than a princess, you would be a queen." I smiled, mostly to myself.

Ryker ran her fingers through my hair and pressed one more small kiss to my lips before she sat up straight. "And that sounds like a lovely dream. Hell, if it wasn't something that had also passed through my mind, I would have thought you were insane."

Her teeth raked over her bottom lip. It created a deep rumble in me and urged me to kiss her again. I brushed her hair away from her face. Her green eyes were glassy as she watched me. Her small admission only gave me further faith in us.

"It doesn't have to be now," I finally sighed. "I'll wait till you're ready if you want. If you want me to court you, I'll do it. Damn, if you want me to sacrifice myself to the gods, I'll do it and come back in my next life for you."

"Don't be so rash. I have to go back to the Heathern Court. I understand that you have a place here, but you have to understand that I have a place there. Someday maybe those places could meet in the middle. It just isn't today." She couldn't hide the hope in her voice. "You saw the way everyone disapproved of me. The stigma isn't going to end tomorrow just because I become your bride."

"I don't care what they think. I've never cared what they think," I said stubbornly.

Someone cleared their throat behind us. I glanced behind Ryker to find Jesseline in the doorway. "Sorry to interrupt, but your parents are looking for you, Dace."

"Gods, can I just tell them to fuck off?" I groaned.

Ryker smiled as I took her hands and gave them a squeeze. I wasn't ready to leave this room just yet, but damn if it wasn't exactly like my parents to ruin a good thing.

"Think about it Ryker," I whispered, unable to stop my wide, toothy smile.

She turned on the bench as I walked out, calling after me, "I'll think about it all night, but it doesn't change a thing."

I shook my head. She was a stubborn one. But I'll take all the time she needs if we have to.

"I'll just..." Jesseline pointed back toward Ryker and vanished from beside me as I rounded the corner and found my parents waiting at the top of the steps. My father was pacing around my mother, who cocked her head and watched me walk toward them with a goofy-ass smile.

"Why are you grinning like that?" he said, slowing his steps. "Are you trying to pull a fast one on us? You think we're going to let you marry a nymph?"

My mother stood still, observing me as I came closer. She was certainly annoyed, but surprisingly, not angry. I'd expected her to already be yelling at me five paces back.

"Care to explain?" she finally asked. "Or is this just simply a ploy to get a rise out of us?"

"Not a ploy. I simply just want to marry whom I wish to marry."

"You didn't even give LaBelle an entire two minutes of your time. You caused a scene with Torrance--" my father started.

"Torrance lost me my crown. Torrance killed innocent nymphs," I interjected.

"You lost your crown, Dace, not him. And now you want to leave your party early. Are you declaring the nymph your bride then?"

"She isn't ready for marriage," I said plainly. "And would it help if I told you I've seen our relationship in my dreams?"

"Did you see your marriage?" my mother said with a coy smile.

No. No I hadn't. But I'd seen everything else, and that had to be enough. I thought back to all the visions I'd had. There were so many more memories to be made with her. I'd never seen a wedding at all.

"No, but I know we are meant to have a relationship."

"Perhaps she is just a side piece. Kings have mistresses all the time, son." My mother placed her hands on her hips. My father was suspiciously silent next to her. "What do you propose we do?"

"I'm suggesting you take my offer of engagement to Ryker Avery. But we wait until she says she's ready. Deal?"

"How is that a deal?" my father sighed.

"Look, I'll marry this one. Promise. And in the meantime... I'll travel within the Twinity Court. I'll talk to the areas that you say have been out of control. I'll get back the control that you want. You'll have your food on the table."

Mother grinned, a dangerous sort of smile, like she might eat me up and spit me out and enjoy every agonizing moment of it. "I'll take that deal on the condition that if Ryker turns you down, or grows bored of you before you are officially wed, you marry the bride of our choosing. Princess Maggie still isn't off the table."

It wouldn't come to that. I had hope. And if that ever did happen, I might be so completely broken on the inside that it wouldn't matter who I married.

"Deal," I nodded. Now I just had to pray that Ryker would always feel the same way about me. I wished Shavarra was here right now. She'd love to hear a rant about my terrible parents and then she'd probably smack me upside the head for taking the deal.

With a frown, I slipped between my parents and headed back into the party. Guess I'll continue to play the role of host and finish these damn dances.

Rebecca Grey

TWENTY

Dace

Nymphs were cleaning up the empty glasses of fae who drank far too much. Many of the guests still danced and cheered with the music. I rubbed at my eyes, blinking, and wondered why I hadn't drank more.

"Are you tired?" Ryker's soft voice said from behind me.

I twisted to face her and ran my fingers through my hair hoping I hadn't ruffled it too much. "Just who I wanted to see. I'm doing okay, thankfully I've finished the last of the dances, which is good. They all seem to be having a good time."

Ryker followed the direction of my finger to the swaying drunkards. Torrance danced sloppily next to a woman with an incredibly low cut gown on the edge farthest from us. I'd made a point to keep him on the opposite side of the room from me. Parents wouldn't be happy if I popped off like that again.

"Hmm, makes me miss my friends." Her arms wrapped around her, her hands rubbing the exposed skin. "I was actually thinking I would call it a night and head back to my room."

"Let me walk you back." Stepping forward, I offered her my hand once more.

Skeptically, she leaned away from me. "Don't you think it will look bad if we walk out of here together like that?"

I hummed, "I don't know how many times I need to say this, but I don't give a fuck what it looks like, what anyone here thinks, or that it's technically too early for me to leave my own party. If you're comfortable holding my hand, the simplest of acts, then nothing else matters."

"You know this isn't an invitation into my bed, right?"

Her hand slipped into mine, and I brought it up to my mouth, placing a gentle kiss on her knuckles. "I won't touch you like that until you ask. Though," I added with a wink, "I'll be waiting, oh-so-impatiently, until you do."

Heads turned to watch us walk together up the stairs. Ryker tried to smile at me as we took our time. In my head, this wasn't just about what my court needed to see. Though the sight of fae and nymph hand in hand was necessary, this was one of the small moments

254

where I felt like I was who I was meant to be. Life came at me in overwhelming waves, but Ryker somehow slowed them down and brought them into perspective for me.

The smile she gave me wasn't without the sadness that still touched her eyes. Her back, her very scarred back, was in plain view for all to see. More eyes were trained on her than on me, for once. I hoped they saw the beauty in her like I did. I hoped they saw the wicked in them.

Together, we stepped around the corner and out of sight. Ryker let loose a long breath, like just walking up the small flight of stairs had been painful to bear. Her pulse still raced, I felt it in the grip of her hand and heard it thudding in her chest.

Another small shiver ran down her spine. Tentatively, I let go of her hand and reached to put my arm over her shoulders and hold her close as we walked. "May I?"

"I'm honestly surprised you even asked."

"Have I not been anything but polite?" I wrapped my hand over her cold skin and brought her up against my body. The smell of her drifted in intoxicating waves up to my face. It took all of my strength not to bury my face in her hair.

"Polite, but assertive," she thought aloud, "Cocky, and full of assumptions."

"Damn, I thought you were starting to like me."

Her gaze traveled from my head to my toes as she smirked up at me. "You may have convinced me that you have *some* admirable traits."

"Mmm, say more things like that," I murmured. The silk of her dress was just a thin layer of material between us. My mind couldn't quit thinking about it as I felt her frame shift with each step against me. "You must be great at talking dirty."

She chuckled awkwardly, "Your version of talking dirty would be hurtling half hearted compliments at each other."

"Sorry, years of crippling mental damage will do that to a guy."

A few posted guards bowed slightly at the waist as we passed. I'm sure many assumed that she wasn't the queen-to-be, but a pawn in a game, since she was a nymph. It would take time to untrain their minds to think that way.

"You're not the only one damaged," Ryker said, watching the guards.

"Two peas in an unstable pod," I whispered.

The door to the suite she was staying in came into view. I unwrapped myself from her and took her hand again. Once we reached the door I turned to face her. I couldn't quit looking at her, touching her, and getting high off the reality of her.

"May I kiss you again?" I leaned forward.

Rykers back reclined against the door. Her lips pressed together, her eyes darting from my gaze to my mouth.

"Yes, please," she breathed.

That was enough. The space between us evaporated. Both of my hands held her face, tilting her chin up toward me. Excitement ballooned in my abdomen, the ecstasy of her embrace spiking desire that traveled straight to my cock.

Her lips parted for me. She opened her mouth wider, the kiss deepening as if we couldn't get enough of each other. I couldn't breathe, I couldn't think. All I could do was want and taste and enjoy.

Her hands ran down my torso, settling along my hips. Her fingers gripped me tightly to her, digging sharply into the fabric of my shirt.

I pulled away just enough to press kisses against her tan skin, trailing down along her jaw and onto her neck. The briefest of scents caught my nose. Two small white dots had yet to fade, and still contained the smell of another man. My tongue flicked out over the spot. I wanted to claim her. I wanted to be the one to sink my teeth into her. If you did it right, if she wanted as much as I did, pleasure would spike wildly. It would make her legs tremble.

I paused, brushing my nose along her neck, trying to fight the primal urge that grew as the smell of her arousal filled the air. "I know you didn't ask for that," I said, pressing a kiss to the mark. "I could cover it up for you, if you'd like."

One hand rose and she cupped her neck, pulling away to watch me. "It's almost faded. It will be gone soon enough."

Absently, her other hand brushed my hair out of my face, trailing over my scalp, around my ear. She watched me, still trying to catch her breath as I was.

"Our attraction to each other is... undeniable."

"The problem is, it isn't logical," she laughed.

"Maybe to you," I mused with a sigh. "I want to kiss you all night and into the next day."

"I'm not sure I would be strong enough to say 'no' to more if you did that." The hand at her neck slipped over my body, her fingers drawing a line where my belt sat.

"Don't tempt me like that," I growled, wishing we could. Taking a long, shaking breath, I stepped away from her. I tried to focus on filling my lungs and releasing the air back out to clear my head. If we kept up like this I wouldn't be able to stop. Ryker wasn't ready for this yet. She had set the boundary and I needed to respect it.

"Will you father be available to take me back to the Heathern Court tomorrow?" She cocked her head.

MADNESS

Everything inside me wanted to crumble at her statement. I wanted her to be with me, but I had made the commitment to finally accept my responsibility as prince.

"Uh, yes. He can be. Though, I wish you would stay." I'd have to talk to my father in the morning. At least it was better than my mother using her magic to take Ryker back and forth. That would only be filled with cutting remarks about how much of a disappointment I was and how she thought we shouldn't be together.

"It's complicated, remember?" She reached for the doorknob.

"I'll just have to visit you then." I purred. "For practice, you know."

"Practice?" she blushed.

I leaned down to her and kissed her cheek. My lips moved against her skin as I spoke. "I was talking about training, but I'll happily practice anything you'd like in your bedroom."

The way her breathing hitched made my toes curl. I wheeled myself back, taking a few steps down the hallway. She touched her face where my mouth had just been and twisted the knob behind her.

"Good night, Ryker," I sang.

"Goodnight." She waved and inched inside her room. Even as I turned my back and headed for my room, I could still feel her gaze on my back, her door not clicking shut until I was nearly out of sight.

If I wasn't careful, Ryker would consume me. Not that that was a bad thing.

With every step, my mind replayed every moment of the night. Some bad, some good. But nothing could stop the high of finally getting to kiss her, to embrace her so freely, for her to return the attraction that I'd contained for so long.

Some guards watched me, confused as I walked back to my room alone. They expected me to party hard and do as I pleased, without respecting Ryker's wishes, because she was a nymph. They had me all wrong. I wasn't like the rest of this godless court.

With a smile still on my lips, I slipped into my room. The smooth material of my jacket felt almost suffocating as I slipped out of it. My fingers were already working the buttons of my shirt. Under my pants, I could feel the fullness of my cock pressing against the material. I tried to think of something else, anything else to ease the desire, but the impressive firmness of it didn't go away.

Growling under my breath, I undid my pants and tossed them into a waiting basket. Silk pajamas were already laid out for me on the bed. The smooth texture reminded me of Ryker's dress and the way it hugged her body. That did little to soothe the growing erection in my briefs.

Despite the spark that had erupted between me and Ryker, a few not-so-good things still had come from the day. The weight of them caused exhaustion to beckon me toward the bed. When Ryker left I would still have Torrance and my parents to deal with. I wondered if Jesseline would stay though. I was surprised she had followed, but it seemed that she was certain there was a price on my head. A little extra guarding didn't hurt anything, I mused while I pulled back the covers and climbed into bed.

For the first time in a long time, it felt like being awake was better than my dreams. I longed to be able to pick the moment of the future I could live in while I slept, but it never came like I wanted. More often than not, my dreams would be the opposite of what I was craving.

Closing my eyes, I smiled to myself and began counting to divert my thoughts and lull myself into sleep. Numbers passed in visions under my eyelids, until the next moment, they were no more.

White fog swirled inside my head, giving way to the frosted Twinity Court. Snow crunched beneath me as I appeared within the walls of our courtyard. The snow on the ground wasn't as white as it should be. Red was splattered and large puddles stained the once-pure earth.

Rapidly, my gaze traveled over the ground. Bodies of guards were slumped over in death. Fear made my body stiff and my mind sharp. Was someone in the castle? Were my parents okay?

Slipping in my haste, I ran to the bottom of the steps that lead inside. A strange body, not dressed in our guard's armor, was stretched over the stairs. Wind rustled a ragged black cloak, revealing grey skin with black veins underneath.

I took a deep breath. It didn't smell like fae, it didn't smell like nymph either. It smelled ancient. It smelled deadly.

Repressing the part of me that wanted to flee, I crept forward. My fingers trembled and I struggled to keep them steady. I was a prince, nothing should scare me like this. My powers would rival so many.

Still-warm flesh was soft under my skin as I pressed two fingertips against the body's throat. The wind picked up the torn hood and pushed it away from the face. A woman. Long, black hair was bound in a low ponytail, black veins ran in splintering lines over her cheekbones. A faint heartbeat registered beneath my fingers.

Recognition of just what I was touching startled me enough that I snatched my hand back. A burgundy witch? They had long since been thought to be extinct, and they were not friends of the fae. Blood coated her bottom lip, sharp teeth extended, ready to feast on fae flesh.

I knew what I had to do. This thing couldn't stay here. It couldn't stay alive.

"Guards?" I called, looking for anyone still alive, or a sign that the castle hadn't been breached.

The front door opened, the helmet of the attending guard poking out to see me. His eyes grew as he took in the sight.

"What happened here?" I asked.

"I don't know," he stuttered. "We didn't hear anything. No one sounded any alarms or anything." The guard inside next to him pushed the door open farther and gawked at what his comrade was looking at.

"Sound the alarm, then! Scour the castle, and for the love of the gods, send someone to check on my parents."

"Yes, my prince," the one guard said quickly, before he bowed and darted away.

My hand was already on my waist, a knife slipping quietly from its sheath. It couldn't be allowed to live. To keep myself from stopping, or letting fear take over, I hurried. My fingers intertwined in her hair as I lifted her head to expose her throat. The knife slid easily across her skin. Blood gurgled, as she tried to inhale, and splattered around her. I wiped the weapon on her cloak and slipped the knife back into my belt.

Rebecca Grey

TWENTY-ONE

Ryker

I returned to the Heathern Court the same as I had left, in the silence of King Henrick's presence. He didn't speak this morning either, as he swiftly took my hand and slung me through time and space, back to where I truly belonged. The briefest of nods was all he gave me once we returned. Nausea was still spinning strongly in my stomach when he used his travel manipulation and returned to the Twinity Court.

Part of my heart had stayed behind in the Twinity Court. The part of me that begged to ignore everything I'd worked for thus far to run away with Prince Dace was frantically screaming in my head. That voice left me no choice but to leave without saying goodbye. Worry had me thinking that if he would ask me to stay one more time, I'd strip all my clothes off, let him take me right there, and I'd never return again.

You're so fucking weak, Ryker, I snarled to myself. A few nymphs called from the valley as they saw me appear. Their friendly smiles made me feel so much more welcome than Dace's parents ever had. I waved back, scanning the small crowd for my friend, for Daethian. Instead, Graceson's red hair bobbed into view.

Already on his way up the hill toward the steps, Graceson waved in greeting. Sweat left the stray hairs near his face clinging to his cheeks. His scarred wings opened and closed like a small fan behind him as he fell in step next to me.

"So, are you the queen of the Twinity Court yet?" he clicked his tongue.

"That's a no. And how do you always know things before I tell them to you?" I shot him a bewildered look, taking the steps two at a time. "You haven't said anything to Daethian, have you?"

"I have friends far and wide." He chewed his lip, his eyes watching anything but me, as he spoke. "Was I not supposed to tell Daethian? It's good news, isn't it?"

"Damn it, Graceson. How did he take it?"

"He didn't really say anything."

Okay, maybe it wasn't as bad as I thought. Maybe this time had done what it needed to do and he had realized we were just better as friends and that this was all for the good of everyone. *Including my own personal interests.*

"I hope that's a good sign. Everything still standing here?"

"Some of the nymphs have taken to calling me 'bastard' instead of my real name. A few minor complaints from some nymphs who want to use the same training weapons, and someone learned they are allergic to bees, but apart from that, it's been business as usual, I would suspect."

My gaze traveled over the doors we walked by. The noise of sex-crazed nymphs was still noticeable in the air. I scrubbed my face and tried to ignore the noises. Graceson walked along next to me, happy as can be, oblivious, with his cheeky smile and casual stance. My plan was to jump in the shower, try and wash off a fraction of Dace's scent before I hunted Daethian down. Even with the dread of our impending conversation, I missed him dearly.

"Have you heard anything from Hattie?" I asked hopefully, as we started down my hallway.

"Oh, yeah, actually a messenger stopped by and dropped off some sort of crystal. She said if you wanted to talk, all you'd have to do is hold it and say her name? Sounds like witchcraft to me, but I put it in your room on top of your wardrobe so no one would find it."

"Thank you," I murmured and twisted the handle on my bedroom door.

"Here, I'll follow you in and get it down for you so you don't have to climb the wardrobe for it," Graceson said, stepping with me over the threshold.

"You don't have--," I started to say, but realized we weren't alone. My body jolted, making me stumble backwards into Graceson's immovable chest.

Daethian sat up on my bed, his hair ruffled and eyes dark. The scruff of his stubble had grown in more, like he hadn't bothered to care for it the past few days. "Should I congratulate you now or later?" Daethian said.

"I'll just step outside for a minute," Graceson whispered, and slipped from the room.

Watching him, I fiddled with a loose strand of hair, trying to come up with something to say. My hair was still pressed into the elegant curls. It was a nice change from my natural frizz.

Daethian leaned back into the shadow under the canopy of the bed. It made everything about him look nefarious as his frown deepened. He surely didn't look okay to me.

"You let them change your hair? It was perfect the way it was."

"I don't know what you want me to say, Daethian," I finally managed, meeting his half-slitted gaze.

"Hmm." He stood, ducking to miss the drooping fabric above him. The floor creaked with each slow step he took toward me. Static made the black fabric of his shirt cling to his abdomen.

Daethian took a deep breath as he brought his boots to my toes. His spine straightened, his chin tilting down to watch me with some shade of disgust. "Why can't you say that you choose me?"

"I thought we already had this conversation. I'm not choosing him over you. You're my best fucking friend. That's not how this works."

"Then how does it work? Because from where I stand, you're running off with him and leaving *me* alone."

"You're not alone right now." I pushed a finger into his chest. I could feel anger flooding my body. I wanted to scream at him, like *really* scream at him. Things had never been like that between us.

"You're so stupid," he yelled, spit showering over my face. I flinched away, bumping against the wall behind me.

"Don't talk to me like that," I snarled and stood taller, refusing to back down. Daethian was wrong and his anger was unjustified and unnecessary. Rage made me spit out the words I knew would cut the most. I wanted to say them. "Maybe we shouldn't be friends either, if you're going to act like this."

Daethian growled. I expected his cheeks to brighten in fiery red fury, but instead they only looked more ashen. His hand shot out, grabbing me by my neck and slamming me against the wall. Plaster cracked behind me, the shock of my head bouncing off the wall made the room spin. Both hands rushed to pull at Daethian's hands, wrapped so tightly around my throat. But he only squeezed harder as I wheezed, and my legs scuffed against the wall to find some sort of purchase.

"You don't get to tell me what I can and can't do anymore, you bitch." Black flooded his irises until there was no difference between his pupils and, what used to be, a lovely brown color. Dark waves of smoke began uncurling from his back, tiny tendrils of something unnatural reached off of him. The air filled with the strong scent of something burnt, something wrong.

"Daethian, stop," my voice squeaked out. Inside my chest, my lungs begged for reprieve. I pulled and scratched at his fingers, but he only tightened his grip and leaned closer. This wasn't him. Suddenly, guilt plagued me for my angry words.

"Stop telling me what to do," he bellowed.

The thought to reach for my magic came to mind. But even though he was trying to hurt me, I couldn't bring myself to want to hurt him. The space between us was too small, whatever I did to him I would also be doing to myself.

In a desperate plea to save myself, while also saving my friend, I slammed my fist against the wall.

Magic, like extended limbs, reached into the walls. Within the castle, I could feel every support beam, every piece of stone, and every place I could hit that could make the building come crashing down. The building shook at my rage. I didn't need the castle to fall. I just needed Graceson's attention. I could feel his weight through the floorboards he stood on outside of the room. Pushing, I popped them up under his feet to bounce him forward. Black was beginning to form on the edge of my vision, my body feeling weaker. The limbs of my magic quickly rushed back toward me, no longer tethered to my thoughts.

Graceson pushed the door open, stepping into the room. "Is everything oka-- Goddess above! Daethian, let her go!"

He rushed forward, but Daethian kept his hold. I could feel my body growing more lethargic, my hands getting weaker and weaker as I tried to pull myself free. Graceson hissed under his breath and pushed himself between us, his arm slamming into the crook of Daethian's elbow.

Pressure was finally released from my neck and a distant pain vibrated through my body as I crumbled against the old floors. I tried to blink up into the light to make out the scuffle between the men. Each breath was ragged and rough as it burned down my throat.

"What's wrong with him?" Graceson called, pinning Daethian's arms behind him. He shifted away from the snaking black fog that still drifted off his skin.

"I don't know," I coughed, my hands pushing up off the dusty floor.

Daethian laughed, the noise sounding like an off-key chord, "I'm fine, Ryker. Clearly, I'm fucking fine."

Forcing myself to stay still and keep my distance from him, I looked at Graceson. I shook my head, unsure of what to do. "What should we do with him? He needs to see Suzetta."

"He can't see her like this," Graceson grunted, while Daethin snarled and thrashed in his arms like a wild beast. "He'll hurt her."

He was right. I couldn't have him getting to anyone else the way he had to me. Along with that, I didn't want anyone to see him like this. How would they react to something so unknown? Just as much as I didn't want him hurting anyone else, I didn't want someone to hurt him either. There had to be a way to help him.

There was only one place that the nymphs made a point not to visit. The pits of the dungeon. Would taking him down to someplace with so many bad memories make this worse on him?

"Can you take him down to the dungeon without being seen? I'll go get Suzetta."

"Everyone is out practicing and I'll stick to the less frequented halls. No one here likes to walk by the dungeons."

"You can't save me, Ryker," Daethian cooed. "You've already ruined me."

A passing feeling of horror rattled my thoughts. Leaving had been the wrong answer, and I had left him alone to deal with whatever it was that was happening to him. I didn't want to blame myself, but something about the way he said it rang true.

"Shut up." Graceson drug him forward. "Mind if I gag him?"

"Please do," I nodded, pulling the door open for him as the two wrestled forward.

"Damn it. He's strong. Tell Suzetta we may need to sedate him," Graceson huffed as he struggled out and down the hall with Daethian pressing his feet into the ground and pushing off of him.

Fear and urgency nipped at my heels. I tried to push down the waves of dizziness that still plagued me from the sudden rush of not breathing, to breathing, to standing, to running. Nymphs watched me, confused, as I sprinted past them without a word. I caught their twisted expressions as their faces followed. Every tick of their surprised, gaping mouths or upturned eyebrows filtered through my brain. Doorways came and went, inching away at an alarmingly slow pace. Everything moved, but never as fast as I needed it to. Even the air around me felt heavy, thick with guilt and worry, and hard to navigate.

Daethian was going to be okay. I just had to keep repeating it in my head. The heel of my shoes slid across the floor as I slid into the white, clean infirmary. Suzetta and Shavarra were hovering over a patient, delicately wrapping the man's arm. Both looked up, wide-eyed at my sudden appearance. The air was full with the bitter scent of the products Suzetta used to keep the room as sterile as possible.

"You're back!" Suzetta paused, "What's the matter? What the hell happened to your neck?"

"Here, I can finish this," Shavarra whispered and nudged Suzetta toward me with her elbow.

The healer looked down behind her at the patient even as she crossed the room. Her gentle hands reached out, brushing over my neck. "Who did this to you?"

I hadn't had the chance to look, but I'm sure his hand left large, mean bruises that would rival those that Ganglin had once left. It hurt to speak, and air still plagued my chest as I tried.

"Don't worry about me. Something is wrong with Daethian. Can you come with me?"

Suzetta nodded eagerly, leaving Shavarra to finish the work she had started. The healer easily kept pace next to me as I basically ran down the halls once more. Questions bloomed out of her like petals of a flower that faced the sun.

"What's wrong with him?" she began.

"I don't know. His eyes are black, black smoke is literally fuming off of him, and he just tried to kill me," the words came out in a tumble, on top of each other. "It's like he is possessed."

"By a demon of Havala? Has he done anything else out of the ordinary, other than just now? It is a tad worrying. Daethian loves you."

"Only a tad worrying? I almost died!" I laughed to keep from crying. If I thought too hard, hot, wet tears welled in my eyes. "Uh, he has been argumentative lately. He has said some really mean things, but I've just assumed we were going through a phase or something. There has been this tension between us and... and I'm talking too much you don't need to know that."

"Either way, black eyes and oozing black smoke isn't natural." Suzetta stroked a beaded necklace that hung from a belt loop on her loose pants. Her thumb rubbed over a worn pendant, faded to a bronze, the olive branch symbol of Mother Nature.

"Graceson thinks you'll need to sedate him."

Suzetta hummed as she thought. The door that opened to the stairs that lead down to the cells was still swinging on its hinges. Muffled shouts and bitterly yelled curse words echoed up to us.

"Oh no," I mumbled and jogged down the stairs.

Graceson leaned heavily against a cell door, his hands fumbling with the jingling keys as he tried to keep it closed and lock it. Daethian pushed on the other side. His long fingers gripped the bars with white knuckles. Curling strands of fog reached out around him like deadly arms.

"Fuck you *and* your fucking smoke," Graceson hissed, dodging a strand that reached for his cheek. The key clanked loudly, the lock clicking in place. Daethian's fingers grazed Graceson's shirt, trying to grab him through the bars, but Graceson was already shaking his head and walking toward us.

The metal door rattled on its hinges, Daethian's large hands rocked the bars. An uninviting scent still filled the space. I breathed through my mouth trying to ignore the stench that reminded me of rotting flesh. Blood still splattered the floors. Visible claw marks from nymphs who tried anything they could to withstand torture, or to break free of the cell, were scratched against the walls.

"No one saw you?" I asked, chewing on my nails.

Graceson held out his arms, "What can I say, I'm blessed by the gods."

"Well that doesn't look good." Suzetta stepped closer examining my best friend. "Daethian? I'm Suzetta, the healer, I just want to take a look at you and make sure you're doing okay."

"I know who you are, you idiot." Daethian pressed his face between the bars, pulling from either side.

"So you're clearly semi-lucid, a good sign. I'm just going to place one hand on you, okay? Just to test your vitals."

"Don't you dare touch me."

"Come on, friend, won't you just..." Graceson stepped up to the door. In a flash, he grabbed Daethian's shirt and yanked him against the bars, "Listen to the lovely lady."

The black around Daethian flared. His eyes narrowed to thin slits as he glared, his chest rising and falling in panting breaths. Unsuccessfully, he tried to pull away. Nearly rabid, Daethian was moments away from foaming at the mouth.

"Suzetta, be a dear and sedate the man," Graceson purred.

Suzetta carefully laid a hand on Daethian's exposed neck. Daethian's eyes glazed over as he fought to keep them open. Between long blinks, brown began to return to his eyes and the black magic around him drew back into him. I swear his eyes ticked up to mine and he held my gaze for the briefest of moments before his body dropped against the bars and floor. Graceson lowered him slowly to the ground by the straining material of his shirt.

"Okay, I'll take a better look at him now." Suzetta snaked her hands through the bars and gripped Daethians open hand. Pink was returning to his flesh, the sickening grey color finally becoming a healthier tone. Her eyebrows furrowed. She closed her eyes in concentration and after a moment pursed her lips.

Graceson poked Daethian's body with his boot. Satisfied that he was out, he turned to look at me. "Don't tell your future hubby about this. You might find yourself friendless."

"Dace wouldn't hurt him," I mumbled. I could hardly take my eyes off of Daethian's face. He was looking better, he was looking like himself again. But was his mind his again?

"I wouldn't be so sure. Fae are awfully possessive, and Dace has all but put a mating claim on you."

"Can we not talk about that right now? I've already got a lot on my mind."

"Mum's the word, sweetheart." He smiled sadly. If he talked too much longer I was going to break at the thought of what had happened to Daethian in my absence. I was selfish, and because of that something bad had happened to my friend.

Suzetta leaned away from Daethian, sitting back onto her heels. Her ponytail of dirty blonde hair brushed against her back. "Well, good news or bad news first?"

"Good news," I snapped.

"He isn't physically sick. Which, now that I'm saying it, doesn't sound like good news so much." Suzetta chewed on her lip between sentences. "Bad news is, I don't know what it is. It's bad, I can tell you that. My magic though, just bounces off of whatever it is that has settled in his mind."

"What does that mean?" I rasped. Graceson took a step closer, but I waved him off. "Do you think he is actually possessed by a Havala demon?"

Those were old wives' tales, stories of religious fanatics. While my belief was that my magic was gifted from Mother Nature, I had yet to fully embrace the idea of the dark side of the creation of the world. Could they even be real?

"I've never heard of a possession ever actually happening in my lifetime. But the sad point is that I don't know how to help him, Ryker. I'm sorry."

"There has to be something we can do. We can't just let whatever this is keep tormenting him like this."

"I can do some research, but it just isn't something my magic recognized," Suzetta offered, quietly, glancing up at Graceson. He rocked on his heels, watching our nervous exchange.

"But you'll find an answer, right?" Tension built in my chest, making my voice squeaky and shrill.

"I can't promise you that, truthfully."

"Damn your honesty," Graceson whispered.

"But what do we do if we can't find anything? Is he just supposed to live down here now? In a cage? Like an animal? He just earned his freedom." My hands shook at my sides. Graceson took another step toward me. His warm hands gripped my shoulders and he made me face him.

"Look, I'll make a trip back to the Acture Court. I'll take Randsin back with me, because goddess knows he needs to get out of that damn room. Windre knows a lot of odd information; he owns a lot of weird old books. I'll do what I can. We will fix him."

Suzetta shot him a warning glare, "Your lies will do her no good."

"Okay," was all I could manage.

Graceson prodded me toward the stairs. "Don't stay down here stewing on this. I'll make sure he gets what he needs in the meantime. Go upstairs, get something to eat, take a shower."

Everything in my body felt numb and nervous all at once. It felt like history was doomed to repeat itself. History was making a mockery of the present, *of what could be my future*. Every step I took off the staircase felt like a terrifying step into the unknown. Daethian's limp body remained in view for a short time. Then suddenly it felt like I was never going to see my dearest friend in the same light again.

TWENTY-TWO

Milo

Dearest Milo,

I appreciate your letter. More so, I appreciate that you refrained from sharing all aspects with my father. Additional knowledge puts me at an advantage. You are a valuable asset, friend. Since you have been honest with me, I'll share one nugget of suspicion I have. My father did receive your letter the other day, but the envelope remains sealed. If that doesn't suggest to you that to him this is a meaningless errand, I'm not sure what else will.

Truly,
Maggie

I crumpled the paper in my hand. A fresh breeze drifted in from the window, still open from when the bird had arrived and left. Fresh flowers bloomed year-round in the Acture Court, making the air smell fragrant with the pollen. That did little to help my churning annoyance.

If I was not acting the part of the spy, if I was just a boring errand runner for the king, what was even the point? Why send me and Red away if he didn't care for the information?

The days here had come and gone with little peace for either me or Red. She experienced torture and I had to live with the guilt of it. None of it was pleasurable for me, not like I wanted. Windre remained brutally cruel, mildly apathetic, and mainly elusive. It made the thought of conversation with him so daunting, that at dinner I'd often chosen not to speak.

Red was always there, watching us eat. She was already skin and bones, and the food that I could sneak her was barely the minimum to keep her alive. Something had noticeably changed between us, though when it had happened I wasn't sure. I could openly admit to myself that I wanted her safe, I wanted her out of this court. I wanted Red to be free. Maybe I had picked the wrong side of this brewing war.

Servants in the castle halls whispered, unaware of how often I was listening. Red's rebellion wasn't the start. Many, many more were blooming all over Stylica. One successful in the Heathern Court. If Randsin was there, had he even survived the onslaught the nymphs gossiped about? As much as I hated the man, I didn't want to be the person who had to tell Eydis about his death. Though it would make my task of finding him pointless... making my personal mission to rid the world of that token a million times easier.

Hastily, knowing I was going to be late for dinner, I tossed the paper in the small trash bin near the desk. Standing, I turned, only to stop as pain made my back arch in surprise. The mirror that hung on my wall glowed an eerie red. Pain dissipated as quickly as it had struck, in a long tingling sensation.

I fought the growl on my lips as I stared into the mirror at the reflection of my queen. Queen Atarah smiled, the thickness of her red lipstick easily apparent, even through the crimson tint of her image.

"I need an update," she said, her fingers drumming loudly against the glass.

With a deep breath, I began. "I've moved on to another court, trying my hand at finding him here. There is a new king here, but I don't suspect he would divulge any information, if he even knows it."

"You are taking too long, Milo. If you cannot get it done, I will send Barthalow into that realm to find him. You're running out of time."

"I apologize, my queen." I dipped my head. I wanted to make excuses or to tell her about the richness and size of this realm, but the more I did that, the more I would be planting the seed of greed in her heart. I already needed to save my realm from Atarah. I didn't need to add an entire new realm to that also.

"I've missed you," she finally pouted. "I've made plans for us when you return."

Heat coursed through my veins. Atarah often fancied her guards, and used them for her own pleasure. At one time in my life I hadn't minded being used like that. But that had changed after I found my love for Eydis. Even without Eydis's love, the desire for Queen Atarah's bed hadn't returned.

Clearly, she only wanted what she could not have. Because I wasn't around right now, the appeal of having me became greater in her eyes. Selfish bitch.

"I'll look forward to those," I said stiffly.

A knock came at my door, the guards who were to accompany me to dinner ready to leave. Windre wasn't fond of lateness, I'd been told, and it wasn't hard to believe.

"My queen," I whispered. "They are calling me for dinner."

"You are dismissed, but remember your time will be ticking away," she sang, running her tongue over her teeth. She adjusted the crown that rested on her head and then the red of her image disappeared.

A large sigh of relief left me. I dipped my head down. There was so much to be thinking about at all times, so many layers to the lies I was spinning every day. With one hand, I tried to wipe away the feeling of dread my queen had given me, and I opened up the door with a tense smile.

"About time, I'm starving."

Jerydin clasped his hands in front of him. Somehow I never got used to the wings, every time I saw him I had to fight to keep from staring. He never cared, he was used to it, but it was rude nonetheless. Jerydin didn't speak and turned toward the dining room, giving me the best view of his wings. I wonder how easily he would notice if I touched them? Maybe if I had wings I could fly away from Queen Atarah, never to be seen again. Then someone else could be fighting this battle instead of me.

King Windre was leaning back in his seat holding a half-full glass of wine. His face remained neutral, void of any emotion. Instead of the braid I'd gotten used to him sporting, his hair was loose, pooling in his lap.

I bent slightly at the waist as I entered and let a nymph pull back my seat for me. "Tired of the braid?" I cocked my head watching him.

A small smile lifted his chin. It nearly startled me right back out of the seat. Windre didn't smile unless someone was crying in pain. Sometimes not even then.

"I woke up with quite the headache this morning. I thought relieving some of the tension might help it go away." He took a long sip of his wine, watching me.

The savory scent of our meal filled the room as nymphs walked in, setting the plates before us. I looked over Windre's shoulder, hoping to see Red. She wasn't there.

"Your nymph had a longer session with my torturer this morning. She was still dripping too much blood for me to want her to drag herself over my freshly cleaned carpets."

"I'm surprised by that," I said.

"How so?"

"She's bled so much. How does she have any left to give?" I cracked a smile.

Windre chuckled quietly, slipping his fork into his hand, "You can be funny sometimes."

Except for the fact that I wasn't funny. I had never been a funny guy. It was just the only way to say the words of my concern without him taking them so seriously. A small moment of truth that needed to be said.

I turned my head away. It was sort of a relief not to have Red watching me eat. It made the knotted feelings of guilt within the pit of my stomach loosen, just a little.

"I've heard your nymphs whispering," I started, popping a crisp piece of broccoli into my mouth.

287

"Gossipy little things. Have they said anything worth noting?" Windre's gaze flickered from me to Jerydin, who had placed himself quietly by the door.

"I've just heard a lot about some sort of rebellion. The Heathern Court isn't doing well? From the sounds of it, their king has fled and is currently missing. Just curious what the truth in that is and what your opinion may be."

"Ah, yes, a pesky problem that one is." What was a tiny ghost of a smile faded away to a dark scowl. "I have men already working on that issue, but it's information that I can not freely disclose. I apologize, but your loyalty to me is none."

Well, that lot of information did me absolutely no good. I wanted to avoid the Heathern Court. I wanted to avoid Randsin. But... Red needed to be there. If there were nymphs there fighting, as Red had attempted to do, she needed to be with her people. It was only safe. Even if that meant that she wasn't with me. No matter how I wanted to keep her close, it seemed that I only brought her misfortune.

A door on the opposite side of the room opened with no sound. The movement caught my eye, my hand drifting to the knife at my belt. Had there been a door there a moment before? I didn't think there ever had been. Behind me Jerydin was already shifting from his position and walking toward the door. Windre set his glass down and perched on his seat like he was ready to jump out of it if need be.

Red hair poked through the door, a fae man who looked around with an apologetic smile, "Hate to interrupt, I really do." He stepped fully into the room, wings just as Jerydin's, but scarred with long jagged lines, sprouted from his back. The man bobbed his head in regards to me and turned to Windre.

Someone else stepped in beside him. The figure stilled as my gaze traveled to meet the other man. Cropped black curls, large brown almond-shaped eyes, and the trained, perfect military posture.

"Windre, could we borrow you for just a moment?" he continued.

My body went stiff. Fighting the urge to bolt up from my seat, my hands gripped the table. I could feel magic burning through my veins. The call of the blood oath demanding to be fulfilled stung my skin like a thousand poison-dipped needles.

Randsin's eyes were wide as he stared at me. The wood of the table groaned under my hands. Trembles shook my boots against the floor.

"Do you know each other?" Windre asked, looking from me to his guests.

My will was dwindling away with every passing second. "Randsin," I said, my words just a growl on my breath, "You're a wanted man. You need to get out of here before I can't control myself anymore. You need to leave. NOW."

I didn't need to say anything else. Randsin sprinted away and out the door. The last tie to my will dissolved with one final effort. With both hands, I pushed the table with all my strength, throwing it toward the red-headed fae and the open door. The fae jumped out of the way, food, dishes, and wine crashed and splattered across the floor, across the walls. The table was the only thing blocking the door now. The only obstacle I could make for myself to delay the rush to capture him.

My voice rang out in a deep bellow. Every movement was stiff with the pull of my queen's words. *Find the thief. Get the token. Find the thief. Get the token. Find the thief. Get the token.*

I knew he had it. Eydis has spelled it into his skin, like every other tattoo he had. Objects bound into his flesh. He was a walking storage bin of monsters and ungodly power.

"Milo!" Windre yelled, throwing his hand out before him. Magic made the atmosphere thick, holding me in place like cement.

Mentally, I was relieved by the sudden stop. Physically, I panted as agony built and strained under my skin. I was able to tick my head to the side to watch Windre stare at me in confusion. Jerydin and the other winged fae were already at my side. Bony fingers dug into my arms as Windre dropped his magic and his men pulled me away.

"You can't stop me," I shouted. "I can't stop myself until what Randsin has stolen has been returned."

"The world has really gone to shit now, hasn't it?" the red-haired man said.

Jerydin laughed as he tugged me through the door. "You have no idea."

TWENTY-THREE

Ryker

Hattie skipped in front of me. Her braids, that mother had tightly done behind either ear, bounced against her shoulders. I followed closely behind her as she ran in circles, arms outstretched, and singing at the top of her lungs.

"Hattie, I don't want to play this. I'll race you to the top of that tree," I shouted, already turning for the nearest tree to climb.

A gentle breeze drifted between us, pulling the single daisy behind Hattie's ear toward the ground. Hattie snatched it out of the air with a pout. "I climb trees with you all the time. You could play my game at least once."

"Your games are boring."

Both of us turned toward our mother who sat on a fallen limb, sewing a patch over one of the few pairs of pants that I owned. She didn't look up from her task as she responded.

Everything felt like a distant memory, and somewhere in the back of my mind I wanted to cling to the image of my mother. Ten year old me, though, looked away. No, memorize her face. Take in every laugh line, take in her soft, flowing, straight hair, take in the tender love in her eyes and the gentle care that she handles her project with.

"Why don't you play a game that you both want to play?" she said with a small smile.

"What about hide and seek?" I snickered, leaning against the tree. Bark transformed and molded over my skin until there was no part of me left to be seen.

"You have an unfair advantage," Hattie said, sourly.

"Fine, you pick something else then." The pout was evident in my voice.

Hattie plucked a couple wildflowers from the ground and held them up. "Let's weave together some flowers and make crowns. Then we can play the princess and the queen. I call being the queen!"

"No, because then you'll just boss me around the entire time. I want to be the queen."

My mother shuffled behind us, setting down her work quietly as my father walked toward us through the trees. His hands were clasped around a small wooden box, his face pale and grim.

"Ibarra," he whispered to mother. *"The spell is complete. We just need to bind it."*

Mother glanced at me and Hattie. Hattie was already knotting the ends of the flower stems. My fingers interlaced with the grass as I grew white, delicate flowers around us. I kept my gaze on the dirt before me and so did Hattie, but we both knew we were listening to our parents. They knew too.

"How long will we have with them, Calton?" she asked, her voice heavy with sadness.

"A year at most." His rough hands stroked down the length of her face. Mother's gaze drifted between the box he held against him and us, playing cluelessly next to them. "It's important we do this. The Mother didn't give us this to let it fall into the wrong hands. It's meant to be used with its other half, should we need it to protect her holy lands against the other realms of the gods."

"I know, I know." She gently pushed his hand away. "I just worry about leaving them alone in this world. I don't want them to feel burdened by this, just as we have since your family passed this down to us. I wish they would never have to know what this was."

"And they won't."

"What do you mean?"

"I made a deal with the burgundy witch who spelled the box. All we have to do to wipe the memory of this

from their mind is to complete the spell with our blood. They will remember nothing, unless the spell is broken. I pray that never comes to pass."

Plucking a few flowers from the ground, I started braiding them together and watched my mother as she pressed a kiss to my father's lips. Hattie hummed in front of me, a crown nearly complete. Her lips didn't lift with a smile, as she continued to listen to our parents with me. I didn't want to forget this box. I didn't want something to be lost to my mind and never even know it. The thought plagued me.

"A year isn't very much time to love someone" Mother said, her tone growing more mournful by the second.

"A year is adequate if you love them fiercely enough. And I will love you and them with all my might, until our last breath."

"Okay."

Father pulled his knife from his belt and slid the blade over his forearm. Blood dripped from his arm and onto the box. Mother extended hers, and she met the blade without flinching as she stared into his eyes with intense admiration.

"This will make this world a safer place for them." Father slipped the knife back into his belt and set the box behind the log.

Hattie and I blinked at each other. We had been building floral crowns. Mother had been sewing and Father had returned from a long walk.

And nothing more.

The canopy above my bed lifted in the slightest breeze from my cracked windows. Urgent breaths, fueled by sickening waves of released magic, tormented my body. Everything was coming back. Every moment that was erased rushed back to me in confusing flashbacks. Images of colorful leaves and the crisp, early morning sun appeared behind my eyelids as I tried to process the onslaught of information. The box lay open, the jagged half of a large circular coin rested inside. Ganglin had opened the box. And this wasn't a good thing.

I tried to slow my breathing, to focus on something other than the rising panic and the shit-show that had become my life. I needed to talk to my sister, because this damn thing had more to do with us than we thought. It was our job, our duty to our family, to the Mother, that we keep the pieces of whatever the coin was out of the hands of someone who could use it outside of its intended purpose.

The air was already warm and muggy. Bright rays of the sun crept over the horizon only to heat the day further. My legs felt sticky with sweat as I pulled the blankets off of me and slipped out of bed. Floorboards creaked quietly underfoot, the wooden planks still mildly chilled from the night. I yanked the desk chair over to the wardrobe, flinching as it squealed over the wood.

The top of the wardrobe was dusty. Stones and the varying materials of the gowns pressed against my stomach as I stretched against them. Under me, the chair creaked at my weight. A thick film of grime made my hands feel dirty as my fingers brushed over the stained wood until they met the smooth, cold surface of the crystal.

I gripped it with a sigh of relief and pulled it into view. Light thrummed through it in a glistening flash as I stared down at it. Dark magic rippled through, and it felt immensely improper. Silver, jagged rock budded in small pillars that stopped at many points. Graceson had said as much, when he mentioned the idea, that it was witchcraft.

All I needed to do was say Hattie's name. Clutching the crystal, I stepped down from the chair and sat in it. I rolled it over in my hand, running my fingers over the sharp points and rough edges. These odd, mystical objects were all that was left of a species some believed to have never have existed at all. It had to be rare and expensive.

"Hattie Avery," I spoke quietly. The crystal grew warm in my hand, and white light glowed around it. Squinting into the brilliance of it, the shine of the points narrowed on my bed. Flares of it danced over my covers, forming into Hattie's figure. She sat forward, her legs crossed, and an excited smile on her lips.

"Oh, Hattie," I nearly shrieked. "It's so good to see you."

"I was hoping Graceson would give you the damn thing sooner so we could talk. What kept him away?" she said, her smile falling slightly.

"It wasn't Graceson. He gave it to me last night. Some things came up..."

"Sounds an awful lot like what's happening over here. Something is *always* coming up."

For once, her curls were not bound in a tight bun on top of her head. Instead they brushed against her cheeks and twisted down over her shoulders. Her hair looked extremely long, a surprising thought. Had it been that long since I'd last seen her?

"Wait, what's going on there?" Genuine concern filled me, accompanied by the small pang of conscience from putting off what I needed to say.

"Ottack sent some keeper with a nymph. Normally, we just collect them, with no witnesses actually in our court. Windre staged his whole castle just to host them. He is paying nymphs to act as servants in the castle, too. But the issue is, he is actually trying to break this poor girl. A ruse to make sure Ottack continues to believe this whole charade. It's wrong what they are doing to this girl!" Hattie's voice grew strident.

"Have you said anything? Have you seen her?"

"No, Windre refuses to let me come to his castle. We got in a huge argument over it," she sighed, balanced her elbow on her knee, then propped her chin in her hand. "What's causing strife in your neck of the woods?"

"Something is wrong with Daethian. Graceson is making a trip back to the Acture Court to use Windre's resources but... it's like he's possessed." I chewed on my lip.

"By an agent of Havala?" Hattie gasped.

"We don't know. His eyes are black, and when he gets angry, black smoke comes off of him. Absolutely terrifying." My hand drifted up to my neck.

Hattie narrowed her eyes, her image stood from the bed and closed the space between us. Light brushed against my neck, but I couldn't feel the touch. "Did he do that to you?"

"Yes."

Any semblance of a smile melted away to a dark scowl. "That can't be true."

"It is," I started, trying to keep my thoughts on track. There were so many things I could say about the problem with Daethian. Too many worries to even list. "There's more I need to share with you, too."

"Oh, great. Hopefully it's better news than what you just told me."

"Dace wants me to marry him," I blurted before I could talk myself out of saying it altogether.

She took a step back, her eyebrows knitting together. "Do you want to marry him?"

"You make it sound easy," I scoffed. "There is more at stake here than just if I want to do it. Isn't there?"

"It sounds simple enough to me."

Everything always seemed so simple to Hattie. Her life was a series of choices, all of which were either black or white. But my choices all felt murky and grey, no easy difference between the good and the bad of what I should and shouldn't do.

"I would have to live in the Twinity Court. And what of this advantage we took here in the Heathern Court? What of Daethian? What of the war?"

"We can figure it out together." her voice was motherly. "Honestly, I'm more surprised you've made it so far with Dace in such a small amount of time. I've been flirting with Windre and going on these dates, for five years, and the man still refuses to kiss me. I'd marry him in a heartbeat. If only he wasn't so stubborn."

"I knew you two had a thing!" I smiled.

"As do you and Dace. You like him, don't you?"

My heart raced at the thought of him. A small space inside of me missed his company. "I like him," I said slowly, in an attempt to speak some part of my muddled thoughts. "I mean, mother above, he is beautiful, charming, revolutionary in his political stance, he cares for me, and we get along so well. But he is also cocky, vain, and fae nobility."

"What is so wrong about that?"

"I'm a nymph. I'm just barely not a slave, I don't have any wealth, and I'm living out of an estate that I stole. Dace is a prince. Totally opposite ends of the spectrum. You should have seen the fae at his bridal proposition. They hated seeing me. They hated seeing us together even more."

"Stop worrying so much about everyone else. Worry about you. Does Dace make you happy?"

"I mean, yes, I'm interested. The spark between us is everything to me. But don't you think it's too soon? You even said it hasn't been very much time."

"Stop overthinking," she laughed. "Yes or no answers only. Do you like Dace?"

"Yes."

"Do you want to marry Dace?"

"We need more time before I'm ready to marry him. That's a huge commitment, a scary one at that."

"Yes or no only," she tsked. "Do you want to marry Dace, maybe not tomorrow, but someday in the future?"

"Yes," I finally said, weakly. It felt like giving in. Like I was finally admitting the extreme amount of feelings Dace made me feel.

"Then you have an answer." Hattie's gaze was soft as she looked me over.

"Daethian hates it," I whispered, touching my neck once more. "It's why he did this."

"You don't really know that. There is something very wrong with him, and it has nothing to do with you and Dace."

I nodded like I agreed, but my stomach still felt heavy. Something was very wrong with Daethian and it felt so much like it was partially my fault, like my body was going to cave into itself to fill the gaping hole the divide in our friendship had caused.

"What else did you want to talk about?" she pressed.

"Did you have any dreams last night?"

"None that I recall. Should I have?"

When we were young it wasn't unusual for us to wake up and have gone on the same adventure together in our subconscious. It was one of the fun things that made us feel closer as twins. It didn't happen every night, but sometimes we would both wake up excited. I hoped this had been one of those moments.

"I had a dream... but it felt more like a memory... about that box Ganglin had."

"Oh?" Her voice was soft.

"It contains half of a coin thing, a token, is what our parents called it. They said that it contains unthinkable magic, and it was created by mother nature to protect us against other realms of the gods."

"I know." Hattie took a step back, her eyes squeezing shut, like she was anticipating that I would smack her or scream at her. Part of me wanted to.

"You know?" I didn't yell, but any trace of humor, joy, or concern had left my voice.

"I never forgot."

"How?"

"I don't know. The spell never worked on me. After mom and dad died, I kept the box in my bag that I always carried. You asked about it a few times, but always forgot about it less than ten minutes later, no matter what I told you about it. The magic clearly worked on you."

"Why didn't you say something after you knew Ganglin had it?" A hint of anger now tainted my words.

"I didn't want to burden you. You already seemed so stressed out with everything else, I thought I could manage this one thing alone."

"Since when are we not doing things together?"

"Don't try and guilt me, Ryker," she whined.

"I'm not," I lied. "I'm genuinely concerned. I think there's a chance Ganglin is in the Acture Court, too."

"How? I followed him to the Obtune Court."

"I don't know. It's just a feeling. A glimpse I saw, once the magic released my memories. I saw the box and the background... it looked like the Acture Court. Maybe he is traveling."

"I better tell Windre." Hattie chewed on her nails, her attention drawing to the floor.

"I need to check on Daethian anyway. I can contact you like this whenever, right?"

"Yes, it goes to the necklace I'm wearing." She pulled a smaller crystal pendant out from under her shirt.

"Perfect. Now how do I make you go away?"

"That didn't sound rude at all," she lifted a brow. "Just let go of the stone and I'll vanish."

"Easy enough. I'll reach out again soon, promise."

"Okay. Love you, Ryker." Hattie took a step back waiting.

"Love you, too." I set the stone on my desk. The light faded from the crystal and Hattie's image evaporated. As she disappeared, a desperate loneliness gripped me. A shiver ran down my back and I tried to shake off the terrible feeling.

I needed to go check on Daethian. But what kind of condition was I going to find my friend in today?

MADNESS

TWENTY-FOUR

Ryker

Light didn't make it to the dungeons like it did the rest of the castle. There were no windows to offer reprieve from the darkness. Fae firelight still glowed at the end of torches that lined the rough rock walls. Daethian was in the largest of cells, his door only bars. When I was brought down here, I was shoved into the smallest cell with a thick iron door.

Cold seeped through the stones that never seemed to warm, no matter how long you curled against them. Some things, like that, came back like haunting nightmares as I walked down the narrow staircase. My fingers brushed against the cut stone walls, my mind wondering how many times Daethian had thrashed and pushed against them on his descent to his cell.

At the bottom of the steps, I took the glowing torch and touched it to the two wooden sticks on either side of his prison door. They lit, a sunny hue of orange that shifted to a soft yellow-white glow. Both of his muscular arms hung through the bars, leaning down against one of the few bars that ran horizontally. Big brown eyes looked up as the sudden brightness illuminated his dirt-covered features.

"Ryker?" he whispered, pulling himself up with a groan. "Why am I here?"

The urgent need to hug him, to soothe his confusion and fear, tormented me. Silently, I wrapped my arms around my body and stepped closer to him. There weren't any sickly snakes of dark black magic curling off of his skin, and his eyes were a somber bronze color.

"Do you remember anything?"

"The last thing I remember is heading to my room. I was going to visit with Randsin while I waited for you to come back home." He rubbed at his tired eyes, smudging more dirt in messy rings against his skin.

Home. He used that word so sincerely. And in some ways he was right. The Heathern Court had become my home. It housed terrible memories, but it also contained good ones, filled with friendships that felt more like family.

"You tried to kill me last night," I finally said. I just needed to rip the sticky bandage right off, no need to let the anticipation build. Carefully, I reached out and

307

touched one of his hands, calloused and scarred, but still familiar.

"No, that's not possible. No, no, no," he said on a fading breath. He took my hand in both of his through the bars. Water gleamed on the edge of his eyelids, the whites tinted with red.

I nodded, closing my eyes and squeezing his hand. Just seeing him in this cage, and feeling the strength of his panic, made me nervous to open them again. I didn't come down here to cry. I'm stronger than this, I can cry alone in my bedroom later. Daethian didn't need to see how badly this affected me too. He didn't need any more guilt.

"I love you Ryker, I would never hurt you." His hands ran roughly over my palm, the back of my hand, and up my arm. Trailing fingers filled with remorse. His touch became static closer to the top of my shoulder as he took in the bruises that had already faded a bit from yesterday, on my neck.

"No, no, no," he quietly cried, pulling back into the cell. His forehead rested against the cold bars. Fisting his hands, he beat against the door. "What the hell is wrong with me?"

"Stop." I grabbed his hands to keep him from hitting the metal anymore. He was already in rough enough shape. "Suzetta already looked at you and she doesn't know what's wrong. What's in you is... unnatural."

"What does that even mean?"

"I don't know." It wasn't the answer he wanted. Confusion and fear became clear on his features.

"What will you do with me? Keep me in here?" The pitch of his voice broke.

"Suzetta is looking into it more. Graceson took Randsin back to the Acture Court and he will be working on it too, with Windre. Until then, you have to stay in here. You're a hazard to other people, a hazard to yourself."

Daethian's gaze fell to the floor. I couldn't help but want to touch his face, to offer him some sort of comfort in the midst of all this distress. The hair on his cheeks had grown so long, it wasn't nearly as scratchy and rough to the touch as it had been.

A growl rippled over his lips, his hands shooting between the bars and clamping against both my arms. "I don't have control anymore," his voice dipped into a deep, taunting tone.

"Let me go!" I pushed off of him.

He titled his head back, his pupils murky, his skin draining to an unhealthy, ashy tone. "Next time, I hope you get close enough for me to eat." He snapped his teeth at me.

"Who are you?" I hissed. Without thinking, I took a step away.

"I am Daethian, clearly. I'm just the side he normally suppresses. Everything I say is a thought that passes through my head. But now I can no longer pretend like it doesn't exist."

Every ounce of his anger for me was real. Everything he said had been some sort of thought that, until now, he hadn't vocalized. I mean, that was one way to be more honest. But one thing didn't ring true. Daethian wouldn't want to hurt me.

"He would never lay hands on me like that. He would never hurt anyone like that."

"Oh, how you're wrong," he snickered. "I want to hurt people. There are lots of people I've wanted to inflict pain on. It's just sometimes I can't help it if it's you, or one of the keepers that I happen to unleash my fury on."

Daethian dipped his head lower watching me through the bars. "There is so much love for you in here." He tapped a finger against my chest, his tongue darting out over his lips. "So much passion. So much *lust*. Tell me, *Ryker Avery*, have you ever thought about touching me like I've thought about touching you?"

This was wrong. Everything he was saying felt painfully like an insult. His intention to get under my skin was clear, and unfortunately, it was working.

"I don't have to sit here and listen to this," I pointed out.

"Yet, you stay," he purred. "Just admit it. Just admit that your love for me is as great as my love for you, and I'll shut up."

We'd had this conversation, what felt like a thousand times. Every time I said it, every truth that I told, only seemed to break him even further. I didn't want to push him off the edge he was already teetering on.

"I'm not staying." My feet stumbled over the stone as I turned quickly and headed up the stairs.

His voice called after me, an eerie song that bounced off the walls and echoed through the space and followed me, "I love you, Ryker Avery, and you love me too." The last sentence was a menacing growl, "Just say it already."

The door slammed shut, a powerful force fueled by my frustration and powers that itched to be released. Behind me, the door and the wall shook with the effects of a mild earthquake that I couldn't contain. I needed to talk to someone before it all carried me away.

Suzetta had wanted me to return to see her so she could take another look at my neck. It was probably nothing, but she wanted to double-check anyway, she had said. Might as well get that trip out of the way now. She'd gladly listen to me.

Hopefully, whatever Daethian had wasn't contagious. We didn't know anything about what was happening to him, and that was almost as terrifying as the words that kept coming out of his mouth. Not to mention the violence.

I made my way through the halls, waving in passing as nymphs went on with their day, unaware of Daethian in the dungeons below them. Injuries had healed and the rate at which people were hurt had slowed. No noise was carrying from the infirmary, which was quite slow compared to the days after we first took the castle over.

My gaze washed over the empty beds and the crisp clean walls. Suzetta wanted a sterile room and she kept it that way. But I didn't see Suzetta now. No, instead long blonde hair and violet eyes blinked up at me. Shavarra lifted her nose from the book she read, curled up on an empty cot.

"I'm looking for Suzetta," I mumbled. Shavarra was Dace's best friend and if she was anything like my best friend... well the thought of her harboring any feelings for Dace made me want to vomit.

"She stepped out for something to eat." Shavarra closed her book with a smile.

I stepped away to leave with a bob of my head, I could always return later, but Shavarra spoke as I tried.

"I could help you, though."

"Oh, she just wanted to take a look at my neck. It's probably nothing." I ran my fingers over my throat as I turned back to her.

She smiled softly. "I'm sure if she wanted you to come back, it's probably not nothing. Here." Shavarra patted the bed next to her.

Quietly, I joined her, sinking into the thin mattress, watching her with intense curiosity. They were lovers, her and Dace. The thought rose, along with bile inside my throat, an angry, jealous feeling along with it. *So don't think about it, Ryker.*

Her fingers were gentle, as she lifted my chin and felt along my neck. "Can you tell me how this happened?"

"Daethian did it. But it wasn't him, not really. Or maybe it kind of was…" I sounded ridiculous, even to myself.

"And Daethian is… your friend?"

Staring straight ahead, I wondered if she asked the question for context or if she was wishing I was interested in someone other than Dace. The sentiment wasn't very clear. Either way, I answered.

"Just a friend, yes."

"Why would he do this to you?" She pressed her fingers along my windpipe. The pressure was uncomfortable, but surprisingly painless.

"Some sort of dark magic, Suzetta thinks. His eyes turn black, and this ugly, stringy fog crawls off his skin. Then he starts sputtering about how much he loves me, but he also hates me, how much he wants me, but he also wants to kill me. I talked to him this morning... He implied that his actions, though cruel in nature, grew from thoughts that he was already having when he wasn't in this state. Watching it makes me feel like I'm being stabbed in the gut with a thousand long swords."

"Black eyes, you said?" Her hand dropped back to her side with a nervous chuckle. "That sounds like a children's story my parents used to tell me."

"Your parents told you scary stories?" I watched her lavender eyes flick up to my face.

"It was supposed to scare us into staying in bed. And it's based off of a species that doesn't even exist anymore."

That was peculiar. An odd magic that Suzetta couldn't identify, symptoms of darkness that we were going to have to search through books for. I mean I'd listen to a children's story if it meant we had a chance to figure out what this thing was. But they weren't real, right? It was just a story?

"What's the tale? I'm sure it's worth a listen."

"It's silly, actually. Parents would just tell their children that if they got out of bed at night that a burgundy witch might find them. Burgundy witches were not fond of the fae, even though we often made deals with them. Or so it's said, I've never met one, they were gone before my time. If you made a deal with them and crossed them, they would come back to eat the meat off your bones. Or as my parents told the story, if you got out of bed and they found you, they would put a powerful curse over you." She raised her eyebrows. "The curse would change your eyes black, and dark magic would seep from your soul."

I snorted, "You think Daethian has been cursed for getting out of his bed at night, by a species that doesn't exist any longer?"

"No, I'm just saying that all stories come from somewhere. It's very interesting to me that his symptoms match that of a burgundy witch curse."

I laughed, like I was going to shrug off the idea, but I knew I wouldn't. I'd look into it, even if it was a dead end. "So how does my neck look, doctor?"

"Your neck is fine. I suspect Suzetta wanted you to come back because sometimes the wounds remain under the surface." She tapped her head. "Anytime you need to talk, you'll have a friend in me."

"Dace seems to think you're pretty special, so if he trusts you, I suppose I could too," I mumbled, as I returned to standing.

"He is...something special," her voice was riddled with a harmony of love and sorrow, a feeling that I also recognized. "Dace has loved you for *so* long. We may have had something at one time, but it was never love. I have resigned myself to be happy as long as he is happy."

"You use the word love so freely." Maybe it was something wrong with me. Was there some sort of fear that seized me deep down that kept me from being so open to it like everyone else was? I was the odd nymph out.

"That's the funny thing, though." She clasped her hands in front of her. "I don't."

A surge of emotions welled within me. My life was turning into a series of emotional whiplashes. Between my pain for Daethian, and my growing feelings for Dace, I was at war with more than just the evil fae rulers. I was at war with myself.

TWENTY-FIVE

Dace

I had arrived in the late evening after pardoning myself from dinner early to retire to my bedroom. My parents didn't need to know that I really was excusing myself to visit my friends in the Heathern Court. Silverware scraped against plates, squealing in a way that made my teeth ache. The smell of ham was prominent in the dining room. Chewing mouths froze, and content gazes shifted to me and melted into confusion by my sudden appearance.

Their looks didn't bother me so much though. If I wasn't used to my family materializing in front of me like that, I'd probably stare too. A nymph girl with flowers blooming over her cheeks smiled at me as I leaned against her table. The curling petals stained red the closer I came. The few around her watched me with awe. Missing these looks had finally begun to fade into a memory with my title back. Their longing gazes filled with the idea that I could give them something; money, power, romance with someone who has both. It felt like I was in control once again. People who wanted something from you could be bargained with. They could be governed.

"Where would I be able to find Shavarra?"

She opened her mouth to speak, her eager lips spreading into a small smile, only for the girl next to her to lean forward and blurt, "She's in the infirmary. Suzetta is teaching her the art of healing with tonics and medicine."

I hummed, righted myself and patted the poor girl's shoulder as I passed. "That will do. Thank you."

I shouldn't have been surprised that their answers had led me back to the infirmary. Even if she didn't have the magical gift, there was plenty she could learn without it. It didn't surprise me that she busied herself with learning something new that would help her help others. It was very Shavarra of her.

"Hello, my dear friend," I sang as I sauntered into the room.

"Dace?" Shavarra's face lit up as she poked her head out from behind a curtain. "Just a minute, let me wash my hands and I'll be right there."

"I would say take your time, but I only have the evening to visit before I have to return home, and I was hoping to visit my future bride while I was here, too."

She nearly squealed, "Oh, I had heard rumors like that and I didn't know if they were true. She was here earlier today, but I didn't want to ask her directly yet. She's still a little hesitant."

"It's not set in stone yet, so let's not get too excited." But I couldn't keep the goofy grin from my cheeks. "I made a deal with my parents. Ryker gets time to fully commit, and if she decides she doesn't want to, my mother gets to pick my bride. I'll be stuck with LaBelle likely, so let's pray Ryker will take the offer."

"We both know she will," Shavarra deadpanned as she shook the water from her hands and crossed the room with her arms stretched out for a hug.

Breathing her in, I pulled her close. My eyes closed at the comfort of my friend. "I've missed you."

"I've missed you too. It gets quite boring without you coming around to complain about your life of luxury every five minutes."

"Oh, shut up." I playfully pushed her away.

Shavarra adjusted her green shirt, that she had probably dug out of some closet in the castle. The color clashed with her frosted skin tone, but brought out her vibrant purple eyes.

"So I had a weird dream last night," I began, with a tentative smile.

"Ah, here it is, the real reason you came." She rolled her eyes, still grinning at me.

Easing myself onto one of the available beds, I leaned back onto my arms. Shavarra sat across from me on another bed, pulling her legs up and crossing them in front of her.

"I, uh, I had a dream that I found a Burgundy Witch on the front steps of the Twinity Court."

A cough rattled her chest like the wind had just been knocked out of her. Shavarra patted her heart and shook her head. "You did what, now?"

"I dreamt I was coming home and I found dead guards everywhere. But the witch had killed them quietly. No alarms had been rung and the castle doors had not been breached. But she laid on the steps, barely alive."

"What did you do?"

"In the dream, I slit her throat. She shouldn't exist and she's a danger to all of us. I'm not about to get cursed or have the flesh eaten off my bones," I said with a nervous laugh.

"This doesn't make sense. Burguncy witches don't exist anymore. They are extinct." Her hands scrubbed at her face. "Ryker was literally just in here telling me about Daethian. The only symptoms he has reminded me of the stories of burgundy witch magic. You don't think there is a witch running around cursing us, do you?"

"Daethian? What's wrong with him?"

Shavarra patted my knee as she heard the obvious distaste for him in my voice. It wasn't really a dislike for the man himself, more like their closeness made me uneasy. "Something about odd behavior, black eyes, and magic that oozes off his skin."

"Okay," I tried to take it all in, because there was no way this was all a coincidence. "Don't say anything about the witch, yet. I mean I haven't found her, so it could not even happen for days or weeks or years. It could mean nothing, and I don't want to freak Ryker out about it if it's not even a thing yet."

"We hardly even see each other around here, so I don't think that would be very hard," she said slowly.

"Thank you." I sat forward and pressed a kiss to her cheek as I stood. "I'm going to see where Ryker is at. It doesn't sound like she is having a very good time here since she has returned."

"Go woo her," Shavarra waved. "Come back and say goodbye before you go though."

I nodded my head as I backed out of the room. Carefully, I pulled an apple out of my navy jacket and tossed it back and forth between my hands as I strolled the halls to Ryker's room.

Her door was closed, as it usually was, so I knocked on it gently. There wasn't a call to come in from the other side or any shuffling of activity. Maybe she wasn't there or maybe she was taking an evening nap.

I knocked louder. "Ryker?"

A door down the hall cracked open, the door that had belonged to the room I had stayed in. Ryker's green eyes peered down the hall. As she saw me, she opened the door wider.

"Dace? What are you doing here?"

"I came to visit. I told you I would. What are you doing in my room?" I left her door behind and made my way over to her. She leaned against the doorframe with a slight crimson blush.

"I wanted to make sure I was left alone. I came to hide," she laughed quietly, stepping away and allowing me inside.

The room remained as I had left it. Mostly clean, with the few items of the previous occupant still sitting as they were left. I hadn't felt the need to move them since it didn't really feel like any of that was mine. Inside the room, I turned on my heels tossing the apple at Ryker.

"Want a snack?" I asked.

"I don't really feel like eating right now." Ryker closed the door, pressing her back against the wood, the apple held between her hands. Soft curls tumbled down her shoulders, just asking for me to run my fingers through them.

"Do you want to talk about it or be distracted from it?"

She thought for a moment, clearly debating it as she chewed on her lip. An uneven breath filled her lungs. Her attention finally settled back on me. If she kept biting her lip like that there might be an issue, I thought as a lust-filled pang of desire shot straight through me.

"Distract me," her hushed voice trailed to my ears and rose goosebumps over my arms.

With a sly smile, I answered, "I was hoping you would say that."

"Oh no, maybe I should have picked the other option." Ryker pushed off the door and drifted over to me. "It doesn't have anything to do with the apple does it?"

"Not if I'm to distract you properly." I slid across the floorboards, easing my way around her. Her face turned, her eyes following me as I stepped behind her. My fingers traced up her arm running over her smooth, bare skin and stopping along the sleeve of her shirt. "I need to practice my power, but I was thinking you could offer more of an incentive."

"Mmm?" she hummed. "What kind of incentive?"

"If I can make progress..." I paused, wishing to draw out the suspense. I could see her interest tweek her upturned lips. Full and round, the teasing smile made my pulse quicken.

"Out with it," she breathed.

I nuzzled my nose into her neck, taking sips of her scent like she was expensive wine I needed to savor. Pressing my lips against her neck, I caught sight of the bruises I somehow hadn't seen before, and pulled away.

"What are these?"

Ryker cupped her hand to her neck, looking away from me. "It's part of what I need you to distract me from."

An urgent, pressing fury built tightly in my chest. I smoothed my button-up shirt down, trying to rally my self-control. If Daethian did this to her, I was going to freeze his heart.

"So will you tell me the incentive now?" She twisted and looked up with me. Something like hope shined in her gaze.

She really wanted to be distracted. And maybe, so did I.

"If and when I make progress, you take an article of clothing off."

Ryker smiled like she thought I was joking, then laughed with a small shake of her head. I could feel the slight chuckle vibrate through her arms where I held her. "You don't think that's too tempting? I won't have sex with you, Dace. Not till I'm sure."

"Not yet, you won't." I kissed her forehead. "I won't touch, only look. Unless..."

"I won't change my mind."

"Okay, okay. It's just an option... that's available. It's literally always on the table, you just have to ask." I winked and took a couple steps back. Simple chairs and decorative pillows filled the small living space. I turned, looking around for ideas of anything I could try and take with me that wouldn't be so terrible if I ruined them. Happily, I grabbed one of the incredibly dusty novels, clearly only used as a prop, off the side of the desk and held it in my hands.

"What do I get out of it then?"

"Set your terms, Ryker." I waved my hands in front of her.

Both hands planted on the curve of her hips. "Every successful turn, I pick a new, bigger object. Anytime you fail... you take off some clothes."

"Oh, look at you." I feigned surprise. "What a negotiator you've become."

"Take it or leave it."

The air felt thick. Tension, both good and probably at least a little bit bad, churned between us. Gods, I hoped I could pull this off. Even underneath the plain clothes she wore, I knew the figure of a woman was there.

"It's a deal" I stretched a hand out. She took it firmly and shook on the bargain. Clearing my throat, I set the book back on the desk and lifted up a pen. "Better start small then."

"That feels a little bit like cheating," she said.

My laugh disappeared in the void of space as I vanished from in front of her and reappeared a foot behind her. She turned and watched as I held out the full pencil.

"Okay, then." She slipped out of the boots she was wearing and kicked them over to my feet.

"*That* feels a little bit like cheating."

"Hardly," she snorted, as she snatched the pencil out of my hand and began walking around the room for another object. Her sock feet were quiet on the floor as she padded through the room. She disappeared into the bathroom and reemerged holding a wooden paddle-brush. "Now try this."

"Easy enough," I smirked.

"Don't get too excited." She pointed at her sock covered feet. "These are next."

Huffing a growl, I took the brush. Magic tingled over my skin, swelling to consume the additional object it wasn't used to. I kept her image in my mind's eye as I wasted no time manipulating my travel and returning a few feet from where I started. I held the brush up with a triumphant grin.

"Fuck yes! Take the socks off." I danced.

"You don't have a weird foot fetish, do you?"

"You think foot fetishes are weird?" My smile grew as she slipped one sock off and waited. "The other one, too. They are a pair."

She rolled her eyes and pulled the other one off, tossing them over by her shoes. She pulled the brush from my grip as she passed, and moved toward the table. The book I held earlier sat crooked and half off the edge.

Air passed in a whoosh over her lips as she blew the dust off the cover. Particles of the powdered dirt misted into the air before her. "Now that you've had two freebies, let's try this."

"Done." I took the book and stepped through the pockets of space that didn't exist for other people and appeared in the desk chair. I opened the novel and flipped through it's pages. Boring, blah blah blah, some fantasy tale filled with humans and violence.

"Have you been practicing without me?" Ryker almost looked offended at the idea. Her fingers skimmed over the edge of her shirt.

My eyes lingered on the skin above her pants, trailing over the dip of her tapered waist, and up to the nude colored bra as she lifted the shirt over her head. Her gaze narrowed.

"Is this prize enough for you?"

I blinked. Every time I saw her, her curves filled out even more. The more she trained, the more her muscles grew, the more nutrition was filling her body, the less ribs I could see and the greater her bust filled out. She was everything, and she was only half naked.

"You're beautiful." I smiled. Honestly, I could be content to look at her for the rest of the day.

Ryker brushed off the comment and looked around the room. I set the book down on the desk curious as to what she could find that was the next step up. She jerked to a stop as she looked around the dresser and pointed to the bed.

"Moving the bed is quite a big jump, don't you think?" I laughed.

"Not the bed." She bent down to her knees and reached under the bed. "This." She dragged out a small chest from under the bed. She held up over her breasts, hiding the nearly naked bit of her as best she could.

That would be harder to move... but if I could do it, she would have to lose one more bit of clothing. I'd gladly take another chance at worshiping at every subtle curve of her body. Sighing loudly, dramatically, I walked across the room and took the chest. Not only was it large, it was quite heavy too. A testament to her growing strength.

"This could be tricky," I mumbled. Then I looked at Ryker and the way she folded her hands over her chest. She might be feisty, she might have good banter, but she was not confident about her body. A shame considering she was so pretty. Maybe my prize for progression wouldn't do her much good.

I gripped the edge of the chest and held it to my stomach. The familiar static-y magic feeling danced over my skin and I willed it over the box. The magic could have easily stretched I found, but I didn't let it.

As I shaped back into reality next to her, I could hear part of the box clatter to the floor where I once was. Letters, weapons, and worthless knick knacks spilled out the side of the chest into a pile at my feet. I set it down with a fake frown.

My fingers reached for the button of my jacket. Ryker's gaze snapped from the chest, to my face, to my hands. I lifted a single eyebrow as I shrugged the jacket off.

"Well, this won't do me any good anyway," I whispered and began unbuttoning my sheer shirt underneath. "Two for the price of one."

With a laugh, I threw my shirt at Ryker. Her attention had begun sweeping over my body, greedily taking me in. She made it hard to contain myself. "Stop looking at me like that."

"Isn't that how you look at me though?" She took a slow step forward. Her hand lifted, calloused and scarred, she ran her fingers over my chest and the dip of my abs. "Your skin is flawless."

She saw every nick of her skin as a blemish, where I saw it as just another piece of her. Another perfect piece. It made sense that she hated the markings, since she hadn't asked to be punished with such severity. Despite the roughness of her hands, the feeling of them tracing over me was pure luxury.

With my hands, I ran my finger over every scar. As delicately as I could, I traced their lines on her torso and the top of her shoulders. Her mouth parted, her breathing quickening.

"Do you not think you are lovely?" I asked.

She smiled softly. "I'm not ugly, but I'm still not sure how I snagged the attention of someone as handsome as you."

"Is it the scars you don't like?"

"I hate them. They ruined my body."

The quiver in her voice made me squeeze my eyes shut for a moment. I wanted her hurt to be erased. Watching her, I lowered myself to a scar along her shoulder, the place where a whip had come too high, and pressed a kiss to it. "How can I convince you otherwise?"

I could feel the slightest tremble that traveled through her at the touch. I wanted to chase that excitement, I wanted to make her scream in pleasure. But not yet, I reminded myself. First, she needed to love herself like I loved her.

With the tip of my nose, I ran my face over her skin to another scar. "It would appear that every inch of you has been made for me. Like you were carved out of the likeness of a goddess." I kissed the spot and took a deep breath of her warm scent.

"I don't believe in the gods. Nymphs believe in Mother Nature," she whispered and cupped my face as I leaned closer to hers.

"Maybe they both exist. Maybe neither. Or maybe they've chosen to combine their creations with the likes of us."

Ryker's teeth ran over her bottom lip, holding in the slight grin. I toyed with a curl near her face.

"I love the kinks of your hair. I love the fierceness and the vulnerability that somehow coincides in your evergreen eyes. Your lips," I brushed my finger over her mouth. "They were made to fit mine, I believe it."

"You've probably said that to a thousand girls," Ryker said in a hushed tone, but her attention remained on my mouth.

"Never." I lowered my face to hers. Our lips brushed so closely, her eyes fluttered shut.

"Kiss me," she eventually said.

With her blessing, our lips fully met. There was a fierceness to the kiss, a desire that had to be met. Tentatively, her tongue traced along my bottom lip. But as my fingers drew circles over the jagged skin of her back, her arms wrapped around my neck, pulling me closer, each kiss grew more frantic.

Her heartbeat raced against my chest, every breath fanning over my face. The taste of her only made me want her more. Together we stumbled back toward the bed. Her body was pinned beneath mine as the mattress dipped with our weight and the soft blankets wrinkled.

I pulled my hands out from underneath her, stroking down her face, down her neck as our kisses grew and we swallowed each other. There was peace in this moment. Every worrisome thought melted away. Ryker's body, typically so filled with tension, loosened as my fingers roamed her skin.

Slowly, I ran a line over the swell of her bust over the top of her bra. A small moan escaped her against my lips. I could smell her wetness in the air. The feeling of my own desire pressed between us. Slipping my hand over her bra, I could feel the point of her nipples under the fabric. I caught the peak of her bust in one hand, gently tugging before I took her whole breast with the fullness of my palm.

She moaned, grabbing my face and pulling me roughly against her. I lost the feeling of my own uniqueness and my own identity. It was no longer me, but we. We were a single entity that made the idea of what I was before her feel so foreign and wrong.

My hand caressed down her body. I cherished the thought of what it would be like to feel whatever slickness had formed between her legs. A literal, tangible, reaction to her desire. I drew a line over her bare skin above the waistline of her pants.

Ryker shuddered at the touch. I stopped, breaking the kiss, and panting.

"This is where I draw the line." I rolled to the bed staring up at the ceiling as we listened to our heaving breaths next to each other.

"Thank you," she finally said, turning to look at me. Her curls had fanned out around her and her full lips were red and practically swollen.

Closing my eyes, I reveled in the feeling that still swelled in my heart. With one hand, I reached for hers, the other tucked my erection away as best I could. I turned to her and held her gaze.

"It isn't my job to convince you with lust to bed me. If you aren't ready mentally, you aren't ready at all."

A smile grew over her lips. "How did you become so sweet, Dace?"

I laughed, because sweet... I was not. "I've waited a long time for you, Ryker Avery. I can wait as many more days as I need to for you."

Rolling to my side, I took her hand and laced our fingers. "Whatever is enough for you is enough for me."

The look she gave me, her large hope-filled eyes, her cheeks the slightest rosy red, and her mouth still pink from our kisses, burned into my memory in the very best of ways. One day she would love me too, I reminded myself.

Because sometimes the waiting hurt.

TWENTY-SIX

Milo

As the distance between me and Randsin undoubtedly grew greater, the roar of magic inside me became a throbbing ache instead of the fire-storm it had been. I didn't bother to fight as the two winged males carried me off to a cell. Ungreased hinges screamed in protest as the door was shut and locked behind me.

Red looked startled when she saw me coming. Her hand wrapped around the bars nearest mine as she pressed herself forward. "What's happening?"

Jerydin and the other man exchanged a look. "What are we supposed to do with her, Graceson?"

Graceson, as he was called, shrugged his shoulders and headed back up the stairs. Everything was left how it was as I had last seen it. All the blood splattered tools and the table with cuffs remained, no new occupant within them. My gaze traveled the cells I could see. Still empty.

As the men's steps faded away from my hearing, I walked to the corner where Red's hands could be seen. The metal bars were cold where I pressed my face to them.

"Damn it, Milo, if you don't tell me what is happening I swear I'll find a way out of the cage just to kill you myself."

"Do it, it's probably better than what they have in store for me," I sighed, rubbing my temples and lowering my voice to a whisper. "He is here."

"Who is here?" she snapped.

"Randsin, the man who stole from my queen. The entire reason I'm in this gods-forsaken realm. I tried to fight the urge as best I could, but it's so damn painful. I told him to run and if my queen ever finds out that I've betrayed her like that, she'll hang me."

"What are they going to do with us?"

There was a growing fear in the tone of Red's questions. Some sort of urgency built within her to find some way to survive, to get herself out of here. But I didn't have any answers, and I didn't know how I was going to survive. If they were smart, they would try to get information out of me and then they would kill me.

"I don't know," I managed.

Voices rose far past the stairwell. Two people argued as they walked down the hallway above us toward the stairs. Their words were muffled at the distance, until they reached the door.

"Well if the ruse is up, I'm setting her free," a female voice said stubbornly.

"We don't even know what's happening, yet. Would you just listen for once?" Windre's voice growled.

"Maybe next time," she said with a snap as she took the final step. Her dark green eyes made contact with Red's, her jaw falling slightly ajar. "Windre she looks awful," the girl cried, a curly ponytail swung behind her as she ran toward the cell with her keys.

Windre stepped quietly down the last step, watching her. Every word she said left him flinching. He didn't bother to give me any of his attention.

"I told you not to do this. I told you this was wrong."

The woman's scent filled the air. Not fae, but nymph. She looked very free, and very much like she had some sort of control over Windre himself. It was becoming more and more apparent that Windre wasn't who he said he was. But maybe that made him more empathetic, maybe I could plead my case.

"I'll get you cleaned up," she whispered as she held Red and guided her up the stairs, keys still in her hand. She narrowed her gaze on Windre. If looks could kill, he would be dead a million times over.

A new set of feet came down the stairs, stopping before the person could be seen. Windre sighed and finally turned to face me. He didn't look cruel anymore, he just looked tired. Behind him, Randsin stepped off the last step.

The bars of the cell rattled loudly as I pushed against them. Magical urges consumed me, burned inside my bloodstream, and forcefully moved my muscles against my will. I cried out in pain.

Randsin palmed the wall next to him. I could feel the magic running through from him and into me, some of it trickling away toward Windre. Windre crossed his arms, his long robe folding in front of him. Randsin had learned some new tricks since the last time I saw him and he lost his ability to speak.

"Why are you here, Milo?" His voice carried inside my head.

I tried to hold in the sob of pain, but it still managed to tumble from my lips as my whole body pressed against the metal trying to find some way to him. "You know why I'm here, Randsin. My queen wants the token back, and she's using my blood oath to make sure that it happens."

Windre's eyebrows knitted, one hand rose to his chin with a finger over his lips. "This can't be anything good."

"No," Randsin said to the both of us. "It brings back unpleasant memories."

Heat seared up my spine. I gritted my teeth. "Please. Please leave, your presence is so painful."

"You gave me the token to take from her. Now you want to take it back."

"I don't want to take it back," I yelled. "She's forcing me to. Can't you see I'm not in control of my own fucking body?"

My muscles twitched. Every inch of my skin flushed every shade of red imaginable as I fought against the iron bars. I could withstand this pain, I tried to tell myself. I could do it as long as I knew the token remained out of my hands.

"Randsin, go, and I'll talk to him." Windre pointed back up the stairs.

Randsin's lips twisted into a scowl, his eyes staying trained on me until his body was no longer in view behind the wall of the stairwell.

A couple more sobs shook me as the pain sat at the surface, still plaguing my brain and my muscles. He has gone. I told myself. He has gone. But it still took time for the blood oath to settle once more. As it did, I let go of the bars and sat down on the floor.

Windre pushed his robe behind him and sat on the dusty floor outside the cell. He tilted his head. "Why did you come from the Acture Court?"

"Don't you want to know who I serve? Don't you want to know which wicked queen really sent me?" I drew lines in the dirt next to me.

"No, I know enough of that. I've been to Tierasia once myself."

My attention snapped to his face. When and how? He even knew the name of the land I hailed from. "How?"

"I followed Randsin's call for help. Found myself falling up a hole instead of down. An odd trip, to say the least. But I sought the voice that kept calling in my head until I found him fleeing for his life. From your queen. My question is why now? Nearly seven years later?"

He really did know it all. No doubt Randsin and him had lengthy discussions about it. I leaned back into my hands.

"After I helped Randsin escape, a witch, a relation to the one who had announced the prophecy that he had fulfilled, bound the portals closed. It wasn't until Queen Atarah found her and killed her that the spell was undone, and she sent me through."

"What of this token you say Randsin has?"

"He hasn't told you?"

"Randsin is a private man who keeps a lot of secrets. The weight of them, I'm sure, is a hefty price to pay." Windre folded his hands in his lap.

I could still smell Red's blood in the air. It was weird how the roles had switched so quickly. She was free from the cell, and here I was, locked up with nowhere to run. The tears that had welled in my eyes finally dropped over the edge as I blinked. I wiped the at them quickly. I was better than that.

"If that token gets into the wrong hands, like Queen Atarah's, and she finds its other half, the world will not be the same. The owner of both halves will have more power than any other being on this earth. What would someone so evil do? I shudder to think."

"So the question remains," he smiled.

I couldn't help but gawk at his smile. There was nothing joyful, or happy about this. Perhaps I was wrong, and he was deranged and sick.

"What am I going to do with you?" he continued.

Suddenly, I didn't want to die. I never really did. Logic told me that they would likely kill me and I wanted to be prepared for that, to meet my fate like a man, but I certainly didn't want to die if another option presented itself. Was this what it was like to be Red? Was this something else we seemed to have in common? It felt like it.

"If I don't go back, she will send another." In truth, it had always been between me and Barthalow, but I had subtly suggested it be me. Barthalow was savage and would cut his way through this world. If I went, as I had,

I could undermine her at every step. For the most part, it had worked, up till now.

"When does she expect your return?" He crossed his legs in front of him, propping his elbows on the edge of his knees and resting his head in his palms. After he asked, he hummed a light tune, as if he couldn't contain himself.

I squinted at him, but otherwise ignored his odd behavior. "Not long. Last we spoke she said if I was not successful, and soon, she would send another. He won't be trying to fight her commands as I do. Barthalow is loyal and wholly evil, like her."

"So what do you think I should do?"

"I think you should let me live."

"Okay," Windre nodded. He pushed himself off the floor and dusted his billowing pant legs.

"Okay?" I looked up. He had to be fucking with me.

"You'll have to understand though, that I'll need to keep you down here. I can't have you running off with Randsin in the middle of the night." He gave me a flashing smile that was so beyond different from the sly, wicked ones he had given me before. "My sincerest apologies for the poor living conditions. You understand, right?"

I nodded my head, but truly I didn't get it at all. He turned his back to head upstairs, but I scooted myself forward, drawing his attention again.

"What will happen to Red?"

His robes gathered dirt from where he had sat and along the edges that trailed the floor. He dusted them further as he spoke. "Hattie will take care of her. I can promise you that. She'll be given something that will give her her powers back, and she'll heal quickly after that."

"You don't break nymphs here, do you?"

His smile grew wider, slightly crooked and his eyes sparkled with something mischievous. "No, I do not."

"Are you not afraid I'll convey that message back to Ottack?"

"Should I be? I thought you worked for that queen back in where? Tierasia?"

I pursed my lips. Even though the princess bothered me, there was some odd sense of loyalty to her that I felt, even now. Some weird connection from trying to help her get out from under her father's nose, free from her own oppressor, that made me think she'd like to hear this news.

"Either way," Windre waved his hand before I could respond. "You'll be down here with no way to communicate with the outside world. I don't know what you know about our war, but Ottack isn't the good guy, you don't want to be on his side. It's the losing side."

"I'm not on his side."

Windre's smile fell on one side, a single eyebrow quirking in a way that made his face look crooked too. "We'll see. I hope not, for your sake."

"Can I see her?" My question was barely even a whisper, but I kept my chin up.

"This is why I think somewhere inside there is a good guy." His hands clapped loudly together. "She may be allowed to visit at her own will, when she is up to it."

His cloth shoe-looking slippers spun in the dirt as he turned away and disappeared up the stairs. Silence echoed around me. The ringing sound of silence surrounded me in an uncomfortable blanket.

All my life, I had clung to my gut feelings. Now my gut was muddled and confused. This wasn't my war, I wasn't here to help or to imprison nymphs. My mission was Randsin and to destroy the token. I shouldn't have any feelings of loyalty to the fucking princess. I shouldn't be worried about Red.

"Focus on Tierasia, Milo," I said to myself.

The singing call of my queen burned me. I groaned, ready to admit defeat, ready for my queen to put a price on my head. All the torture devices on the wall glowed crimson. The image of her face appeared in all of them in some way, until together they made up a single image of her face.

"Well that doesn't look good," she chuckled.

"I'll get out of it soon enough," I groaned, trying to wipe any dirt away from my face and look presentable.

"It's too late for that. I'm sending Barthalow."

I sucked in a breath, knowing what was coming. Stylica didn't know it yet, but a butcher was about to walk through their lands, cutting down anyone in his path. And I was likely to be tossed aside like an old, used toy.

"But," Atarah said, holding a finger up. "I'm making deals today. I'm feeling generous."

"Thank you, my queen." I bowed my head. Anticipation built in the following silence as she watched me.

"I will grant you what you want most, Milo. If, and only if, you get that token before Barthalow."

"And what do you think I want the most?" *To be rid of you.* The thought crossed my mind and I prayed it didn't show on my face. I wanted Tierasia to have the rightful king on the throne. I wanted the myths of his survival to be true and I wanted Atarah tried for her crimes against the kingdom.

"Freedom," she hissed the word, and it stung me directly in my chest, ringing through the blood oath like a promise. "I'll end your oath. No sacrifice will be needed."

It had never been spoken before that she could end it at her will. Everyone knew that for the oath to be broken you had to give up the closest being to your heart.

"You're lying," I stuttered. "It can only be broken one way."

"I never lied." She fanned herself. "I merely omitted part of the truth. The oath can be broken both ways. Either by sacrifice or by my will. Do we have a deal?"

I was still here. I was so close to the token already. But if she had it she had a chance at all of the power that could destroy everything. However, if I was free I could leave. For once Queen Atarah wouldn't have to be my problem. I didn't have to stick around to feel the need to free all of Tierasia. I could just free myself.

"It's a deal."

As soon as I said the words, Atarah smiled and her image flickered away. The emptiness of the room felt heavy on me. Slowly, I leaned back and laid down on the ground, tucking my hands under my head. The ceiling was carved stone and not much to look at, giving me mental space to think about my racing thoughts.

I didn't know if Windre was telling the truth, I didn't know if he was a good guy. What I did know is that I wanted to be free. Since I had arrived I was only trying to stop myself from getting the token, to fight the urges that welled from the oath. Now with independence in my foreseeable future, I was going to change everything.

And no one here needed to know that.

TWENTY-SEVEN

Dace

Leaving Ryker was the hardest part. Now that I had her, I didn't want to spend a second without her. She had finally fallen asleep after talking for hours. I knew I was losing my own chance at rest, but didn't care. I'd just have to be tired in my meetings tomorrow. It was worth it to hear stories about her childhood and the smallest good memories she had here in the Heathern Court with Daethian. I'd listen to her talk forever if I could.

Carefully, I brushed the slightest bit of hair from her face and listened to her heart beat slow and steady. My lips brushed her cheek, a final kiss before I left, but I dared not wake her up. The slight bruising on her neck was starting to fade already; it would be nearly gone, if not completely, by morning. If Daethian wasn't her best friend I would be hunting him down and ripping him to shreds right now.

Instead, I focused on my magic. I focused on the Twinity Court. The power covered me, taking me over miles of land in the briefest of moments.

Something was wrong. I hadn't opened my eyes yet, and I could smell blood in the air. The crisp, copper tang of something amiss in my home. Both eyes snapped open and the hairs on my arms stood on end. Bent limbs and bloody bodies were everywhere.

Blue armored men were face first in the fresh snow, white already covered their backs as it continued to fall. Just as in my dream, large red puddles had oozed out around everybody. Sprinkles of blood dotted the snow farther away.

Ice crunched under my boots as I spun, taking everything in. "No, no, no," I whispered to myself. Men were slumped over in death, leaning against walls or folded over the high walls that surrounded our castle. Panic, worse than the fear I remembered in my dream, welled inside of me. The witch was as silent as she was deadly, and she had left the castle completely unprotected as she took out every perimeter guard.

Pushing forward, my feet slipped on the icy ground. The witch's body lay as it should be, stretched out over our steps. A stench stronger than I remembered greeted my nose. Some mixture of old, molding books and an acidic scent of toxic herbs managed to cover the smell of the fae blood that had been spilled.

An icy breeze lifted her holey cloak. Even though I knew what she looked like, had heard stories of their death-like appearance, and had seen them in the dream, the shock of it still hit me. Her skin was grey, every vein that ran underneath was black and bold in web-like lines.

The familiar feeling, the desire to run in the other direction, coursed through me. The unwanted urge to flee made my fingers quake. I struggled to keep them steady. I was a prince, I reminded myself, nothing should scare me like this. My powers rival so many.

Shavarra's question still repeated in my head as I bent and pressed two fingertips against the witch's throat. *What if this was the witch that had caused whatever was wrong with Daethian?* A heartbeat still pulsed under my fingers.

Wind swirled snow around us in tornadoes of white, it picked up her torn hood and pushed it away from her face. Strands of her long black ponytail lifted with the breeze, the black veins that ran over her cheekbones were particularly unsettling. I tried to breathe through the panic that wanted to grip me. This was the burgundy witch. A real, no longer extinct, species was right in front of me.

Even with the blood that covered her mouth, and the sharp teeth extended for breaking through fae flesh, I knew what I was going to do.

I was going to save the witch. She would help us with Daethian. She would tell us how she was still alive. For all I knew she was the last of her kind and I couldn't be the one to end their entire race, even if she was dangerous.

"Guards?" I called. Cold, wet snow clung to my forearms as I scooped her up into my arms.

The front door opened, the dark blue helmet of the attending guard appearing. Warning flared in his eyes as he tried to take in the sight.

"Should I sound the alarm, my prince?" he stuttered.

"No, no," I shook my head. "Quietly, I need you to scour the castle to make sure no one else has been harmed. No need to cause a panic."

But panic was already settling on his face. The guard inside next to him leaned over, pushing the door open farther, and gawked at the mess of bodies behind me. His eyes cut quickly to the witch in my arms, all color draining from his face.

"What is that?" the second guard said.

"Something straight out of your nightmares." Pushing forward between them, I stepped into the hallway. "Go," I growled at the first guard. Pulling himself from his fixation on the witch, he stumbled backwards to gather others to help search the castle. I prayed he wouldn't spread fear and hysteria with him. The other guard walked next to me.

"What do you plan to do with her, Prince Dace?"

"I plan to ask her questio--" But I couldn't finish my sentence. A deep, stinging ache didn't register in my mind until after the guard next to me quit screaming. My body froze in shock as the teeth of the witch sank into my neck. The squelching sound of flesh and blood being shredded and sucked was a distant noise inside my ears.

She was meant to be out cold. Instead, she was pushing off of me. Her long, bony fingers with sharp pointed nails interlaced into the guard's hair as she yanked his head to the side. His blade had been drawn and caught in the witch's hand. Not a single drop of her blood was spilled. But his was.

It was all I could do to remain conscious. My fingers rose to the gnarled skin on my neck, the warmth of my own blood covered it. Pain radiated through my knees and up my legs as I fell forward.

My guard was already dead. I was well on my way. The black cloak of the witch blurred in my vision, the distance between us growing as she darted down the castle halls.

Get up, Dace. Get up. I screamed at myself.

Had I only made it through the front hall I would have had the magic binding cuffs that would keep her from doing the most damage. I needed them now, even more. I just needed to make it there.

Grunting, with the taste of blood on my tongue, I pushed myself up to stand. My legs wobbled underneath me, the muscles fatigued. To this day, I had lived a mostly easy life. I hadn't fought on the front lines of any prominent wars. My life had never been at stake, nor something I had to often fight for, though it was becoming oddly more regular since I announced my support for the nymphs. Was this struggle to stand, to focus through the pain, what it was like to be injured during combat? To use your mental strength to force your body to move despite its instinct to be still?

Blood dripped down my arm and off my elbow onto the floor behind me. Screams began to echo down the hall. They all ended nearly as abruptly as they started. The walls around me tilted, the floor sloped, and the lights danced as my head felt light and my body heavy.

Focus on your magic, Dace.

Pinpricks dotted my skin, power that grew covered me from head to toe. Every blink felt like it was too long, and if I closed my eyes while I manipulated my travel, I feared I wouldn't open them again. A rush of colors streaked my vision, everything going out of focus, then a new room appearing.

My stomach lurched. One hand held my neck and the other held my throat as I bent forward, blood and the remnants of dinner in my stomach spewed onto the floors. The mess didn't matter. All that mattered was that I had the handcuffs.

Taking a ragged breath, I ripped them off the wall. Screams continued to meet my ears. The direction of the sound stirred me to forget about myself. She was heading for my parent's room.

The chains were heavy and long, but not larger than the chest that I could have easily moved with me in my practice with Ryker. It would work now. It had to.

This time the surge of my powers washed over me, burning as it went. It extended through my fingers, but stuttered over the magic stopping cuffs. I stuttered, letting go of the tendril of powers that I had extended. I wouldn't be able to manipulate travel with these.

Somehow I was going to have to make it to her before she made it to my parents, on foot. I blinked trying to clear my spotty vision. My boots scuffed against the ground, my legs not picking them up. Turning down the hall, my eyes fell over three bodies. Blood pooled around them, just like the men who had died in the snow.

I sprinted, sliding through the thick, sticky puddles, leaving behind dark crimson footsteps in my wake. Nothing could make me move any faster. Not my fear, not the impending sense of doom, not my regret, and not the foundation of love I had for my parents. I was moving as fast as I could.

The cuffs crashed loudly against my parents' open wooden door and I threw myself into the room. Bile rose in my throat as I took in the scene, as the gore met my eyes. My knees threatened to buckle underneath me. Guards rushed down the hall, I could hear their echo approaching. But it was too late.

My mother's face was frozen in shock. Her nightgown was stained red, her outstretched arm still covered ice. The witch had surprised her. She left my mother's body sprawled out on the bed like a tattered rag doll.

My father fought her now. But every punch he threw, she blocked. When his eyes flickered up to me he paused. It was a deadly mistake. The witch darted into his personal space. Her body was covered in the gore she had collected along the way, and my father's blood only added to it as she sunk her teeth into him.

His bellow tore through his clenched teeth. He didn't bother to push her away. Through the pain evident in his tense, twisted features, he lifted his hands, pointing at the chains I held. My name was noiselessly mouthed.

I didn't have time to think about the last thing my parents had ever said to me. Mourning would have to wait.

With a grunt of effort, I threw the chains into his waiting grasp. With one hand, he pulled the witch off of him, skin tore away following her mouth. The metal clicked into place, and ice was already spiking out of my palm. Effort to control myself only made the room spin more.

Dark spots in my vision blurred into large black flowers that expanded over my vision. My legs stumbled forward, my arms outstretched for anything to catch me. The thud of a body, then another, was the last thing I heard before I collapsed.

Thoughts no longer connected in tangible sentences inside my head. My eyelashes fluttered against my cheekbones. My gaze pointed ahead, and through the darkness my father's lifeless eyes stared back at mine.

What had I done?

Continue reading this series with book three, Heartsick.

Coming soon!

Also by Rebecca Grey

Ruined by Fae Saga

Ruined

Madness

MADNESS

Rebecca Grey

About Rebecca Grey

Rebecca Grey leads a busy life. Somewhere between working a day job, raising two kids, and daydreaming about being a reality television star she writes. As a reader she enjoys books filled with arrogant boys, who she would never waste her time on in real life, and large fantasy or paranormal novels. Much of her love for these things is reflected in her books.

MADNESS